The Invitation

THE BREWER FAMILY SERIES

ADRIANA LOCKE

UMBRELLA
PUBLISHING INC.

This is a work of fiction. Names, characters, organizations, places, events, and incidents are either products of the author's imagination or are used fictitiously. Otherwise, any resemblance to actual persons, living or dead, is purely coincidental.

Copyright © 2024 by Adriana Locke
All rights reserved.

No part of this book may be reproduced, or stored in a retrieval system, or transmitted in any form or by any means, electronic, mechanical, photocopying, recording, or otherwise, without express written permission of the publisher.

Published by Umbrella Publishing, Inc.

Special Edition Paperback ISBN: 978-1-960355-30-0

NO AI TRAINING: Without in any way limiting the author's [and publisher's] exclusive rights under copyright, any use of this publication to "train" generative artificial intelligence (AI) technologies to generate text is expressly prohibited. The author reserves all rights to license uses of this work for generative AI training and development of machine learning language models.

Cover Design by Books and Moods

Books by Adriana Locke

My Amazon Store

Signed Copies

Brewer Family Series
The Proposal | The Arrangement | The Invitation

Carmichael Family Series
Flirt | Fling | Fluke | Flaunt | Flame

Landry Family Series
Sway | Swing | Switch | Swear | Swink | Sweet

Landry Family Security Series
Pulse

Gibson Boys Series
Crank | Craft | Cross | Crave | Crazy

The Mason Family Series
Restraint | The Relationship Pact | Reputation | Reckless | Relentless | Resolution

The Marshall Family Series
More Than I Could | This Much Is True

The Exception Series
The Exception | The Perception

Dogwood Lane Series
Tumble | Tangle | Trouble

Standalone Novels

Sacrifice | Wherever It Leads | Written in the Scars | Lucky Number Eleven | Like You Love Me | The Sweet Spot | Nothing But It All | Between Now and Forever

For a complete reading order and more information, visit www.adrianalocke.com.

Cast of Characters

parents
    Rory Brewer - matriarch of the family; divorced and dating again
    Reid Brewer - patriarch of the family; in prison for a list of felonies

siblings
    Gannon Brewer - the oldest Brewer sibling; president of Brewer Group
    Jason Brewer [*The Arrangement*] - CEO of Brewer Air; former military/private security
    Renn Brewer [*The Proposal*] - retired rugby player
    Ripley Brewer [*The Invitation*] - exercise physiologist
    Bianca Brewer [*Flame*] - former Interim President of Brewer Group; moved to Florida and got married
    Tate Brewer - Director of Operations at Brewer Group

Synopsis

I *hate* Ripley Brewer.

So why am I cuddling on his lap, peering into his ocean-blue eyes while cameras record our every move?

My best friend needs my help to save her career, and I would do anything for her. Besides, filming a reality show sounds fun ... until Ripley shows up to play the role of my fake boyfriend.

As always, we nearly come to blows within minutes of seeing each other. The playboy billionaire accuses me of a setup, but I insist I'd rather live in a world without carbs than spend a minute with him.

At some point during the melee, we sign contracts. I can't stand the look of his six feet two inches of chiseled abs and broad shoulders. And I loathe his arrogance. But now that he's my pretend beau, I'm stuck acting like I'm falling in love with my biggest enemy.

It turns out that Ripley's a good actor, too. Every soft touch on the small of my back makes my heart thump faster. His sultry smirk feels like it's only for me. I should detest every word that passes his kissable lips.

Is this all a ruse, or does Ripley want to end this episode of *The Invitation* going from enemies to lovers? Because now? I'm not convinced I can despise him anymore.

Chapter One

Georgia

"How did the date go?" Sutton asks, lifting her martini. Despite the low lighting in the bar, the rock on her left hand—on the important finger on her left hand—twinkles. *God, that's a stunning ring.*

The Swill, Sutton's favorite establishment in her new, swanky Nashville neighborhood, isn't what I expected. She insisted it was a dive bar where we could hang out and catch up after two weeks of being so busy that one-word texts constituted our friendship. With that vibe in mind, I wore cutoff jean shorts, an off-the-shoulder top, and my favorite cowboy boots. Purple, of course.

I was met with valet parking and a three-page wine menu.

Make it make sense.

It's no wonder I have trust issues.

"The date last night?" I ask, plucking a toasted ravioli from the plate between us. "I canceled."

"*You did not.*"

"*Yes, I did.*" I pop the appetizer into my mouth. "When I realized I'd rather wash my hair and pluck my eyebrows than meet him for dinner and drinks, I bailed."

Sutton sighs, shaking her head. "I can't believe you canceled on Bennet Copeland. What's wrong with you?"

"Currently? Unemployment, the price of wine, and the fact that you let me walk in here dressed like this."

She grins. "Well, if I had your legs, I'd live in those shorts. All heads turned when you walked in."

"Yeah, probably because compared to the rest of you, I look like I charge hourly and spend a lot of time on my knees."

"Shut up," she says, laughing.

I shrug, swiping another ravioli.

Sutton McKenzie and I met on my first day at Waltham Prep. My parents divorced the summer before, and to suck as much money out of my father as she could, Mom finagled him into paying my tuition at a ritzy private high school that, financially speaking, I had no business attending. I wasn't happy about leaving my friends for my senior year, and I *really* wasn't happy about wearing a stuffy uniform and forgoing nail polish. But Sutton's bright smile and offer to sit beside her at lunch eased my fish-out-of-water fears.

We've been best friends ever since.

"So what did Bennet do to earn the not-your-type label?" Sutton asks.

"I think it was his breathing that did it for me." I chuckle at her eye roll. "Honestly? I don't know that he did anything specifically. I just got tired of feigning interest in his portfolio. That man is pretty proud of himself."

"Listen, I know you're still in your rich-men-are-pricks era, but you need to reconsider. *Trust me.* It's a lot easier working through your trauma while wearing a Siggy's diamond and shopping at Halcyon than sitting at home in sweats eating ramen."

"Sounds like you've had the wrong ramen."

"You know what I mean, smart-ass."

I laugh. "I do. I just disagree."

"You are such a pessimist."

"No, I'm a realist."

"Your reality is what you make it."

Sutton launches into a spiel about how life is like clay, and you must mold it to your liking. I tune her out, letting her voice blend in with the laughter from the tables surrounding us.

I've heard her speeches enough times that I can repeat them verbatim. It's not that she gives awful advice or even that she's wrong. I admire her perspective and how she wakes up in the morning with a clean slate. She doesn't hold grudges. Her negative experiences aren't allowed to taint her future, either. She truly believes that only good things are meant for her.

She might be right since she does live a charmed existence. My grandfather used to say people like her could roll around in pig shit and come out smelling like a rose.

That must be nice.

I'd love to be more like Sutton—a trusting, loving, positive individual who wears a smile and carries love in her heart. But when I try to slide on those rose-colored glasses, the ends poke me in the eyeballs, and I'm reminded that the best predictor of the future is the past.

And my past is filled with rich, manipulative pricks who wouldn't even know what the word love means. *Sometimes, I'm not even sure I know what it means, so I probably shouldn't judge.*

"Hey, what happened with your project at work?" I ask, eager to shift the focus away from my quasi-love life. "You lured me here with the promise of a huge update. So update me."

Her eyes sparkle. "Remember the reality show idea I presented to my boss last year?"

"Of course I do. It was such a fun concept and totally original."

"Well, he took it to the executives a while back. I've spent the past few months building out the concept and trying to attach names to a pilot, just in case." She pauses, her smile growing as my anticipation inches higher. "*And I did it, Georgia.* I was notified a few days ago that it's a go. The football player and beauty influencer we've been courting signed on, and the funding came through."

I squeal, my auburn ponytail swishing along the top of my back. "You're freaking kidding me! This is incredible."

"Thank you." She shimmies in her seat with excitement. "I'm over the moon about it. Because it's just a pilot, we're only shooting with one couple and have a low budget. We start filming next week, which is why I've been so slammed lately."

"Sutton, I am so, *so* proud of you."

I lift my glass to hers and tap them together.

My heart swells with delight. It's incredible to share this moment with my friend and to witness the well-earned pride color her cheeks. She doesn't often pause to revel in her achievements, choosing instead to root for those around her. So I sit back and give her space to toot her own horn.

"I'm pretty proud of myself, to be honest," she says. "I put my heart and soul into this concept, and seeing it come to fruition—knowing others with much more experience than me believe in it, too—it's so satisfying." She spears a ravioli with her fork and drags it through a dish of marinara. "It's also going to be satisfying when I tell Jeremiah's parents, and they realize I am an asset to their family, not just a silly gold digger like they think."

My smile fades. "Do this for you. Not them. You have nothing to prove to those people."

She raises her glass and clinks it to mine again. "Amen."

"Just remember when you're a famous producer that I was the one who supported you when you were a nobody."

"Thanks, I think," she says, laughing. "Now, what about you? Have any of your interviews panned out?"

I down the rest of my martini before flopping back in my chair.

I didn't expect to be job hunting for this long when I got laid off two months ago. I have a bachelor's degree in communications with a minor in journalism. My résumé is solid, and I have great contacts in the broadcasting industry. My references are stellar, too. I've sat for numerous interviews and applied for various positions, everything from a news writer to a weatherwoman—the latter out of desperation. I'm pretty sure it just entails reading the weather report. And, if not, I can guess when it will rain as well as anyone.

The response? *Crickets.*

It's disconcerting.

"I had an interview yesterday at a music label," I say. "And I met a podcaster this morning for coffee. Both went great, but I doubt I'll get a call back from either."

"What makes you say that?"

I shrug. "Gut feeling."

"Okay. Hear me out."

I groan.

"I have an idea," she says.

"That scares me."

"As it should." Her eyes dance with humor. "Remember when I took a weekend alone in Utah last year?"

I nod slowly. I'm unsure where this is going, but I know it will give me a headache.

"Well, I spent most of that weekend setting intentions for my life. I dreamed big. Created vision boards. I took a deep dive into who I am as a person and who I wanted to be. Where did I see myself in my personal life? Professionally? Emotionally? Spiritually?"

"Are those rhetorical questions?" I ask, grinning.

"Tease me all you want because all my intentions came true."

She sits back, crossing her arms over her chest with a smug smile.

"And I'm thrilled for you," I say, noticing an incoming text from my mom. "But it unnerves me to place my hopes and dreams into the hands of ... *does the universe have hands*?"

Sutton's annoyance at my failure to take her woo-woo seriously is written all over her pretty face.

"I love that it worked for you," I say. "But I'm more confident in using actionable items than vision boards and weekend retreats."

"Fair enough. But where have those actionable items gotten you lately?"

I gasp. "*The audacity*." Knowing I can't pretend she's wrong, I sigh. "Also, good point."

"Thank you. Now, humor me. What are your biggest dreams? What would you hope to find if you could see three years into the future?"

"That's easy. Employment. Cheap wine. And a new wardrobe to fit the body I earned by actually working out five times a week instead of sitting in the gym parking lot and warring over whether to go inside or leave to get chicken nuggets."

She narrows her eyes, shaking her head. The server, Bobby, momentarily interrupts her scowl by delivering another round of martinis. Sutton mumbles something that makes him laugh.

The alcohol warms my blood and loosens the muscles across the back of my neck. It's a nice respite from the stress I've been holding on to for the past few weeks.

I ponder Sutton's question while she chitchats with Bobby. *What is my biggest dream*? The straightforward question doesn't warrant the slight tightness in my chest, *but there it is*. If I don't nip this in the bud now, that tightness will grow.

I've considered this often lately. It's obvious that over the past few years, I stopped working toward a dream. Not only did I abandon my ambitions, but I stopped dreaming altogether. Life, heartbreak, and fear will do that to a person.

No one talks about this. There aren't trending books or podcasts for the dreamless crowd.

Someone needs to make that happen.

"Okay," Sutton says as Bobby heads for the bar. "Back to your dreams. Gimme."

"Honestly, I don't know. I could give you an answer, but it would be bullshit."

Her brows knit together. "Do you have any dreams at all?"

"I mean, not really. *I know that's a problem*," I say, cutting her off. "I need to figure out what I want to do with my life, but I'm not going to figure it out tonight. So let's talk about fun stuff like your wedding." I smile. "Did you decide on a date yet?"

Sutton's face lights up, and she leans against the table. "Kind of. We've decided on either September or October next year. I have no interest in sweating my way through a Tennessee summer wedding, and the spring is too soon. Besides, the foliage is beautiful in autumn, and I heard my chances of renting the Knopf Estate for the ceremony are better then."

"Well, I have a lot of time on my hands right now. If you need early planning help, I'm your girl."

"And my maid of honor, I hope."

I laugh. "You'll have a big problem on your hands if you even try to give that spot to someone else."

"Promise?"

"Yeah, of course. Why?" I ask, my stomach twisting as I take in the look on her face.

She rests her elbows on the table and nibbles her bottom lip. "Jeremiah picked his best man."

"So?"

She exhales a long, semi-shaky breath. "So he picked Ripley."

No, he did not.

I bite my tongue before I let out a yelp of protest.

"Jeremiah and I decided we will do everything we can to keep the two of you from having to coordinate on anything," she says earnestly. "But I had to pick you, and he had to pick Ripley. It would feel wrong if either of us chose someone else."

Internally, I scream. Outwardly, I try to look cool, calm, and collected but probably fail.

My storied past with Ripley Brewer began on my fifth day at Waltham Prep. It was a sweltering Friday evening in the West Gymnasium. *The Senior Mixer.* The night that Ripley humiliated me in front of our entire class.

It set the stage for every future interaction between us.

I'm not sure why I'm seemingly the only woman in the universe who can see beyond his sexy smirk and remain unfazed by his boy-next-door act. *No one is that perfect.* But instead of questioning his golden boy persona, our friends accept it. They lean into his storytelling abilities, absurd generosity, and how he teared up while showing us pictures of his new nephew, Arlo.

Everyone is so dazzled by him that it's ridiculous.

Why can't they see the arrogant, argumentative asshole I see?

We once argued for nearly an hour over the number of stairs in Jeremiah's house and had to be separated by our friends. We hotly debated the existence of pickles at a Fourth of July party. Blood was almost shed. Our most famous fight, however, was over a sale flyer from a grocery store that neither of us had ever visited. *Does a ten-for-ten sale mean you have to buy ten of the item to get them for a dollar each?* I called the store to prove I was right, but they were closed.

"Is that why you brought me here?" I ask as Bobby returns. "You wanted to liquor me up before you broke the news of Jeremiah's betrayal?"

"Betrayal?" Bobby asks, eyes wide.

Sutton snorts. "She's being dramatic."

I rest my chin in my hand and look up at the dark-eyed man handing Sutton more marinara. "I'm not being dramatic, Bobby. Her fiancé just chose Satan to be his best man in their wedding. Would I be a good friend if I wasn't concerned?"

"Satan, huh?" Bobby grins.

"Yup. *Satan*," I say, sighing sadly. "Sutton is trying to support her soon-to-be husband, and I respect that. But someone must fight for her."

"And that's you?" he asks.

I scoff. "*Yes, that's me*. Ripley will make this whole thing about him. I've seen it before—a thousand times, really."

"When?" Sutton asks, laughing. "Name one."

"Oh, let's see," I say. "What about when we all went to the hockey game and sat in his family's box?"

"Well, it *was* his family's box," Sutton says slowly.

"Fine. What about when we went to the lake for Jeremiah's birthday, and he brought a yacht—"

"It wasn't a yacht!"

Bobby's brows shoot to the ceiling. "He has a yacht?"

"No," Sutton says as I say the opposite.

I roll my eyes. "Trust me, Bobby. He'll find a way to make it about him. If Ripley isn't the center of attention ... Well, who knows what would happen because it's never happened."

Bobby nods warily, a cheeky grin slipping across his face. "I see what you're saying, but if he has a yacht ..."

I gasp, making him laugh.

"I need to go check on my other less entertaining guests now," he says. "I'll be back in a bit."

"Thank you," Sutton says, flashing him a soft grin as he dashes away.

Then she turns to me. "Look, I know this isn't ideal, but will this be an issue? You don't have to like him—"

"Good, because that's impossible."

"Just play nice. I need you to do this for me."

"Yeah, yeah, yeah," I say, sipping my martini.

Sutton leans to the side, her smile growing. I start to turn to see what she's looking at but stop in my tracks.

The hair on the back of my neck stands abruptly on end. Goose bumps ripple across my skin. Whiffs of expensive cologne—cedar and vanilla, if I'm not mistaken—nestle around me, trying to lure me into a false sense of comfort.

I set my jaw and brace myself.

Speak of the devil ...

"Hey, Sutton," Ripley says from behind me.

"Hi," she says.

A long, heavy pause settles across the table. I hold my breath, refusing to break the ice.

"Hello, Georgia."

Oof.

His voice is warm—rich, and smooth. My name rolls off his forked tongue as if it's being caressed. The two syllables are blurred and lazily sexy, and I hate that as much as I don't want to—he's only putting on a show for Sutton—I like it.

Bastard.

I affix an aloof look on my face and turn slowly. I'm not fully pivoted in my chair when a pair of ocean-blue eyes snatch my gaze and hold it hostage.

Ripley smirks. "Am I interrupting?"

"No, you aren't interrupting," Sutton says, warning me with a lilt to her tone. "We were just chatting."

"Looks intense," Ripley says, his gaze still trained on me. "What was it about?"

I narrow my eyes back at him. "The devil."

Chapter Two

Georgia

"Here we go," Sutton mutters, her shoulders sagging.

"The devil?" Ripley's smirk grows. "How is your family, by the way?"

"You're such a riot," I say, my voice edged in sarcasm. "Don't you have somewhere else to be? Hell, presumably?"

He grins. "I just entered the pits of hell. You always provide such a lovely welcome party. Don't they give you days off?"

A bright mockery invades his stare. My lips part to fire back a sharp retort, but I catch Sutton's silent plea. It begs me to play nice.

The thought of letting Ripley win this exchange is almost painful. If I stay quiet, he'll gloat—quietly, of course, because we're in public. But he'll know he won, and I'll know he won. And he'll know that I know he won, and living with that is unbearable even to consider.

Yet Sutton's hopeful eyes stab me in the heart. I *did* come to The Swill to spend time with her, and to celebrate her new project and engagement. And she doesn't ask much of me. *And* she is important to me; Ripley is not.

Ugh.

I sit back, take a deep breath, and adjust my features into a contrived serenity. The relief in Sutton's posture is immediate.

"It's your lucky day," I say through semi-gritted teeth.

With a deliberate casualness that's really a smug victory celebration, Ripley shifts his attention to a table of women across the room. They swoon beneath his gaze.

Despite my inherent dislike for the man and my frustration that no one ever sees beyond the exterior, I get it. Muscled thighs, a narrow waist, and shiny, copper-colored hair that looks like it's had fingers run through it all day—it *is* textbook appealing. And his whole approachable-gentleman-with-a-glimmer-of-bad-boy vibe is alluring—if you don't know better.

I get it.

I understand it.

I hate it.

He towers over me in tailored gray pants and a crisp white button-up. His sleeves are rolled to his mid-forearms, naturally showcasing his strength from a life of sports and a career in exercise physiology. As much as I don't want to admit it, he's ridiculously good-looking. If he'd keep his mouth shut, he'd be a ten.

"Why don't you go talk to your fan club and leave us alone?" I ask him.

He pulls his attention to me. "Are you jealous? We'll let you join. Don't be mad."

"*Oh, please.*"

"I love it when you beg."

His lips curve into a sardonic smile, and his eyes twinkle with mischief as he waits for me to explode.

I lean forward, ignoring the notes of his stupid cologne, and meet his stare. I give him a little smile of my own.

"Careful, Ripley. Your subconscious is slipping again."

"Is that what you think happened?"

"Of course. But it's okay. Just a little slip of the tongue."

The words are out before I can stop them. I flinch, knowing I just walked headfirst into a trap of my own making.

"Now, whose subconscious is slipping?" he asks, teasing me.

Dammit.

"Can you please leave?" I ask, huffing my displeasure.

"No. I'm meeting my brother Tate here in a few minutes. If you're not happy here, you could leave."

"I'd hate to waste a perfectly good martini."

He reaches down and swipes my glass. Before I can protest, he downs the entire thing—never breaking eye contact with me.

I bite back the string of profanity that's primed on the tip of my tongue because that's exactly what he wants. *He wants me to lose control.* It takes every ounce of self-restraint that I can muster to suppress my anger under an appearance of indifference.

"Why are you such a dick?" I ask.

Ripley leans down, close enough that I can smell the sweet citrus of my drink on his breath. "You really should stop thinking about my dick, Peaches."

My blood pressure rises. I hate when he calls me that—and he knows it.

"You really should get out of my face, asshole."

His gaze settles against mine, practically begging me to blink or to pull away. Instead, I move closer to him.

My senses spin at his proximity, fighting to stay balanced. *And not to throat-punch him.*

"So Ripley, did you say you're meeting Tate?" Sutton asks, her voice a few decibels louder than necessary. "I haven't seen him in a while. What's he been up to?"

Ripley stands tall, ripping his gaze away from mine like a sticky bandage that clings a little too hard.

I breathe deeply, hoping the fresh air settles me a bit. *What's the wedding day going to be like if he acts like this the entire time? Will he be asked to play nice?*

I hate how my heart pounds around him. Fight or flight always kicks in, and it takes a moment to recover. I hate it. *I hate him.*

"He's been traveling a lot. I've hardly seen him much either," Ripley tells Sutton.

"Is he traveling for work or pleasure?" Sutton asks.

Ripley chuckles. "I think Tate mixes the two pretty seamlessly."

Sutton laughs. I manage to eke out a smile for her benefit. It vanishes when Ripley catches my eye so he doesn't get confused and mistake my smiles for him.

"Tate wants my opinion on a few things before we finalize our purchase of the Tennessee Royals."

"The rugby team?" I ask.

He glances at me over his shoulder. He waits, presumably for me to say something more so he can jump down my throat. But I stay silent. I'm playing nice, even if it is giving me chest pains.

"Yes, the rugby team. My siblings and I are purchasing the franchise. My older brother Renn played pro."

"Thank you for assuming I'm one of the few women on the planet who hasn't searched Renn Brewer's shirtless pictures online."

His lips twist wryly.

I've discovered one vulnerability in Ripley's veneer over the years, and it has to do with his siblings. The six of them are known for being as thick as thieves. Ripley defends the others ferociously, whether they're right or wrong. Our friends say that he nearly beat the crap out of his father, Reid, when news broke that the old man had an altercation with Renn's now wife, Blakely. He's loyal to a fault.

But I've noticed that as proud and loyal as he is to them, they're a touchy subject. If I mention that Renn is hot, Ripley tenses. If I comment that Tate is hilarious or their older brother Gannon has freak-in-the-sheets vibes, he becomes edgy. It doesn't matter that Ripley is objectively the best-looking of them all and subjectively funny. He also has a certain sex appeal that's made me curious once or twice. And he knows all of this—except the last part. *Thank God.*

I can't help but poke around a little every now and then to get under his skin.

"If you two will excuse me for a moment, I need to make a quick phone call," Sutton says, standing with her phone in her hand. "It won't take long."

Ripley slides a hand into his pocket and rocks back on his heels, watching Sutton weave through the tables in the bar. The light above hits him perfectly, highlighting his high cheekbones, broad shoulders, and perfectly straight teeth. It's wholly unfair. I can't find a good angle in perfect light, plus a filter. This asshole stands in the middle of a bar, and the good angle finds him.

I reach for my martini, only to remember it's empty.

"You're paying for my drink," I say, flicking a fingernail against my glass.

"Ripley's buying Georgia a drink?" Tate appears at Ripley's side with an exaggerated look of surprise. "What is going on here? I haven't been gone long enough for hell to freeze over, have I?"

"Very funny," I say, smiling at the younger Brewer.

Unlike Ripley, Tate is a gem. There's nothing pretentious about him, and his self-deprecating humor softens his ego. He has a charming way of making everyone around him feel seen, and I've never witnessed him be anything but polite and good-natured.

Clearly, that's not genetic.

"Your brother drank my martini just to piss me off," I say. "So I told him he's paying for it."

Tate lifts a brow at Ripley.

"I didn't drink it to piss her off," Ripley tells him. "She said she couldn't leave because she hadn't finished her drink. I was helping expedite her departure."

"I bet you were," Tate says, shaking his head. "You know, I can't decide whether I'm relieved or disappointed that the two of you haven't turned over a new leaf. On the one hand, it would end a very entertaining era. On the other hand, I'm interested to see what that would look like."

"Well, don't get your hopes up," Ripley says, peering down at me. "She's as incorrigible as ever."

"*Oh, whatever,*" I say. "He's the one who drank my martini. I've just been sitting here."

"In purple boots," Ripley says, his brows arched to the ceiling.

I hold a leg to the side, showing off my boots ... and a bit of leg. "Aren't they cute?"

"Not really the word on the tip of my tongue," Ripley says, his gaze a little higher than the top of my boot.

"I bet not," Tate says, winking at me. "Where's Sutton?"

"Hey, Tate!" she says, reaching the table with her phone in her hand. "It's so good to see you."

An unwelcome blush creeps up my cheeks as I place my foot back on the floor.

Ripley and I glare at each other as Sutton invites them to join us. I scoot farther to my left to keep a respectable distance between Ripley and myself, as I'm afraid I might stab him in the leg with my fork if we sit too close.

Tate stops our server and orders two martinis and a beer for himself and Ripley.

"What's been going on with you?" Sutton asks Tate. "We haven't seen you in forever. Jeremiah said we should invite you for dinner soon now that we're settled in our new digs."

"That would be great. Let me know when, and I'll be there."

Tate smiles kindly at Sutton, and I can't help but wonder why Ripley can't be more like his brother. Sweet. Charming. *Human.*

"I've been on the go for the past three weeks straight, and I've barely had time to catch my breath," Tate continues. "As a matter of fact, I came here straight from the airport." He runs a hand through his hair that's a touch lighter than Ripley's. "I'm ready to spend some time at home and return to a routine. I miss my bed. I miss the gym. I even kind of miss Gannon."

Ripley chuckles.

"Speaking of the gym, did you ever run that 5K we were talking about at Jeremiah's birthday party?" Tate asks me.

"Good memory," I say. "But no. It turns out that I'm not a runner."

"I could've told you that before you bought your first pair of trainers," Sutton jokes.

I make a face at her, then turn to Tate. "I did start weightlifting after you told me to give it a shot. But can I ask you a question?"

Ripley rustles beside me.

"Sure," Tate says.

"I had been doing light weights at high reps, but a trainer in the gym told me to do heavy weights at low reps," I say. "Now I'm not sure what to do."

"I'm an exercise physiologist, you know," Ripley says.

"I know," I say, giving him a smile that anyone watching would think is friendly. "Anyway, *Tate,* I'm the maid of honor at an upcoming wedding and want to look exceptionally hot. And since I'm not a cardio girl, I need to figure out this weightlifting thing."

Tate's smirk sets deep in his cheeks as he watches Ripley from the corner of his eye.

Sutton laughs, wagging a finger across the table. "Weren't you just telling me a few minutes ago how I needed to ensure *I* get all the shine on my wedding day? And now you're saying you want to look exceptionally hot?" She shakes her head. "You little hypocrite."

"Look," I say, trying not to giggle. "I didn't say I wanted to outshine you. That's not possible, even if I tried. I only want to be irresistible to the single men wandering around the reception."

"Aren't you still dating Donovan Templesman?" Tate asks.

I take my drink from the server and thank him. "We ended things—*I ended things*—a couple of months ago."

"What happened?" Tate asks.

Ripley tips back his beer and pretends not to listen.

"Yeah," Sutton says, fighting a grin. "What happened, Georgia?"

I take a drink, letting the warmth of the alcohol flow through my veins. A nice buzz softens the edges of my irritation and helps me relax.

"To put it simply? He let the cookies run out," I say.

"He *what*?" Ripley asks, dumbfounded.

"He let the cookies run out," I repeat. "I know it sounds bizarre and silly, but it's important to me."

Tate tries to understand. "You broke up with a man because he ran out of cookies? Actual cookies, right? That's not a euphemism?"

I sigh. "Just listen. I love white chocolate and macadamia nut cookies, okay? They're my absolute favorite—especially the soft-baked kind. And once Donovan learned that about me, he always had them in his kitchen. Always. Without fail."

"Cheap date," Ripley mumbles.

I roll my eyes at him before continuing. "Donovan started talking about me moving in with him, and I fought against it. It was too soon, and I don't know, I didn't really feel like we were at that point. That made him mad. Shortly after, he stopped buying cookies."

Sutton nods, an approving smile on her lips.

"It wasn't the cookies that made me break up with him," I say, swirling my drink around in my glass. "It was that he ... I don't know, wanted to punish me?"

Donovan was so quick to take away something small that showed me he cared about me. It wasn't a big thing, really, but it showed me something fundamental about his character. There couldn't have been a bigger, redder flag.

"Anyway, I wasn't going to stay with someone who acted so childish simply because he didn't get his way," I say with a shrug.

Ripley's brows pinch together. The way he studies me makes me uneasy, so I look away.

My phone buzzes on the table, and my mother's name flashes on the screen. I know she wants to talk about her Charity Club drama, which can wait. But it's an excellent excuse to leave—especially because Sutton will be looking for a reason to go soon, too.

I down the rest of my drink and then fish a few bills from my wallet.

"Sutton, I know you said you needed to be out of here by seven thirty," I say. "It's about that time, and I need to get going, too."

She checks her watch. "You're right. Jeremiah will be home from work soon and promised to take me for Thai tonight."

I plop some cash on the table.

"I'll pay for your drinks," Ripley says.

"Oh, I know you will," I say. "It's really the least you can do for barging into our girl time and drinking my martini. I'm just chipping in for the tip."

Tate chuckles. "Okay, I'm glad you two didn't make peace. Watching you bicker is free entertainment."

"Happy you enjoyed the show," I say.

I stand, tugging the ends of my shorts down. It doesn't help much —there's not much length to work with—but it's better than nothing.

Ripley stares straight ahead, intentionally not looking at me. *Good.*

"I'd say it was good seeing you again, Ripley, but that would be a lie," I say.

"Likewise."

He turns his head, catching my eyes with his once again. Something twinkles in his baby blues ... probably bullshit.

Sutton says her goodbyes, and we walk out of The Swill. I sway my hips a little more than necessary in case Ripley *is* watching.

Not that I really care if he is or isn't. But I know my ass looks great in these shorts, and I won't miss the slightest opportunity to make him crazy.

Chapter Three

R ipley

That woman drives me crazy.

Georgia's perfume lingers in the air long after she's gone. The sweetness of honey and the warmth of vanilla are irritating and intoxicating—just like her.

I try my best to ignore her because she gets too deep under my skin. She has since the first day of our senior year. She walked down the hallway to her locker, books clutched to her chest and ponytail swinging behind her. For the briefest moment, her soft, golden-colored eyes met mine, and I wobbled on my feet. I was both drawn to and terrified by the beautiful brunette in a way my teenage brain hadn't encountered before.

That might've been the last time she looked at me without threatening to off me with her bare hands.

"I think she's gone," Tate says.

"Who?"

"Georgia."

I turn to face him and ignore the conspiratorial grin on his face.

"You were just sitting there and staring at the exit," he says. "I was starting to think you thought she was coming back."

I sigh, bringing my beer to my lips.

"I was surprised to walk in and see the two of you talking civilly," he says casually. "It almost looked like you were getting along for a moment."

"Yeah, well, you caught the ten seconds she wasn't being a total monster."

"So what, you noticed she was without her monster vibes and decided to say hello?"

I snort. "Hardly. I tried to avoid her, but Sutton saw me before I could hide."

He laughs. "I love that you hide from Georgia Hayes."

"You say that like you think I'm scared of her."

"Aren't you?"

I flip him a dirty look that makes his laugh grow louder.

"What's going on with you?" I ask, picking at the label on my beer. "Are you back for a while, or will Gannon have you leaving again next week?"

"I think my nonstop travel days are slowing down. The pressure is easing now that Dad has taken the plea deal and has been sentenced. People are starting to move on. Gannon is doing a great job leading the company, and that's helping to gain back investor confidence. We have some work to do, mostly public facing, but we're getting there. I'm not having to fight quite as hard."

I smirk. "Good, because you're a shit fighter."

"*Oh, okay.* You spent some time at a gym in Vegas, and now you think you're a fighting expert?"

"I'm just saying, the president of the world's biggest mixed martial arts studio asked me to help get his fighters in shape."

"Emphasis on *getting his fighters in shape* and not *teaching them to fight.*"

"I sparred a little with some of the guys." I take a drink, remembering how fun the experience was in Vegas. "It made me wish Dad would've let me take boxing when I was younger instead of forcing soccer on me."

Tate's features sober. "In retrospect, it was probably a choice out of self-preservation."

"No shit."

My insides tighten as my mind wanders to our father.

"Speaking of Dad," Tate says, "that's one of the reasons I wanted to talk to you tonight."

"What about him?"

"Well, it's not about him, per se. I got a call from Jonah Spaulding yesterday."

I settle back in my chair and prepare myself for the number of ways this conversation could veer off the rails because Jonah Spaulding rarely calls to chat. Sure, there's the occasional golf tournament or charity event invitation. But as the son of one of our mother's attorneys—the badass woman who brought Dad's counsel to his knees—Jonah was brought up writing contracts and negotiating settlements. When he calls, it's usually to do business.

"And?" I ask.

"He needs a favor."

Interesting. "We owe him."

"I know. And I offered you as tribute."

I chuckle, ignoring the attempts of my *fan club*, as Georgia called them, to get my attention as they leave. "Oh, you did, did you?"

"Trust me. This is one role you can conquer better than any of us. I have complete faith in you."

"That definitely eases all of my concerns."

Tate laughs. "I'll forward you his email with the details. You'll love it."

"Doubtful."

"So how was Vegas, anyway?" he asks before taking a long pull of his beer. "Did you have a good time?"

"Yeah, it was good. There is a lot of talent to work with, but these new guys don't know a thing about taking care of themselves. Their idea of balanced nutrition is massive doses of protein and a citrus-flavored energy drink."

"Did you get them on the right track?"

"I tried." I pause to nod to Bobby that we need another round of beers. "The management team asked me to stay a few more weeks because the guys seemed to respond well to me, but I told him I had to get back."

"I'm assuming you have a full schedule around here."

I nod. "Yeah, the Arrows are keeping me busy. I'm meeting with some of the players for individual assessments tomorrow. The head of baseball operations has some questions about team nutrition, too."

"Great. Renn should control the Royals by the start of next month. Be prepared for that."

We exchange a glance before chuckling.

None of us know what to think about Renn managing the Royals. It might be the best thing ever—the man does understand the ins and outs of rugby. It might also be the worst since he's never managed a lemonade stand. Either way, we'll back Renn because that's what we do ... even Jason, although he thinks Renn is getting in way over his head.

I shift in my seat. *At least he's contributing to the family ...*

Although it was unintended, Tate's mention of Renn and the Royals gnaws at something deep inside me.

Tate picks up his phone and types away furiously, so I lean back and take a long, deep breath.

My siblings are all beasts. Bianca is a genius who, instead of doing what was expected of her and taking over Brewer Group, chose to do what was best for her and walked away. *Such a little badass.* Gannon took over Brewer Group and is successfully leading it out of the mess Dad made. Jason is the CEO of his own airline. Renn is expanding our holdings with the Royals. Tate has been instrumental in helping to restore our family's reputation.

And then there's me.

Bobby hands us fresh beers and carries our empty bottles away.

I love what I do each day. Working with people and helping them become healthier and happier is exactly what I chose to do with my life, and it was the right choice. But sometimes, it's apparent that I'm not as valuable to the family business as everyone else. If you remove any of the others, there's a glaring hole. If you take me out of the equation, life goes on.

The only person to ever mention this fact was Dad, and a part of me understands he was spouting off at the mouth because he was pissed. I *did* have my arm pressed on his throat while pinning him to the wall and threatening to kill him for assaulting Renn's wife. Still, he said it, and I can't quite forget it.

"*Shit*," Tate mumbles, dropping his phone unceremoniously to the table.

"What?"

"Nothing." He runs his hand through his hair. "Carys is just dating an asshole she met at a tailgate party last fall, and she wants to complain about him all the time. I told her I'm tired of hearing it."

I hide a smile. "Well, I'm sure she'll stop complaining now."

Tate rolls his eyes. "She won't stop until they inevitably break up. Then she'll date someone new and complain about him. It's a never-ending cycle with that girl."

Carys has been Tate's sidekick since college. They're essentially the same person in different bodies. Both are good-looking, funny, and surprisingly intelligent once you get past the party-loving exterior. I used to think they'd end up together, but not anymore.

"I need a new best friend," Tate says.

"She tried that once, and *you* melted down. Remember?"

He grins. "I didn't *melt down*."

"That's not what she said."

He glances at his phone screen, then turns it face down on the table. "Are we still going golfing on Saturday?"

"No, Gannon called it off. He has a meeting in Atlanta, and Renn wants to spend all the time he can at home with his family before the Royals acquisition goes through."

"How's the baby, anyway? I need to go over and see that little shit before he forgets that I'm his favorite uncle."

"He can't forget something he never knew." I smile. "Arlo is growing like a weed. Every time I see him, he changes. He has huge hands like Renn and his mama's lips. And he's lost all his hair."

"Really? Is that normal?"

I shrug. "I don't fucking know. They don't seem too worried about it, and Renn worries about *everything*. So I guess it's all right."

"Do you think you'll have kids someday?"

I stretch my legs under the table and think about his question. I always expected that I'd have kids. Holding Renn's son makes me think it would be amazing to have a little guy of my own. But after these past couple of years with our family, I'm not so sure I want to risk it anymore.

"Maybe," I say, wincing. "What about you?"

"I want ten of them."

I snort. "Ten? Really?"

"It's a good even number, and it's just four more than all of us. Think how cool it would be if there were four more of us after me. That'd be great."

"Would it, though? You've lived your life as the baby of the family. Four more, and you're suddenly a middle child. That might change your mind about things."

"Yes, I think it would be great. Phenomenal, really. I've been thinking about having kids a lot lately," Tate says.

"You might want to think in order." I take a drink, enjoying the cool liquid slide smoothly down my throat. "Better find a good woman first." *Someone extremely patient to deal with my brother and his craziness.*

He points at me. "And that's why I haven't gotten started yet. I can't find the right woman."

"Yeah, well, me either, but I'm also not looking."

"I could hook you up with one of Carys's friends," Tate offers. "She has some hot ones, you know."

"Yeah, I know."

His offer hangs in the air between us.

The idea of hooking up with one of Carys's friends doesn't really do anything for me. Sure, they're all gorgeous, and I don't doubt that I'd have a good time. But every time I've hung out with her circle, it's been ... boring. There's nothing to talk about. No spark. Nothing that keeps me up at night.

I don't know what it is that's causing my dry spell, but I'm definitely in one. That's concerning, but it's even more concerning that I don't really care.

"They're not my type," I say.

"Since when?"

"Since ... now."

He nods as if he's deciding whether to worry about me.

"I know that sounds crazy," I say. "But I just don't vibe with that group. They're great girls from what I can tell, but ... maybe I'm getting old."

"You're thirty," he deadpans.

I shrug.

"When was the last time you had a date?" he asks.

"Oh, I don't know. I've seen a few women here and there. It's not like I've vowed celibacy or anything."

"When was your last steady girlfriend?"

"The end of last year, I think."

He watches me pointedly.

"Look, I know what you're thinking," I say with a sigh. "But I'm just ... I'm tired of dating. I'm tired of trying to convince someone that I'm worthy of their time. I'm sick of the entire song and dance of spending time with someone I don't care about when I could be alone doing something I love."

"Like what?"

"Hanging out with Waffles, taking him to the pet store for new puppy toys."

Tate laughs. "I can't with you." He glances at his phone again and sighs. "Okay, I need to go. I haven't even been home yet and am on the verge of crashing."

"Get out of here. I'll get the check."

He stands and clasps a hand on my shoulder. "Thanks, Ripley. I'll talk to you tomorrow. And I'll send you that email as soon as I get home. I don't have my work email on my phone."

"No worries."

He gives my shoulder a final pat before heading for the door.

I settle back in my chair and drink the rest of my beer, taking in the scene around me. The Swill has gotten busier since I arrived. Nearly every table is filled. The music is louder than before, and the customer base has changed from businesslike patronage to a more relaxed crowd.

Georgia's purple boots would fit in perfectly now.

I rub my forehead, wincing at the start of a headache.

The day has been long and busy, starting well before sunrise and going full speed until I walked into The Swill. Meeting Tate here was the last thing I wanted to do this evening ... until I saw Georgia. Dealing with her is always the last thing on my wish list.

Flames lick inside my stomach, still smoldering from the fire Georgia lights when she's around. I exhale in a futile attempt at recentering myself.

I hate that she affects me this way. After all these years, I should be able to manage my reactions to her. It's not that I haven't tried. I've avoided her. Ignored her. I've even reminded myself that reacting to her taunts and glares is exactly what she wants, and by doing that, I only bolster her life choices—mainly to piss me off.

Yet I can't.

I'm caught on this decade-long roller coaster with Georgia Hayes and can't get off.

We're at the same parties. We celebrate the same birthdays. We go to the same weddings. Hell, we're in the same fucking group text.

I can't date women who wear perfume that reminds me of her. I stopped seeing a woman who worked with Georgia because she wouldn't stop telling stories about their day. I returned a shirt my mother bought me for Christmas because it was purple—Georgia's favorite color. I couldn't wear it without seeing her stupid smug smile and knowing she'd like it, and I don't need my days ruined over a shirt.

I hate that she gets so deep under my skin. I hate how damn stunning she is. After all these years, I should be able to manage my reactions to her.

She's already ruined my life in so many ways.

I fucking hate her for it.

And that won't be changing anytime soon.

Chapter Four

Georgia

"And then Eloise acts like we don't know what she was doing in Miami," my mother says about her friend while peering over my shoulder. "Add more cheese."

I unceremoniously drop another handful of shredded mozzarella onto the frozen pizza. "Better?"

"Better." Mom kisses my cheek. "Anyway, Eloise comes waltzing into the club meeting with a glow you only get from one thing."

"The Florida sun?"

"*No.*"

"You said she was in Miami."

"There's more than the sun in Miami, sweetheart." She grins mischievously. "I'm talking about a hot twentysomething lifeguard who doesn't need a pill to get it up."

I chuckle, shoving the pizza into the preheated oven.

My mother was waiting in the driveway when I returned home from The Swill. She walked toward me with a bottle of wine in one hand and a frozen pizza in the other. And on her face? An unmistakable twinkle of forthcoming gossip. Did I feel like listening to her antics? Nope, not even a little bit. But she's my mom, and she's always welcome.

"You don't know if that's what she was doing or not," I say. "Don't spread rumors."

"If I were getting laid by a college-aged lifeguard with a body made for sinning, I'd want people spreading rumors."

Shaking my head, I refill our wineglasses.

"As a matter of fact, if I'm ever in that position, consider it your job to tell everyone you know," she says. "Pretend it's behind my back, though. I don't want to look like I'm bragging. And if you aren't sure about a detail, embellish."

"What is wrong with you?" I ask, laughing.

"Oh, honey. We don't have time to get into all that in one night."

That's for damn sure.

Our laughter follows us into the living room of my small townhome. The blinds are closed, creating a coziness that I crave. Nothing is better than curling up on the couch under a fuzzy blanket and watching a romantic comedy—preferably alone so no one talks while I watch the movie.

We get situated, Mom stretching across the couch and me tucking into my lavender papasan that's seen better days.

"What did you do today?" I ask before taking a sip of wine.

"I worked at the consignment shop for a while this morning, then met the girls for Charity Club this evening." Her eyes light up. "You should see this dress I snatched from the shop today. It's so stinkin' cute."

"Why don't you ever buy me the stuff you think is 'stinkin' cute'?"

She rolls her eyes. "Because I buy that stuff for me. Buy your own shit."

I roll my eyes back at her, making her giggle.

Mom and I have a good relationship, for the most part. It's definitely gotten better over the years. We have dinner together once or twice a week, share clothes—mostly, she steals mine—and talk daily. But our interactions aren't exactly typical.

I pick her up from bars more frequently than she's ever received a drunken call from me. She asks me for advice more often than I go to her. I know her favorite color, band, and the results of her last mammogram. *Does she know mine?* Probably not.

This fact bothered me for a long time, but I've learned to live with it. It's just who she is as a person. I think my father struggled with this aspect of her, and the divorce really stole her sparkle for a while. She's back now, though, and sparklier than ever.

"How was work?" she asks as her fingers fly across her phone screen.

I stare at her. It takes almost a full minute for her to realize I didn't respond.

"What?" she asks, looking up. "What did I say?"

"You do remember that I haven't worked in two months, right?"

Her phone drops to her lap. "But I thought you started work at a music studio downtown?"

"*No*, I interviewed at Mason Music but didn't get a callback."

"I swear you told me you were hired."

"Well, I didn't. I promise."

Her face twists in confusion. "So what are you going to do? Do you have any leads?"

"What do you mean?" I ask, struggling to keep my annoyance at bay. "I'm looking for a job. My job right now is finding a job."

"I know that. I'm just wondering if you've found anything promising. Two months is a long time, Georgia."

No shit.

I swallow my response, knowing it would undoubtedly be thick with sarcasm. That would trigger a melodramatic reaction from her, and I don't have the time or emotional reservoir to deal with a dramatic Felicity Hayes tonight. I have bigger fish to fry ... like finding a job.

The oven buzzes, alerting us that the pizza is ready. I glance back at my mother and find her busy typing away once again. *Figures.*

"I'll get that," I say, dropping my feet to the floor.

I set my glass on the coffee table and head to the kitchen. The wonderful aroma of tomatoes and spices fills the air, making my stomach rumble. I find my oven mitts and remove our dinner from the oven.

Just as I place it on the trivet, my phone rings on the other side of the counter. Sutton's name glows on the screen, instantly lifting my spirits.

"Hey," I say, stacking the mitts next to a vase filled with flowers that died last week. Then I turn off the oven.

"Hey, what are you up to?"

"I just took a pizza out of the oven for me and Mom. I thought you were going for Thai?"

"We're on our way home. I'm in the car with Jeremiah." The phone rustles. "You're on speaker. Say hi."

"Hey, Jeremiah," I say, leaning against the island.

"Hey, Georgia. Thanks for getting my girl out of The Swill on time. Ten more minutes, and we wouldn't have made our dinner reservation."

"That's what I'm here for," I say.

They exchange words that I can't quite make out. Sutton's giggles are the only clear sounds.

"So Jeremiah has to work all day on Saturday, and I was thinking you could come over and hang out by the pool with me," Sutton says. "We could talk about wedding details and make cocktails. It would be fun."

I smile. "Sounds like a plan. What time do you want me to come over?"

The phone disconnects from the speaker, and Sutton's voice is crisp again. "How does noon work?"

"You know I have absolutely nothing going on right now. Whatever time works for you works for me."

"Cool. I'll see you at noon then. *And* if you happen to be online looking at wedding stuff, I'm thinking about going with peach and gold. I think that would be beautiful in the fall."

I laugh. "Is that a hint that I should start looking for ideas?"

"That was definitely a hint that you should start looking for ideas." She laughs. "I'm a terrible decision-maker about things like this."

"Don't worry. I got you."

"I know you do. It's one of the million reasons I love you most."

"Hey!" Jeremiah objects.

Sutton giggles again. "I'll see you Saturday, Georgia."

"Bye."

"Bye."

"Who was that?" Mom asks, making me jump.

"Dammit." I suck in a hasty breath. "You scared the shit out of me."

"Sorry." She moseys to a drawer and pulls out a pizza cutter. "Was that Sutton?"

I grab two plates from a cabinet. "Yes. She wants me to hang out with her this weekend since Jeremiah will be working. Guess we're going to have a pool day."

"When is she getting married?"

I hold out a plate, and Mom plops a piece of pizza on it.

"Next fall," I say. "I'm sure it will be magical and wonderful. I can't imagine Jeremiah letting her have anything but a fairy-tale wedding."

Mom's shoulders stiffen as she takes a slice for herself. I ignore the bubble of uneasiness in my stomach.

Despite all our differences, one thing Mom and I share is our wariness of happy endings. Marriage was tumultuous and constraining for her. Falling in love with my father meant suffering through affairs and making herself vulnerable in a way that wasn't just uncomfortable but also unhealthy. Watching them struggle to like each other when they were supposedly in love wasn't healthy nor fun for me. And then my father turning his back on me post-divorce, *post-tuition*, was devastating. Neither of us has had a good experience in relationships since.

Mom can't talk about weddings and relationships without growing tense, and she's written both off completely. In her mind, there isn't a man in the world worth the risk of being destroyed yet again.

I'm different. I love the idea of weddings and relationships. I'm just not sure either is for me ... and I'm afraid to dream of the possibility.

"I hope she gets herself a good attorney before signing a prenup," she says, heading back to the living room.

"I'm sure she'll protect herself."

"Love can make people too trusting. You should ask her if she has lawyered up. Tell her I know a few good ones if she needs a recommendation."

"I'm not bringing up a prenup with my best friend when she just got engaged," I say, taking my seat again. "If I felt like I had to jump into protection mode, I would've said something to her before now. I wouldn't be a Jeremiah fan at all."

She takes a bite of pizza, chewing a little rougher than necessary. "So you like Jeremiah?"

"Yeah. He's good to her. He's not just her fiancé, and he's not just her friend." I take a bite and consider what I'm trying to say. "They're a team. Equals. He wants her to succeed as much as he wants to be a success himself."

"That's what you think now. Wait until a year has passed, and the sex isn't fun anymore, and real life hits them." She sighs. "I hate to be a Debbie Downer here, but someone has to be the voice of reason."

My lips twist at the irony of Mom being the voice of reason.

"Speaking of fun sex, has Donovan called you?" she asks with a little grin.

Of course, she's suddenly engaged in the conversation. We're talking about sex, not something as silly as my unemployment.

Exhaustion begins to creep into my bones.

"I don't want to talk about this with you," I say, although I'm certain she won't drop the subject.

"So has he called?"

I sigh. "A couple of times, but I didn't answer. Once I'm done, I'm done, you know."

She chuckles. "Yes, I know. And you better be careful, or you'll end up alone like me."

"Who knows? I might."

Mom sets down her plate and picks up her wine, settling back against the cushions. "Is that what you want? To be alone? Seeing your friends marry and start families isn't making you want the same thing?"

She eyes me carefully, almost as if she's afraid of my answer.

My chest pulls tight as I consider her question—one that I've been mulling over for a while. A part of me thinks that if I found Mr. Perfect, getting married and having babies would be the endgame. The idea of having the standard fairy tale like Sutton is exciting ... for a moment. Then it makes me sweat.

Even when I consider having a family, I immediately envision the end. Where there's black, there's white. There's a sun and a moon—a start and an end.

It's the end that stops me from heading down that path.

It's the end that I fear.

"I don't know what I want," I say when I realize she's waiting for an answer. "But it doesn't matter because unless I found the absolute perfect man, I wouldn't entertain settling down."

Her body dips into the cushions. "Good. Now, let's talk about something else. What did you do today?"

Thank God. "I had a couple of interviews, then I met Sutton at The Swill."

"What's that?"

"A little bar near Jeremiah's and her house. She said it was a dive bar, so I went in like this." I motion toward my cutoffs and shirt. "Let's just say there was not one neon sign in the whole place."

She smiles. "Yikes."

"I know. And then Ripley Brewer walked in …"

Mom's icy glare freezes the words as they tumble past my lips.

Shit.

The mention of his last name cools the warmth of the evening. It doesn't matter how fired up I get about him, it won't be enough to thaw Mom's response. I always forget she hated them first—that she hated them before I even knew them.

"Ripley is friends with Jeremiah and stopped to say hello to Sutton," I say.

She hums.

"I'm sorry," I say. "I didn't mean to bring them up."

She places her glass down with a clink against the tabletop. "It's fine. I saw Reid got sentenced and will spend the rest of his life behind bars for his crimes. That made me feel a bit better."

I give her a small smile, but she doesn't see it. She's too consumed by her own memories to notice.

It wasn't until the Friday of the Senior Mixer, the night I came home crying, that I learned that my mom knew the Brewers. But it wasn't until later, well into my freshman year of college, that I realized *how* she knew them.

It was after her divorce, and Reid had given her a fake name and purported to be a bachelor looking for romance. He love-bombed her, and she fell hard. It wasn't until she saw him in the news that she realized he was a billionaire business mogul—a *married* billionaire business mogul.

It was her second heartbreak and too close on the heels of the first. I saw her cry more over him than I recall her sobbing over my father.

It was also the last time she fell in love.

She stands abruptly, taking her plate to the kitchen. "What is he like now? Ripley, I mean."

I stand, puzzled, and follow her into the kitchen. She never wants to talk about the Brewers. *Ever.*

"He's still an asshole," I say. "Not much has changed on that front."

"Well, stay away from him. Trust me. If he's anything like his father, he can be ridiculously sexy, handsome, charming, and hard to resist."

I snort.

"*But resist him,*" she says, staring at me intently. "If you ever do anything I ask of you, let it be this."

I laugh, refilling my wineglass. "Mother, you have nothing to worry about there. Ripley is the only enemy I have in this world."

"Good. Now fill my glass, and let's change the subject again."

"Sounds like an excellent plan to me."

I fill her glass to the brim and then watch her slurp the top as she moves across the townhouse. All I can do is shake my head.

Me? Fall for Ripley Brewer?

"*You really should stop thinking about my dick, Peaches.*"

I snort and take a long, slow drink.

Not in a million fucking years.

Chapter Five

Georgia

Music carries across Sutton's backyard on a warm, gentle breeze. Beads of sweat roll down my chest, catching in my bikini top. I close my eyes, relishing the moment of relaxation, and listen to the fountain splash into the pool in the distance.

"If I lived here, I wouldn't leave this spot," I say, appreciating the buttery-soft chaise cushions. "Are these the chairs that were on backorder for sixteen years?"

She laughs. "Yup. The closest Jeremiah and I have ever been to breaking up was over these chairs. If he has a fault, it's impatience when he *really* wants something."

"Like he wanted you."

"And other things." She wiggles her white-painted toes. "We've been discussing trying for a baby as soon as we're married."

Really? I swallow my surprise. "How do you feel about that?"

She rolls onto her side to face me. "I know I always said that I wasn't in any rush to have children, but I'm slowly changing my mind."

I turn, too, and remove my sunglasses.

"Why are you reconsidering?" I ask.

"I know what you're thinking—that Jeremiah might be pressuring me into parenthood because he's been very vocal about wanting a ton of kids."

Exactly.

"But it's really not that, Georgia. When I thought about having kids before, the first things that popped into my head were negative. I'd have no free time. Traveling would be a pain in the ass. Kids are expensive." She looks down the length of her body. "I've worked hard for these abs, and you know they'd never be the same."

I give her a soft smile. She's given me that list of reasons a hundred times, but instead of agreeing with her, I remain silent. Sometimes she works through things by saying them aloud, and I'll always be her safe space when she needs to navigate life.

"But now, when I think about it ..." Her smile grows. "I imagine Jeremiah's strong arms holding a tiny baby with my eyelashes and his cheekbones. I can see him in the pool with our child, teaching him or her to swim. And I feel like I *belong* in that scenario. When I think about it, I get a lump in my throat in the best way. I can't explain it."

"You don't have to explain it. Sometimes you can't explain feelings."

She wrinkles her nose at me.

"And it's no one's business besides you and your husband's, anyway. You'll know what's right for you," I say.

She holds my smile for a moment and then turns onto her back. "I don't know why I feel better now, but I do."

I chuckle to myself and roll onto my back, too.

My body sinks into the cushion, nice and relaxed from the heat. I haven't had a decent night's sleep since my pizza party with Mom two nights ago. When the townhouse stills for the night and nothing distracts me, my thoughts return to her. *"Two months is a long time, Georgia."*

I've tried not to panic over my unemployment. I've ignored the statistics that the current average rate of joblessness is nine months. *I can't afford to be unemployed for nine months.* Instead, I've been focusing on what I can do to help the situation. But Mom's words dig into my confidence—ruffling my fear that I won't be able to find work and will wind up ... at her house.

The thought makes me ill.

"Things have a way of working out," Sutton says, almost offhandedly.

"What do you mean?"

"I don't know. I was just thinking." She wiggles her toes again. "Two years ago, I was twenty-seven and terrified that I'd wind up alone forever. But look at me now. I'm on the cusp of having more than I even dared to dream."

"It's not that hard to imagine. You met your soulmate."

Her head whips to mine with wide eyes. "Excuse me? Did you confirm the existence of soulmates?"

I roll my eyes. "I've never said I didn't believe in them. I said that I don't necessarily believe that everyone has one, and I don't know that there's one for me. Get your facts straight."

She laughs. "Hey, speaking of soulmates, did I tell you what happened yesterday?"

"If you did, I don't remember," I say, reaching for my iced water.

"Okay, so there was one piece of my project at work that I hadn't quite figured out. We plugged a solution in for it to keep the train moving, so to speak, but it was still wonky to me. I couldn't figure it out. But then, someone in the office said they lost their phone and was terrified someone would find it, break into it, and look at their search history."

I make a face. "Yeah. That's my worst nightmare."

Sutton's brows lift.

"What?" I ask, taking a sip of water, then putting my tumbler down. "I look up some really weird shit when I can't sleep."

"Such as ...?"

"Okay. I was watching a documentary about astronauts, and I wondered how they poop in space. So I looked it up."

Sutton bursts out laughing.

"Don't tell me you haven't looked up odd things," I say.

"I've never looked up the bathroom habits of astronauts." She bites her lip to keep from laughing but fails. "What else do you search?"

"What color is lightning?" I pull my sunglasses over my eyes. "Men speaking in Italian. *So hot.*" I hum while I think. "What sign is most compatible with Taurus? Poisonous flowers. How to spell Mississippi. Do kangaroos really fight people? How long until you bleed out if you cut the tip of your finger? *Porn.*"

Sutton gives up and howls with laughter.

"If someone got ahold of that without knowing me, imagine the picture that would be painted," I say. "They'd think I was an illiterate teenage boy."

"I can't with you." She shakes her head, getting herself together. "But, in that case, you'll hate my idea."

"For what?"

"The one thing I didn't have nailed down was how the two people on the show would be matched. We're handpicking the first two people to shoot the pilot, so there isn't actual matchmaking at work right off. But we needed to have an interesting way to say this guy and this girl are a potential love connection."

My jaw drops. "You are not going to match them by their search histories."

"We are." Her smile is wide and bright. "It's perfect! What you look up is the essence of who you are, right?"

"It's the essence of who I am when I think no one will ever know."

"*Exactly.*" Her amusement at my reaction is written across her face. "We can play this in so many ways. It's fun. It's relatable because everyone fears being judged—and being judged for your search history? *The drama.*"

I side-eye her and frown. "Yeah. Drama is right. Good luck with that. I hope this show is a success, but I'm afraid I'm starting to doubt that anyone will want to participate."

The patio door slides open. Jeremiah steps into the backyard, his gaze going straight to Sutton.

"Hey!" She sits up, beaming. "I thought you were working all afternoon."

"This is my time, dude. Go away," I say, grinning at him.

"Accounting is behind, so half of the work I was trying to do today is stalled until they complete the files," he tells Sutton. Then he looks at me. "I brought sandwiches from Stupey's as a peace treaty. Does that help?"

I pretend to consider it. "It helps a little."

He laughs, but there's an edge to it—one I can't overlook.

The energy around us shifts, swirling around as if announcing something ... or someone. My stomach twists in response, and I sit up, curious. My curiosity grows deeper at the amusement on Jeremiah's face.

"What?" I ask, my brows pulled together.

"Remember that we have a peace treaty," he says.

I heave a breath and drag my attention inch by inch back to the patio just in time to catch Ripley stepping onto the concrete.

You've got to be kidding me.

He runs a hand through his hair. His chin tilts slightly down as he looks at me through his thick lashes and watches me warily.

I keep my gaze trained on his face and not on how his board shorts emphasize his powerful, muscular body. *Asshole.*

He walks toward us with a nonchalance that burns me.

"Jeremiah." I say his name so sharp that it could cut glass. "Consider our treaty null and void."

"But I got you sandwiches," he says, almost singsong-ing the sentence. "And a blondie. I know you love blondies."

"Yes, I do." Ripley stops next to his friend, smiling smugly. "Ladies, I would say that I'm sorry for interrupting, but I'm not a liar."

Sutton stares holes in the side of my face, so I bite my tongue instead of calling him out.

"Are you hungry?" Jeremiah asks. "I'm starving. I got out of here early this morning and haven't eaten a bite today."

Sutton hops to her feet. "*Jeremiah.* You should've woken me up, and I would've fixed you something."

"I'm a grown-up who can fix his own breakfast. And you were sleeping too peacefully to bother."

"Let's get you some food," she says. "Do you want to eat, Georgia?"

"Yeah. Let's head in. I'm baking out here, anyway."

Jeremiah wraps a hand around her and leads her to the house ... leaving Ripley and me behind.

"For the record, I had no idea you were going to be here," Ripley says, his gaze raking down my body as I stand.

I flash him the dirtiest look I can muster. *One that could freeze hell.* I'm sure he renders women speechless when he appreciates their bodies, but not me. I couldn't give a shit if he likes what he sees or not.

But, if he wants to look, I'll give him a show ... and then embarrass him for it.

I bend slowly to grab my tumbler, the weight of his attention heavy on my ass. *So predictable.*

"Staring is rude, Mr. Brewer," I say.

"It's kind of hard to miss."

I gasp, spinning around to face him. My face flushes in embarrassment. "And exactly what is that supposed to mean?"

"What do you think it means?"

"If it means what I think it means, you can fuck off."

He scoffs, rolling his eyes. "It means your ass was in my face with a scrap of fabric barely covering anything. What do you want me to do?"

"Not making assholish comments about it would be an excellent start."

"I ... *no*. Nope. I'm not going there." He grinds his teeth together and shakes his head. A growl rumbles through the air. "You could literally turn anything into an argument."

"I'm not sure what sort of a reply you were after when you basically insinuated that my ass was so big you couldn't ignore it." My eyes narrow. "Does that angle work for you with other women? Or were you simply trying to be a dick?"

He squares his shoulder to mine and peers down at me. His eyes are lasered in on my face, making me gasp from the intensity.

"*Or* let's try this," he says, lifting a brow cockily. "What reaction were *you* after when you intentionally bent over in front of me? Just kidding. I don't have to ask. I *know* that gets men's attention. So am I right to think you were trying to get mine?"

You bastard. I ball my free hand at my side.

"Oh, did I hit a nerve?" His soft voice is mocking. Amusement dances across his stupidly handsome face. "Did you get called out for wanting—practically begging—for my attention?"

"*Please*," I say. "If you want to know the truth, I think *you* wanted *my* attention, and that's why you were staring, which, may I add, doesn't really jive with your fake I'm-such-a-gentleman persona. You should work on that."

My heart pounds as sweat from the heat, anger, and a little embarrassment trickles down my chest.

I'm most angry that the fucker is right—I did want his attention. The problem is that he thinks I wanted it because I think it's a trophy. *The great Ripley Brewer likes my ass.* And while that is a *small, tiny* feather in my cap, that wasn't the reason for my actions.

I wanted to have the upper hand.

"There are many things I need to work on, Miss Hayes, but my *gentleman persona* is not one of them." He rolls his head around his shoulders. "I should've turned around and left as soon as I saw you."

"Why didn't you?" I bring my tumbler to my lips. "Would've been doing us both a favor."

His jaw flexes as he watches me take a sip of my water. The fire in his eyes is met with the inferno in mine.

"You're right," he says.

I drop my drink to my side, flabbergasted he admitted that so easily.

"I'm going to go inside. I'll let Jeremiah know something came up and I have to leave," he says. "Not dealing with your shit is better than ruining my afternoon."

"By all means, please go. Save both of our afternoons. But at least take the blame, *gentleman*."

"You are incorrigible."

"I'm ..." My head spins as I try to find a quick comeback. *Who uses words like that?* "Corrigible."

He smiles. "Corrigible, huh?"

"Yeah," I say, shifting from one foot to the other.

"Do you even know what that means?"

"Yes," I say weakly.

"So you're admitting you can change? You can be reformed from your incorrigible, witchy ways?"

"That's not what corrigible means."

He smiles smugly. "That's *exactly* what it means."

I start toward the house with Ripley on my heels. *Fuck him and his vocabulary.*

"What I mean is that I'm pleasant," I say. "Nice. I can get along with anyone. So the fact that I can't get along with you is very telling."

"Yeah. It means you're an asshole," he says.

"It means that *you're* the problem."

He stops abruptly beside the pool, and I turn and face him. Sweat coats his skin, drawing attention to the ridges of his face and the smooth skin of his neck. He licks his lips as he looks down at me, studying me like a project.

Annoyance rolls through me, intensified by the sun and the heat rolling off his body. I should walk away and leave him behind ... but I don't. I'm stuck in place, waiting for him to speak.

"Do you realize that our biggest argument is over us arguing?" he asks. "We fight the most about the fact that we fight."

"Because we never get beyond that. As soon as your lips part, I want to punch them."

He tilts his head to the side, and I loathe that I notice how much his blue eyes shine in the sunlight.

"What would happen if we stayed silent toward each other when we're in the same room?" he asks. "If we completely ignore the other person instead of going for the jugular?"

I consider this. It might be possible, but I've never thought about it before.

"I mean, you would have to take that stick out of your ass, but I think you can do it," he says.

What?

My jaw hangs open, anger and frustration swirling wildly inside me. It rises too quickly to contain. Before I know it, my hands are planted on his solid, wall-like chest, and I push him backward.

His eyes fly open as his momentum swiftly changes directions, and he loses his balance. He snaps out a hand, wrapping it around my wrist, and yanks me off my feet.

"*No,*" I squeal as I shoot through the air, my tumbler banging against the decking as it falls. Ripley drags me with him, his fingers burning into my wrist, as we sail toward the water.

I barely hold my breath before I plummet into the water.

Two splashes ring through the air as Ripley and I sink to the bottom of the pool. I open my eyes to find him a few feet away, grinning mischievously.

Oof.

Bubbles float from his mouth from what I imagine is a chuckle, just before he spreads his arms—his shirt clinging to every ridge of his body—and heads for the surface.

I swim to the top and gasp a lungful of air, brushing my wet hair off my face. Ripley is treading water an arm's length away. He's cool, calm, and collected—no worse for the wear. His shirt is sucked to his body by the water, like a model waiting for a photo shoot, and that only makes me madder.

But I can't say anything because I shoved him first.

"Hey, Peaches," he says, humor dancing across his features.

"Fuck you."

"Fine. I won't tell you that your tits are hanging out. It's not like I mind."

I look down to see my nipples peaked and pointed directly at him.

I scurry to pull up my top with a full-on blush. He swims gracefully, lazily to the side. Two hands grip the pool's edge before he lifts himself—his arm muscles flexing beneath the sparkly water droplets on his skin—and climbs out.

He walks away without looking back. *I hate Ripley Brewer.*

Chapter Six

Ripley

"I couldn't tell Georgia my phone was in my pocket. She would've taken that as a victory," I say to Waffles, setting his dinner in the built-in feeding station I had added to the kitchen island. "All I can say is that it's good that my phone case is waterproof, and it worked."

Waffles drops a tennis ball at my feet, his little tail wagging back and forth as he peers up at me.

"Eat, and then maybe we can go outside and play," I say, scooping up the ball and placing it on the counter.

He barks in protest but loses his focus once he sniffs his food.

I peel an orange while gazing across the island, over the casual eating nook, and through the floor-to-ceiling windows on the other side of the room.

When I had this house built five years ago, I knew I wanted to be able to stand in the kitchen and look across the treetops to the valley behind it. The lot's dense vegetation and varied wildlife were a huge selling point. Nature has always given me a sense of peace, and I wanted to incorporate that into my daily life—even if only through a pane of glass.

I pop a wedge of fruit into my mouth and savor the sweetness. It's the first thing I've had since breakfast, thanks to Georgia's little stunt making me miss lunch.

A chuckle rumbles from my chest as I think about it ... and her.

I'd find her entertaining if I didn't dislike her as much as I do. She can go from a centerfold stretched out on a lounge chair, to a mouthy pain in the ass, to a sexy siren with the best set of tits I've ever seen. It's as impressive as it is discombobulating. I go from being speechless, wanting to murder her, to wanting to fuck her within an inch of her life —all in the same two-minute span. Yet we always end each interaction at the same point. *Disdain.*

At least I won today's battle. I think.

Another tennis ball strikes my foot, and I find Waffles standing before me with his tongue sticking out.

"Where did you get this one?" I ask, laughing.

He barks.

"Did you finish your dinner?" I ask.

He barks again, this time adding a tongue wag to the mix.

"All right," I say, picking up the ball. "Let's go outside for a few minutes."

He races to the door and sits, waiting for me to catch up. I put the rest of my orange back in the kitchen and shove my phone into my gym shorts pocket.

As I step into the backyard, the evening sun warms my bare chest. The air is filled with a honeyed fragrance from a mystery plant in my landscape design and the bubbling of the pool across the deck. Waffles leaps into the air and barks, redirecting my attention to him.

"Ready?" I ask before throwing the ball across the yard. "Get it."

He zooms after the ball just as my phone begins to ring.

I pluck it out of my pocket. "Hello?"

"Hey," Gannon says. "You busy?"

I take the slobbery ball from Waffles and launch it again. "Not really. What's up?"

"I just read a report that the public perception of our family hasn't fully rebounded following Dad's attempted implosion of Brewer Group."

"Really?" I ask, giving Waffles a look not to jump on me. He sits quickly and side-eyes the ball at my feet. "Tate said he was getting a warmer welcome with the investors."

"Yes, but the investors aren't the public, so to speak."

I pick up the ball and throw it as far as I can. "I saw the financial reports from the last quarter. They looked solid. I thought everyone was pleased with them."

Gannon sighs. "We're happy with where we stand *for now*. We've done a hell of a lot better than I anticipated at turning things back around and cultivating investor confidence. But the public's impression of us is a different battle, and one we don't seem to be winning."

My stomach twists as a dark cloud settles over my head ... because as much as this sucks professionally for Brewer Group, this doesn't directly relate to me. What I do doesn't impact Brewer's bottom line.

Dad's sentence from years ago comes back to haunt me. *"You are completely redundant to our company. You make no contributions to our family."* He laughs. *"If we took you out of the equation, life would carry on."*

"If the public looks at us negatively, it'll undoubtedly bleed into employee morale," Gannon continues. "It'll affect our brand value, and we'll lose a marketing advantage. People want to support exciting, feel-good stories. Thanks to Dad, we might be exciting, but it's for all the wrong reasons."

A year ago, Gannon and I would not be having this conversation. Dad kept me out of discussions about the family business as a punishment for not letting him direct my life. Of course, he never said that outright, but I know it's true. We all do. But now that he's gone, my siblings incorporate me into conversations and decisions, even if all I can offer is a sounding board. We all lean on each other more. We despise what our father did, but I think we're all almost grateful for it in a way. He removed the thorn that kept our family segmented and brought us together.

It's a silver lining in a very dark time. But it's a silver lining, nonetheless.

"What can we do?" I ask, stopping short of asking what I personally can do to help the situation. Gannon sliding over the question or telling me outright that there's nothing in my capacity as an exercise physiologist that I can do to assist the family efforts won't do either of us any favors.

My chest is heavy as I toss Waffles's ball again.

"Bianca is coming home for a few days next week for a big-picture strategy session. Tate is doing all he can," Gannon says. "Jason has put together a PR campaign for Brewer Air. It's getting approved by the legal team now. And once Renn is in the Royals front office, we'll devise a plan for them, too. I have people assessing how we can best use the Arrows and the Raptors hockey team. It helps to have you go to the facilities and interact with the players. They like you. It gives us a very relatable vibe—like we care about people. Which we do, but you know what I mean."

"I do."

There's a long pause. "While we're here, I was going to ask if you've had a moment to call Jonah Spaulding."

"Yeah, I did. I left a message for him yesterday and haven't heard back. Do you know what he wants? Tate acted like it was a big secret, and Jonah's email was pretty nondescript." I pull the phone away from my face. "Leave it alone, Waffles. It's going to sting your tongue."

The puppy turns and lifts one ear on top of his head.

"Jonah might've changed his mind," Gannon says. "I wouldn't worry about it too much if he doesn't return your call. But, if he does call you back with a proposition, I'd appreciate you considering it."

"A proposition, huh?" I laugh. "Is there something I should know? I only like women, Gannon."

He laughs, too. "That's not what I mean."

"Good." I take the ball from Waffles and chuck it away from the insect. "So that's all I get? There's a mysterious proposition?"

"There might be a mysterious proposition, but it was up in the air when I talked to him on Tuesday. He was floating an idea by me, and I thought we might be able to make it work."

"And somewhere along the way, you and Tate decided I might be able to make it work?"

"Well, Tate, Jason, Bianca, and me. Renn was iffy, but we got him on board."

"Fuck you," I say, laughing again. "So everyone knows about this but me?"

A car horn blasts in the background. "It'll probably never come to fruition, so don't worry about it. We're making it out to be more than it is."

I'm not sure I believe that, but I also know pushing Gannon won't net the results I'm after. And I highly doubt that it's anything important, and if it were, he wouldn't have talked to my siblings about it and not me. It's not how we roll.

"I need to go," Gannon says. "I'm meeting a few people at a restaurant for a business dinner, and I just arrived."

"Have fun."

"Sure." He sighs. "Let me know if Jonah calls."

"I might."

He chuckles. "Talk to you later, Ripley."

"Later."

As soon as I end the call, the phone buzzes in my palm with an incoming text.

> Jonah: Are you available for a call in ten minutes?
>
> Me: Yes.
>
> Jonah: Great. Talk soon.

"Can't wait to see what this is all about," I say, sitting on the edge of a lounge chair.

My mind spins with a million possibilities for why Jonah wants to talk to me. Each one is more far-fetched than the next. When I couple it with Gannon and Tate agreeing that I should be the one to handle *the proposition*, it gets me no closer to an answer. It only increases my curiosity.

"I just read a report that the public perception of our family hasn't fully rebounded following Dad's attempted implosion of Brewer Group."

Our family's struggles since Dad's crimes, including the attempted murder of both Mom and Bianca, have only brought us closer together. Before Dad went to prison, Gannon never called me. He and Tate could barely stand one another. Renn didn't bother to come home often, and Jason lived in his own world. But now? Everything has changed for the better.

I only wish I could carry a bigger piece of the load—that I could do something to help ease the burden of Dad's sins on my siblings.

My phone vibrates in my hand. The group chat I share with my friend circle is lit up on the screen.

> 🍑 Georgia: Has anyone seen my sunglasses? I know I had them at The Swill this week, but I haven't seen them since.

> Tate: Nope.

> Jeremiah: Let me look by the pool.

I smirk, my cock hardening as visions of Georgia's beaded nipples rip through my mind.

> Me: Check in the pool, too. She lost a few things there today.

Before she responds, I exit the text app and answer Jonah's call.

Chapter Seven

Georgia

> Ripley: Check in the pool, too. She lost a few things there today.

My face burns as I stare at his text. *The audacity.*

I start and erase ten responses before I throw my phone on the couch. There are a thousand versions of *You're an asshole* that I want to put into words, but none of them feel sufficient. Besides, ignoring him will get under his skin worse than me repeating something he already knows.

Do Jeremiah and Sutton know what happened? Are they aware that Ripley saw me topless? Has he been making jokes to them all afternoon, and now I'll be teased about it until the end of time?

I fake cry as I get up and head into the kitchen.

Only one sliver of satisfaction came from my mishap this afternoon, and that's Ripley's face as I surfaced. It's seared into my mind.

Wide eyes, the color of the pool water.

Brows arched to the sky.

A smile ghosted his lips, as his Adam's apple bobbed in his throat.

For the briefest moment, Ripley Brewer was speechless. I hope I made enough of an impression that he can't stop thinking about it while simultaneously realizing he'll never get the opportunity to see me topless again.

I make an iced coffee and settle back on the sofa with my computer. My inbox is empty. Aside from newsletters announcing sales that I can't afford, every avenue of contact is void of communications. No job offers hang in the interwebs waiting for a reply. No alerts demand my attention with the promise of a new beginning. There are no open doors to lead me out of my current state of unemployment.

The emptiness of my inbox transmits into my soul.

I sigh.

I'm unsure how much longer I can go without finding work. My savings are sparse. There's enough in my account to last a few more weeks, and then it'll be as dry as my sex life. I can't ask Mom for help, as she can barely keep herself financially solvent. And there's no way in the world that I'll ask Dad for a hand. I'd rather eat dirt.

"The way things are going, I might resort to that soon," I mutter, closing the computer.

My phone rings, and I dig it out from under me. Sutton's name and a silly picture of her from a trip we took last summer light up the screen.

"Hey," I say. "Did you find my sunglasses?"

"Sunglasses? *What?* No. I don't know what you're talking about," she says in a rush.

I set my coffee on the side table and sit up, an uneasiness sweeping through me. "Hey, Sutton. Are you okay?"

"I'm trying very hard not to panic here, Georgia, but I'm panicking."

"Whoa. Okay. Slow down. Where's Jeremiah?"

"Downstairs. He's fine," she says dismissively. "This is not about him."

"Then what is it about?" My words are careful—*measured*. Sutton doesn't get panicked often, and when she does, it's warranted.

"I just got a call from Myla—she's directing *The Invitation*," she says. "A huge issue popped up, and everything is temporarily on hold."

"What? Why?" I hop to my feet as panic rises in me, too. I know how much this means to her, and if this show is held indefinitely, it would derail her. "How did this happen?"

"Apparently, Callum Worthington, the football player who signed on to the project, decided to get arrested last night. He can't leave Illinois for the foreseeable future. In the meantime, he started dating the beauty influencer we hired, and now she won't do it without him." She moans sadly. "We already have letters from both of their camps pulling out of the contract, and now we don't have anyone attached to the project, and we're scheduled to start shooting on Monday … and I'm going to lose everything."

The last six words are barely a whisper.

Soft sobs ricochet through the phone, breaking my heart for my best friend. Tears well in the corners of my eyes. I put her on speakerphone and set the device on the kitchen counter.

"Hey," I say, my voice clouded with emotion. "You haven't lost everything. And even if this doesn't go through, you still won't have lost everything."

"I know." She clears her throat. "I know this is me being dramatic, but this project was everything to me. It was my big break. It would give me credibility—prove that I belong in this world. These opportunities are like lightning strikes, and it may never happen again for me."

"Yeah, well, a better one might strike now. Maybe that project would've held you back. You don't know. Aren't you the one who says to trust the universe?"

"Fuck the universe." She laughs through a new set of tears.

I giggle. "That's my girl."

She takes a moment to get herself together. It gives me a minute to gather myself and step back into the Best Friend Role. I have to be strong and rational because she can't be either right now.

"Do you know the part that's bothering me just as much?" she asks. "It's that I've already told Jeremiah's family about the show. They weren't amazing about it. They acted like I was living with delusions of grandeur and was possibly making it up or exaggerating. And now they'll think they were right all along."

And there goes me being rational.

I stand tall. "First of all, Sutton, who cares what they think? I know you do because they're his family, but their opinion of you comes from a very biased background that we'll never understand. All that matters is what Jeremiah thinks of you, and he's made that clear."

"Yeah," she whispers.

"And second, you, my friend, are brilliant. You're a problem solver. You've gotten this far on your grit and grace, and there's no reason in the world why you should stop remembering that." I take a deep breath, letting that sink in. "Now, get a glass of wine if you need it to calm down, but you're going to figure this out."

"I don't know how."

I roll my eyes and dump my coffee down the drain. Then I pull out a wineglass and a bottle of red.

"Yes, you do know what to do," I say. "Let's talk through it. What do you need to make this work?"

"Well, at a base level, I need two people to film who would be a draw *and* available on Monday morning. If they understood the filming process, that would be all the better."

Yikes. I down a huge gulp of wine.

"I had a few leads before Callum and Gia, but I could never reach them, let alone get them to sign contracts by Monday." She laughs sadly. "I'm so screwed. When production halts, the crew signs onto other projects, and we'll lose our teams. I'll never get this back."

The wine warms my insides and makes me slightly ill as it mixes with the coffee in my stomach, but I try to ignore that.

"You don't have to get it back if you don't lose it," I say. "Does anyone in your office know of anyone that could do this? You're all in the industry. None of you know a starving artist who's desperate for a job? And we're in Nashville. There are loads of famous people here."

Sutton pauses, hopefully mulling over my impromptu speech.

"Check out the college campuses," I say after another quick drink. "This city is filled with gorgeous co-eds looking to make it big. Ask your coworkers. Oh! Call Mason Music. Are you still friends with that girl who works there? Ask her."

"Yeah, I could ask someone I know," she says slowly.

"That's the spirit!"

"Now that I think about it, I know someone who fits the bill perfectly."

"See? I told you this was possible."

"I could ask my best friend."

"Yes, you could—*whoa, wait.*" I set my glass on the counter and flinch. "*I'm* your best friend."

Her voice lightens. "Yes, you are. And you're beautiful and *definitely entertaining.*" She takes a quick breath. "Look, I've been listening to what you're saying, and you're right—and you're also the perfect candidate."

The room spins—I don't think it's from the wine—and I also don't think she heard me correctly. *"You're also the perfect candidate."* Sutton has lost a few marbles if she thinks *I'm* the perfect candidate.

I pace the length of the kitchen, trying to make sense of what Sutton is saying. *She wants me to go on her fake-dating reality show? Does she even know me?* I'm not the type of person you put on television. I speak without thinking. I forget to put mascara on one eye. I'm easily triggered by assholes.

I'd rather be home in bed with a book. And snacks.

"Think about it," she says. "You're looking for a job, and you want something on camera. Hell, you applied for a weatherwoman job."

"That's forecasting moisture in a whole different way."

She laughs. "Come on, Georgia. You're perfect. You know how to work a camera. You're hilarious. And you could use the money. This could even be a big break for you, too. You'd be helping me out of a huge hole I'm desperate to escape. You're my only hope."

"Sutton ..." I laugh warily. "You need to think about this."

"No, *you* need to think about this. Filming is set for a month. We have a list of scenarios that need to be filmed. It's nothing wild, just a getting-to-know-you scene, a first date, an adventure—things like that. And, of course, we're footing the bill. Just reframe it in your brain.

You're fake-dating a mystery man on someone else's dime and getting paid for it."

Oof. I down the rest of the wine and refill the glass. I have so many questions, and so many more reasons not to do this. But her *"you're my only hope"* line is doing exactly what it was intended to do—guilt me.

"But what if I don't like the guy?" I ask, my body temperature rising. "What if there's no chemistry? And this is going to be filmed, right? Who will see it?"

"It's just a pilot. So yes, people will see it, but it won't be on television. This is just used to test audiences on the show's viability."

I groan, not sure what to make of this. I don't want to pretend to fall in love with someone. I don't know how. I've never been in love. And I need to look for a real job to keep me from eating dirt.

Yet I'm not getting any callbacks.

"What do you have to lose?" Sutton asks, hope thick in her tone.

"My dignity."

"I think you lost that in the pool today."

I groan again, making her laugh. The sound is more playful and less stressed than before. *Does she really feel that confident in me being such a good fit?*

"We might not even have a guy, and the whole thing might be a no-go anyway," she says. "But if we can find a guy, will you do it? *Please?*"

I close my eyes, ignoring the little voice in the back of my mind that says I'm going to regret this. Instead, I follow the louder voice in my heart that says I must be there for my best friend just like she would for me.

I take a long, deep breath. "If you can't find another woman, and you do happen to find a man, then ... yeah. I'll do it."

"You are the best friend ever." She squeals. "Thank you, thank you, thank you! Let me make some calls, and I'll call you back."

"Yippee." I try to sound excited but fall flat on my face. "I can't wait."

"Love the enthusiasm. Just remember that you might have just saved my career."

"That's me." I swallow hard, smiling weakly. "Career saver."

With each of Sutton's footsteps echoing through the phone as she probably races to Jeremiah to share the news, my grip on the situation slips further away. My heart pounds wildly. My palms sweat around the wineglass that I can't seem to set down.

I want to shout at her and tell her to slow down. The words are on the tip of my tongue. But the thought of doing that and dampening her joy has me biting back my request.

I can't do it. I can't take this away from her despite the irony of me being on a show about finding true love.

Breathe, Georgia. It's only a pilot. The public won't ever see it.

"I love you," Sutton says. "So much."

"You better."

"I'll call you as soon as I know anything."

"Fantastic," I say. "Talk to you later, then."

"*Byeeeeee.*"

She yells for Jeremiah as the line disconnects. I start to shut off my screen when the text thread from earlier catches my attention.

> Ripley: Check in the pool, too. She lost a few things there today.

For once, I'm too bothered with someone else to argue with him. That's a first.

Chapter Eight

Georgia

I can't believe I'm doing this.

The elevator doors open, and the lobby of Canoodle Pictures comes into full view. The room is light-filled, and large potted plants dot the space. The walls are a buttery yellow, giving off happy vibes.

I vaguely wonder if this is because most guests are as nervous as I am.

"Hi," I say to the pretty blonde at the reception desk. "I'm Georgia Hayes. I'm here to see Sutton McKenzie."

"Yes, Georgia, hi. It's so nice to meet you. I'm Juni. Congrats on the new show, and welcome to the Canoodle family."

I hum a little, wishing I was as chipper about this as Juni. "Thanks."

"Head down that hallway," she says, pointing to her right. "You're in the conference room at the end. I'll let everyone know you're here."

"Fantastic."

If the word is edged in sarcasm, Juni doesn't pick up on it. I'm happy for that. My anxiety surrounding this whole thing has nothing to do with her.

I make my way down the long hallway, pausing to peruse some of the many pictures hanging on the walls. Some are from awards ceremonies, others appear to be still photographs from film sets, and a few were taken in cafés and fancy offices—beautiful people in beautiful locations.

When I enter, the conference room is empty. It's about the size of the lobby and not too ostentatious. A table runs down the center of it, and a sideboard table is tucked against one of the two walls without windows. Two extra chairs have been placed beside a projector screen.

I turn to sit when I glimpse my reflection in the glass.

My tanned skin is thankfully not orange after the self-tanning job I performed at home last night. The A-line dress I found in the back of my closet creates an hourglass look that's a bit deceptive, but I'm not about to argue with it. It accentuates my bust and hips, and the purple fabric lifts my confidence. I brush a strand of face-framing hair out of my face before adjusting my high ponytail.

"Not bad," I say, breathing in through my nose and out my mouth. "Just try to have fun. You're getting paid, and it's better than sitting at home and hoping for a call from a prospective employer."

The door behind me opens, and a red-haired spitfire enters the room. "You must be Georgia." She shoves out a ring-laden hand my way. "I'm Myla. It's so nice to meet you. Sutton sings your praises."

I smile and shake her hand. "Sutton is too sweet."

"I'm one of the directors on *The Invitation*, and I'll coordinate with you and the male lead as we go. Speaking of the male lead, have you had a chance to meet him?"

"No." I exhale. "I haven't, but I'd love to."

She glances at her watch. "I believe he's in the building." She places a file folder on the table. "This is a copy of the contract sent to you yesterday. Did you have a chance to have an attorney look at it? I know this is the epitome of *last minute*."

Yes, thanks to Jeremiah. "I did."

"Super. When we get to the signing portion of the afternoon, we'll bring in a notary and get it all squared away. Do you have any questions? If not, I'll go find our other actor, and we'll get started."

The other actor. That makes me laugh. But, hey, *they* asked *me* to do this.

I squash a bubble of nerves from rising in my throat. "I think I'm good."

"Okay, then grab a seat and make yourself at home. I'll be back shortly."

"Great."

"Welcome aboard, Georgia."

She gives me a quick smile before darting out the door.

I heave a breath and fall into a chair when she's gone.

The past thirty hours have been a whirlwind—a nonstop set of movements from when I agreed to participate in this show until now. Contracts, which Jeremiah thankfully had an attorney look over for me pro bono. My hairdresser squeezed me in for a cut and color. I visited my nail tech and had to coordinate with hair, makeup, and wardrobe late last night. Thankfully, since this is fairly low budget and just a pilot, I have the option to create my own looks.

At least I can feel like me in this very non-me scenario.

"Our hero is on his way," Myla says, bursting into the room again. "And, let me tell you, you lucked out."

I lift a manicured brow. "Really?"

She sits across from me. "Trust me. This could be a lot worse. He's handsome and charming. That's not always the case."

"That's a relief." I blow out a steady breath. "Thank you for telling me that. It helps."

"Of course. Now, I want to go over a few things with you because Jonah has already gone over these things with your counterpart." She whips an iPad out of nowhere and turns it so I can see the screen. A bullet point list of items is clearly delineated. "The show's premise is to see if two people can be matched by their search histories."

The blood drains out of my face. "Wait. You're not actually looking at my search history, are you?"

"We will need to film a shot making it look like you were one of several applicants and were chosen based on your results. We don't have to do that today. Actually, we'll probably shoot that more toward the end so we can angle it to match the scenes you've captured."

Thank God. That'll give me time to search for regular people's topics.

"We've created a list of scenes for you to film," she says, pointing at the second bullet point. "Some will be filmed by our crew, and you will film some on your own. We'll give you cameras and review all of that with you this afternoon. You'll be required to film confessionals."

"Excuse me?"

She laughs at the surprised yet concerned look on my face. "I just mean you'll sit for solo interviews where you'll record yourself. I'll send you a list of questions after each scene to get you started."

I nod warily.

"This is going to be a lot of fun, Georgia. Do you have any questions for me?"

I did, but now my brain feels like scrambled eggs, and I can't think straight.

"All right." She glances at her watch again. "Our hero should be coming. We'll do introductions, discuss any questions you might have, and then we'll sign the contracts. Once that's finished, we'll take you both in separately to film intake interviews."

"Sounds good."

The door creaks behind me. Myla's attention shifts in that direction, and her face breaks into a wide smile.

"Hey, Georgia," Sutton says, bounding into the room. Her eyes are wild as she sweeps her gaze from me to Myla and back again. "Myla, could I speak with Georgia alone for a moment, please?"

The uneasiness in her voice set off alarm bells in my head. My palms sweat as they grip the arms of my chair, and my freshly painted nails dig into the soft material.

"Sure," Myla says, hiding her confusion well. "I'll be back in a bit."

"Thank you," Sutton says.

Myla slips through the door, closing it softly behind her.

"Sutton, what's wrong?" I ask.

"Georgia, I'm so sorry. I didn't know. I swear to you that I didn't know."

Every fiber in my body warns me of danger—to get up and flee from the scene of a crime I can't identify. But before I can even question her regarding her apology, the door opens behind her.

"*Please*," Sutton pleads, her gaze holding mine. "Please believe me. I didn't know."

"You didn't know what?" I ask, my heart pounding so hard that I can hear my blood pulse through my ears.

Goose bumps prickle my skin as I slowly turn to my left.

No. No, no, no.

"Georgia?" Ripley's voice is a note too high. "What are you doing here?"

I avoid his eyes and keep mine glued to Sutton. "Is this a sick joke?"

"*I'm so sorry.*"

My hands press against the cool stone table, and I shove away from it. I stand, wobbling for a split second on my heels, and send a bewildered look at my so-called best friend.

"What is this?" I ask, my voice rising. "Why is he here?"

Ripley steps into view. "Someone needs to explain."

His eyes capture mine and attack the small amount of composure I still have in my grasp.

"Look, you two, this is a wild, crazy coincidence," Sutton says, holding her hands in front of her.

"How wild?" Ripley asks, his eyes never leaving me.

"Sutton, I need you to tell me that Ripley is here to drop something off for Jeremiah," I say. "And he wandered into the wrong room."

Sutton's chuckle is almost convincing. "Would you believe that the head of Canoodle Pictures is Ripley's friend, Jonah Spaulding?"

"Sure," I say, knowing the story doesn't end there. "I don't have a problem believing that."

I hold my breath, certain that I won't like what's coming next.

"And Jonah happened to ask Ripley if he would be interested in—"

"*No, he did not*," I say before she can finish. My attention whips back to Ripley. "Are you here to film *The Invitation*?"

An arrested expression crosses his face. "Are you?"

"Let's sit down and talk," Sutton says carefully.

"I can't believe this." I spin on my heel and put some distance between us. "There's no way we can do this now."

"Georgia ..." Sutton begs my name. "Please. *Please, please, please.* Don't bail on me. I need you to do this."

"With *him*?" I point at Ripley and try not to actually look at him. "You want me to pretend to date *him*? Pretend to fall in love *with him*? Are you kidding me? I'd rather live in a world without carbs than spend a minute alone with him."

Sutton flinches, her face paling. Tears well up in her eyes.

"Can you leave the two of us alone for a minute, please, Sutton?" Ripley asks like the gentleman he is not.

"Did you not hear what I just said?" I ask. "I said I'd rather live a life without bagels than be alone with you."

Sutton ducks out the door, taking all the oxygen with her.

My chest burns as I watch her disappear. I know how much this means to her and how helpless she must feel right now. I want to chase her and promise her everything will be okay—that I will do everything in my power to make this happen for her.

But I don't. *Because it's him.*

Ripley moseys through the room, rolling the sleeves of his white shirt up his forearms. His legs are clad in dark denim, and his face is freshly shaven. He's rested, ravishing, and the devil himself.

"For the record, I'm not any happier about this than you are," he says, his voice strong and full of authority.

"I expected no less."

"But arguing isn't going to get us anywhere."

"Agreed."

He puts his hands on his hips and faces me. "You need to go out there and tell Sutton you're pulling out of the project."

I blink in disbelief. "Excuse me?"

"As much as I'd love to back out of this, I can't. I gave my word to Jonah and ..." He rolls his head around his neck. "Let's just say there's more to this for me than just doing a favor for a friend."

"So you think *I* can just bail on *my* friend because that's what's easier for you?"

"Frankly, yes."

I scoff, glaring at him. "You're such an arrogant asshole."

"Why? We cannot pull this off without killing each other, and I can't back out, so I'm an asshole for expecting you to be the one to exit quietly?"

"Frankly, yes," I say, mocking him. "Sutton is my best friend, Ripley, not just an acquaintance like Jonah is to you. She needs this job. That means you should be the one to walk away."

He growls, looking at the ceiling. "What did I do to deserve this?"

I move to the other side of the room to evade his cologne.

What the actual hell?

My face is flushed, and I ball my hands at my sides. The tips of my pale pink fingernails dig into my palms. The chill snaking down my spine starkly contrasts the heat of my blood.

"I'd say this is karma, but I think karma will come for you a little stronger than this," I say.

He barks a laugh. "As if you know a damn thing about me."

"I know all I need to know about you."

"Great." He shrugs. "If you know so much, then walk away." He motions toward the door. "Trust me, if there were any possible way for me to do it, I would without hesitation. *But I can't.*"

"*I can't either.* I'm not going to leave Sutton hanging out to dry. She's like a sister to me. If this show fails, it won't be because I tanked it."

Ripley moves through the room with purpose. "Then what do we do? We're at an impasse."

I groan loudly, letting my frustration get the best of me.

"One of us has to quit," he says. "And it's not going to be me."

"One of us does have to quit, and it's not going to be me."

Ripley stops in front of me, his eyes drilling into mine. The intensity steals my breath, and my vulnerability to him makes me even madder.

We stare at each other, neither of us backing down. We've done this many times because we're both too hardheaded to give in. There's no way I'm breaking for this jerk. Not ever.

Finally, a slow, calculated grin slides over his lips and paints him like a villain. I shiver in response.

"Okay," he says with a casual shrug. "I'm telling you right now that I'm not walking away. Are you going to change your mind?"

I shake my head.

"Then it looks like we're doing it together," he says.

"That's impossible."

"Well, apparently, it's not. You are more than welcome to change your mind, but I'm certain where I stand. But let me tell you one more thing, Miss Hayes." He leans closer, his minty breath filling the air between us. "I plan on fulfilling my end of the bargain for Jonah. I'm going to pretend to fall in love with whomever they put in front of me, whether that's a random woman off the street ... or you."

It's a warning—a threat. An attempt to get his way like he always does.

Sorry, buddy. Not this time.

I want to poke him in the chest, but I know better. Instead, I narrow my eyes and appear as menacing as my five-foot-two-inch frame will allow.

"I'm certain where I stand, Mr. Brewer. And let me tell you one more thing. I'm going to do everything in my power to make Sutton look like a genius, whether that's with a man off the street worthy of me ... or you."

He snorts. "Better be sure you can handle this, big girl."

"Oh, little boy, you don't know what you're getting yourself into."

Our gazes are electrified, the air crackling between us. In the distance, a door opens, and Sutton's and Myla's voices break the silence.

"I see you two have met," Myla says. "Are we ready to move on to the contracts phase?"

Ripley grins. I smile, too.

I lift a brow, and so does he.

"You sure you're up to this?" he whispers.

I wink at him, a sign of indifference, but meanwhile, my legs wobble beneath me. *This is going to be an absolute disaster, but I'm not going to back down.*

I'm not letting him *win.*
"Myla, where is the pen?" I ask.
His eyes sparkle back.
I'm so screwed.

Chapter Nine

Ripley

"Hey, Waffles, my man!" Tate crouches, catching my puppy mid-leap. "Did you get a new collar? You're looking good. The red makes you look ferocious."

The red makes you look ferocious? Whatever, Tate. I march past the love fest and head straight for my brother's office.

"Bad day?" Tate asks.

"Oh, you could say that."

I fling open his liquor cabinet and find his most expensive bottle of bourbon. Two fingers are poured into a glass before Tate and Waffles find me.

My body is hot, and I can't decide if my blood is actually boiling, or if I was so distracted on the drive over that I forgot to turn on the air-conditioning. Pain emits from my jaw from clenching my teeth, and I struggle to keep my breathing under control. *How did this happen?*

Since leaving the Canoodle office this afternoon, I've replayed Saturday's conversation with Jonah a hundred times. It was straightforward.

He explained that a production he felt could be the next big thing for his company was in limbo. He suspected this could happen, and when he reached out to Tate initially, it was to gauge interest. *Would any of us be interested should Jonah need a backup?*

Jonah contacted our family because we owed him a favor and because he knew we could use the boost in public opinion. Word travels fast, and Jonah would definitely be saying lots of good things about us if we help him out.

Both were true. There was no way I could say no.

But there was no mention of Georgia; it was simply a note that his team was in the process of securing the female lead.

No one ever said that I would be fake-dating *her*.

"I'm not judging you when I say this," Tate says. "But isn't it a little too early on a non-holiday Monday evening to pour bourbon?"

The liquor is sweet and smoky as it goes down. I pray that its effects hit me hard and quick.

"Or not," Tate says, setting Waffles on the floor. "I'm guessing the meeting with Jonah today didn't go well?"

"Oh, my meeting with Jonah went fine. It was the rest of the afternoon that was suspect."

Tate's brows pull together. *He doesn't have a clue.*

"So I get to the Canoodle building and go inside," I say, recounting the day before it went to shit. "I meet with Jonah. He thanks me for helping them out of a bind, and we review the show's details again. My attorney calls and clears me to sign the documents, and we're good to go."

Well, as good to go as one can possibly be when they're told they'll be fake-dating a stranger in front of a camera. I've studied hours of footage of athletes moving to work on their gait, batting positions, and range of motion—all the things for work. I'm excellent on that side of the camera. *But in front of it?* Not my forte.

My brother pulls out a bag of beef jerky from his desk.

"Jonah sends me to a conference room to get started, and that, my guy, is where it all fell apart," I say, watching him offer Waffles a piece of jerky. "Hey, don't give him that."

"Why not? It's meat. Dogs eat meat."

"Because it's not for dogs. What is it—teriyaki flavored?"

Tate nods.

"He can't have that shit. Think about it. It'll hurt his stomach."

Tate rolls his eyes, tossing the bag on his desk again.

I pause long enough to give him a look so he knows I'm serious and won't sneak a piece to Waffles behind my back.

"Guess who was in the conference room?" I ask, my heartbeat picking up.

"I have no idea."

I tip back the rest of the bourbon and let it settle in my stomach before responding. Licking my lips, I feel the burn sweep through my gut and sigh. "*Georgia.*"

"Georgia?" He blinks. "Georgia Hayes?"

"How many fucking Georgias do you know?"

Tate freezes. He grabs the back of a chair, his eyes widening as he blinks. His surprise is obviously genuine as his mouth drops open.

Then, suddenly, he bursts into a fit of laughter. "No way."

I stare at him as he revels in my pain.

"Your empathy is appreciated," I deadpan.

"I'm sorry." He cackles. "I just ... you're serious?"

"Do I look like I'm in the mood to joke about this?"

He clears his throat, choking back his amusement. "No. No, you don't."

Waffles paws at my leg, so I bend down and pick him up.

"You're the only person I like today, Waffles," I say. "It's you and me against the world."

He licks my hand before twisting in my grasp until he gets his face nestled against my shoulder.

"So ..." Tate says, choosing his words carefully. "You and Georgia are pretending to date for a reality show?"

My insides tighten so hard I grimace.

"How did this happen?" he asks. "What are the odds?"

"From what I can tell, Jonah had floated the idea to you early last week just in case something fell through. Then it did fall through. They lost both actors or characters or whatever you want to call them." I sigh, my surge of anger starting to wane thanks to the bourbon. "He returned my call on Saturday night, and we discussed it in theory. Shortly after we hung up, he called again, saying they had found a female lead and wanted to know if I would sign on. At some point between his calls, Sutton must've talked to Georgia."

"*Wow.*"

"Yeah. *Wow.*"

Waffles begins to snore on my shoulder.

"So what now?" Tate adds a finger of liquor to my glass before pouring himself one. "How did it go when this all came to light today?"

I chuckle in disbelief. "Not well. We had a pissing match, both of us trying to get the other one to quit. She wouldn't walk away because of Sutton, and you know how much we owe Jonah." *And I can finally do something to help our family.*

"And you're both hardheaded as hell."

"Well ... that, too." I sigh heavily. "She just drives me crazy, Tate. Her smart little mouth. Her temper. The way she stomps her size six shoe and expects me to bow to her. *Fuck. That.*"

I turn to my brother and catch him smirking.

"What?" I ask, unamused.

"Not a thing."

I pace Tate's office, my mind reeling.

Georgia's going into this not only trying to make Sutton look good but also trying to make me look bad. I know her—too well. She will strap on her angel wings, flutter her thick lashes, and try to make everyone fall in love with her. And they will because they don't know her like I do.

The thought alone eats through me.

"Do you two have a plan?" Tate asks.

"For what?" Waffles jumps at the sound of my voice. I pet the top of his head until he falls asleep again. When I speak again, it's quieter. "Do we have a plan for what?"

He grins. "How not to kill each other primarily."

"No, but we need one." *I* need one.

How am I going to navigate this and come out unscathed?

Our exchange echoes through my brain as I gaze out the window.

"Better be sure you can handle this, big girl."

"Oh, little boy, you don't know what you're getting yourself into."

It's like a light goes off—a big, bright light that shines directly on the path I need to travel.

A slow smile splits my cheeks. "I know what I'm going to do."

"I thought I wanted to know, but by the sound of your voice, maybe I don't."

I turn to him. "I'm going to beat her at her own damn game."

"Meaning ..."

"If Georgia's anything, she's predictable," I say, still working out the details in my head. "As much as I hate to admit it, she's good at what she does."

Tate lifts a brow.

"Not like that." *Probably like that, but I wouldn't know.* "I mean that when the cameras are on, she will play her role to a *T*. She'll think in her pretty little head that she's getting to me and making me fall for her. She's just arrogant enough to believe that."

"And you won't be falling for her?"

I scoff at his question. "Are you serious?"

"I'm just saying that while I don't know what all this entails, if the idea is seeing if two people will fall in love, then I imagine there will be some talking, touching—maybe a little kissing."

My pulse quickens, but I ignore it. "Tate, I take offense to your suggestion that I would be weak enough to actually fall for her."

"I apologize."

"No, you don't."

He laughs. "Okay, so you're impervious to her. You're just arrogant enough to believe she'll fall for you."

"Don't be a smart-ass, giving my words back to me."

"Did I do that?" He plays oblivious. "I had no idea. I was calling it as I see it."

I roll my eyes. "Listen, I don't have a choice in this situation. I've given Jonah my word, and I will see that through. I might as well have some fun with it and establish the upper hand with Georgia once and for all."

His chest shakes as he struggles not to laugh again.

"What?" I ask, sighing.

THE INVITATION

"I just hope you win."

"Asshole."

He glances at his phone. "I need to take this. I'll be back."

"Sure."

As Tate leaves, Waffles wakes up and squirms out of my hands. He follows my brother out the door and down the hall.

My body vibrates with energy, still pumped with adrenaline from earlier. But unlike before, I'm finally starting to see things clearly. My emotions are falling by the wayside, and reality is easier to untangle.

I pull my phone out of my pocket and find Myla's email with the filming schedule. We're set to film our first date on Thursday night.

I slide out of my email and to my text app. Then I find Georgia's name with the peach emoji beside it.

Me: First date is Thursday.

Georgia: I'll file this under Texts I Never Thought I'd Get From Ripley.

Me: It's a dream come true, isn't it?

Georgia: Keep telling yourself that. Is there a point to this communication? I might have agreed to do Sutton a favor and pretend to date you, but I never agreed to random texts.

I roll my eyes.

Me: We need to lay out some ground rules.

Georgia: Do we, though?

Me: Think about it …

I stare at the screen for a minute and then two. Finally, her message pops up.

> 🍑 Georgia: Fine. Ground rules meeting tomorrow night at The Swill?

> Me: Seven?

> 🍑 Georgia: Fine.

> Me: Fine.

> 🍑 Georgia: You're paying.

> Me: Fine.

I almost expect her to text *fine* again just to get in the last word, but she doesn't.

Tate waltzes back into his office with a tennis ball, and Waffles jumps high, trying to take it from him.

"I promised Waffles I'd take him outside and throw the ball around," Tate says.

"You hungry?"

"I'm always hungry."

"All right. I'll order a pizza and meet you outside."

Tate opens the door to the back patio, nearly tripping over my dog, who is entirely too excited to go outside and play. I meander through Tate's house and stare at my text exchange with Georgia.

"I imagine there will be some talking, touching—maybe a little kissing."

My muscles tighten as I hear Tate's voice repeatedly in my head.

"Touching—maybe a little kissing."

A slow, mischievous smile slips across my lips.

I might have been wrong to focus on the inconvenience of this setup. Because this? This might just be a hell of a lot of fun.

Georgia Hayes is going down.

I chuckle.

Better keep that visual out of my head.

Chapter Ten

Ripley

The Swill is calm when I walk in. I find a table in the back corner, nestled in the shadows, and sit with my back to the wall so I can watch for Georgia to arrive. I'm early—not only because I was anxious to get this over with but also because establishing oneself early is the best way to take control of a situation.

And God knows that won't be easy with her.

I've contemplated this scenario all last night as well as today while I worked with a couple of athletes at the Arrows training facility. I've gone back and forth about how to approach this meeting. Do I go with the flow, feel her out, and adjust my game plan? Or do I come out swinging with my charm and wit and throw her off her game?

One thing is for sure: she won't make a fool out of me. Again.

"Hey, there." A woman with a name tag reading *Vanessa* slides up to the table. "Can I get you something to drink, or are you waiting on someone?"

Vanessa is pretty with big brown eyes and curly blond hair. Her smile is friendly, too.

"I'm waiting for someone," I say, noticing the wash of disappointment filter across her features. "But I'll go ahead and order a whiskey neat for me and a lemon drop martini for my ... friend."

Weird.

"Great," she says. "I'll be back with your drinks."

"Thanks, Vanessa."

She smiles at my use of her name, a personal touch that always goes a long way with people, and heads toward the bar.

My stomach churns with anticipation as I flip my attention to the front of the building. On cue, as if she were poised outside the door waiting for me to look, Georgia steps into the bar. Her eyes find mine almost immediately.

Every man in the establishment's eyes finds her.

My God.

She moves through the room as if she's walking on air. Her hips, wrapped in light denim jeans with strategic holes in the knees, sway sexily with each step. Her shoulders are bare thanks to a corset-style top that highlights the tops of her round tits. The ridge of her shoulder is soft and smooth. If I didn't know she was a nightmare, I'd make it my mission to get her number.

Get your head together, Brewer.

I clear my throat as she approaches, breathing in her trademark vanilla scent moments before she slides into the booth across from me. Her tits jiggle as she gets situated. Now that I know what they look like without a shirt, it's hard not to stare.

"Perfect timing," Vanessa says, placing two drinks on the table.

Georgia looks at me, confused.

"Do you two need anything else?" Vanessa asks.

"No, I'm good," I say. "Would you like anything else, Georgia?"

She shakes her head, a loose tendril from the pile of hair on top of her head dusting her shoulder.

"Great. I'll check on you two later," Vanessa says before scooting away.

Georgia sets her purse on the bench beside her. "I see you ordered for me."

"I figured a martini was safe."

"What makes you say that?"

I pull my whiskey toward me. "Well, you had several of them the other night when we were here, so I figured it was safe to say you liked them." *And I finished yours that night just to piss you off.*

"*Oh.*" She brushes the errant tendril out of her face. "That's fair, I guess."

"Did you think I just threw a dart at the menu and got lucky?"

"If anyone could do that, it would be you."

"What's that supposed to mean?" I ask.

She takes a drink, watching me over the rim of her glass. Her lashes are long and thick, and her skin sparkles under the light hanging above us.

All she's missing are the wings.

"So ... ground rules," she says, placing her drink on a napkin. "Let's get this over with."

I shift in my seat. "Tate pointed out that we might find ourselves in precarious situations that would make sense for people actually dating but would be more than awkward for us."

"Yeah, that thought has crossed my mind, too."

She holds my gaze long enough to make me question exactly which thought she's referring to. But I don't ask. It doesn't matter.

"Did you get the revised shooting schedule today?" I ask.

She settles back against the seat. "Yes. Thursday is a getting-to-know-you scenario now. I didn't see where we were supposed to meet, though."

"It's at a restaurant called Ruma downtown. Since the crews are filming, they had to get permits and permissions."

"Ruma, huh? I've heard that place is amazing and also ridiculously expensive. Can't say I'm mad about getting to try it on Canoodle's money." She takes another drink. "They have us scheduled for our first official date on Friday. We're supposed to let them know our plans on Friday morning."

"That's what I read, too."

"Well, seeing as though we got the same email, that would make sense," she says.

I narrow my eyes as the frustration I've tried so hard to bury rises to the top.

"Don't look at me like that," she says. "I'm not getting paid to be nice to you yet."

As much as I want to do this for Jonah and need to do this for my family's reputation—*who doesn't love a man bending over backward for the woman he's falling for?*—the possibility that Georgia fails to cooperate and this entire production fails becomes apparent.

"You know, if it pains you that badly to pretend to like me, you need to rethink this," I say, clenching my jaw. "If you walk away now, little time and money has been spent. If you wait and let this blow up in your face, it will be expensive. That'll make Sutton look even worse."

"*Don't.*"

"*Don't what?*" I fire back.

"Don't try to talk me out of this. Yes, it will pain me to be nice to you—even if it's fake. But I signed a contract, didn't I?"

I shrug. "You signed a contract to be professional about this, but you're acting like an asshole."

"Coming from you, that's rich."

We sit across from one another, each holding a proverbial white flag under the table. We both know we can't do this and make our agreement work. Yet neither of us is willing to raise the flag first and surrender.

I fold my hands on the table. "I'm no happier about this than you are, Peaches."

She rolls her eyes.

"I'd rather listen to Gannon talk about stocks and bonds than do this with you," I say. "If you want me to be honest, I don't know that you can do this."

"Oh, really?"

"Really." I pin her to the seat. "You're too busy pretending to be a bad bitch to even allow me to be remotely nice to you. Why is that, Georgia? Are you scared it'll taint whatever fucked-up version of yourself lives in your head?"

She leans against the table, anger rolling off her in waves. "Fuck you, Ripley."

"Does the truth hurt?"

"It hurts about as much as your ego will hurt when you realize I'm not melting at your feet when we're alone, and I sure as hell won't believe every word that comes out of your mouth."

I withdraw a bit, studying the guard that just slid across her eyes. I'm unsure if this is a new thing or if I'm only noticing it now. But it doesn't matter because I don't have time—or the energy, or the desire—to figure it out.

"I'm approaching this like I would any business contract," I say, my voice unwavering.

"Same."

We're not getting anywhere ... I sigh.

"So ground rules?" she asks. "You go first."

I glance at a table of men in suits by the bar who keep glancing at Georgia. "We shouldn't date other people until our contract is up. It's just to maintain the integrity of the job."

That doesn't even really make sense, but that's what I get for thinking on the fly.

"What happens if I fall madly in love with someone mid-shoot?" she asks.

My teeth grind against each other. I know she's just fucking with me—her lips pressed together in a faux pout give her away. Still, I can't give in.

"We'll address it if it happens," I say. "I want to keep my options open in case I meet the future Mrs. Brewer, too. But even though we're fake-dating and this is just a job, I think having a real-life significant other could cause problems, and we're both dedicated to helping our friends succeed."

"Fine. Deal." She flashes me a fake-ass smile. "I also have a demand of my own."

"What is it?"

"I know this is supposed to look as real as possible when we're filming, but I don't want anyone to think we're actually dating in real life."

"You think I want people to think I'm dating you? Funny."

Her features sober, and all levity has left the building. She picks up a small amethyst stone hanging from a chain around her neck and toys with it between her fingers.

I can't help but notice how vulnerable she is at this moment. Her caramel-colored eyes shine with a soft defenselessness that changes everything about her. I've only seen her like this once before, which was so long ago that I forgot about it until now.

"I mean it, Ripley. It's important that no one thinks this is really happening, okay? And if for some reason you're picking me up and I tell you not to come to my house, you can't. All right?"

Huh? "Fine, but why?"

My mind races, coming up with a multitude of reasons she wouldn't want me to come to her house unannounced. Not that I would've anyway, but her determination about this single point makes me curious.

She takes a long drink and licks her pink lips. Her glass touches the table with a soft thud.

"I don't know why I feel awkward talking to you about this because it's not like I did anything wrong, and you might already know, anyway," she says.

"I might already know what?"

She sits tall in her seat. "After my parents divorced, my mother dated your father."

What?

"And, if you do the math, which is what you're probably doing right now, your father was married to your mother at that time," she says.

"That motherfucker," I say in disbelief. "Are you serious? How do you know this?" I shake my head. *Why am I shocked that the son of a bitch could surprise me from inside a prison?*

"I know because my mom told me. She didn't know your dad was married. I'm sure there are two sides to the story, but she claims she saw him on television with your mom under his real name and realized she was being played. She ended things immediately."

"Did my mom know?" I ask.

She shrugs. "I have no idea. I only know because …" She looks down at her lap. "I found out when I started at Waltham Prep, and she realized you guys went there, too. I think if she'd known that before, she wouldn't have made me switch schools. She avoided every PTA meeting and school event like the plague for fear of running into your mother."

"It's a good thing Dad is in prison because, if he weren't, I'd beat the fuck out of him right now."

She smiles sadly. "I'm sorry for telling you that. And, again, there are two sides to every story."

"Not this story. I believe your mom."

"Well, believe me when I say that she still carries absolute disdain for your father to this day."

"She can join the club. But what does that have to do with me?"

She laughs nervously. "I might have taken a blood oath that I'd never date a Brewer. And although she didn't specify, I'm pretty sure the vow I repeated covered fictional situations."

"Are you kidding me?"

"Afraid not."

I raise my glass to my mouth to try to hide my bewilderment.

The air between us is awkward. The silence is heavy. It's unusual for us to sit in the stillness without trading barbs, but here we are.

Vanessa swings by to see if we need anything. We both decline quietly.

"So ..." Georgia says, adjusting the bottom of her top. "How real is this supposed to look?"

"What do you mean?"

She looks up to catch me staring and sighs. "I'm not talking about my boobs, Ripley."

"Trust me. I know they're real. I've seen them, remember?"

Her cheeks flush, turning the same color as her lips. The memory of her topless rushes through my mind—because, unfortunately, Georgia Hayes has a fucking spectacular body—making me hard instantly.

Fuck, you better not think about her tits when you're in front of the camera, Brewer.

"I mean this relationship while we're filming," she says, giving the top a final tug. "Is our connection supposed to be immediate? Is it supposed to be a slow burn?"

"A slow *what*?"

She sighs like I'm a fool. "*A slow burn.* Meaning it's immediate chemistry, but it takes a while for it to burn. We're coy with it. We make the audience crave it."

Don't think about her tits. Don't think about her tits.

"Jonah said it's a strangers-to-lovers kind of thing with an instant connection. We're supposed to demonstrate the best-case scenario when people are matched based on their internet search history."

"I'm not showing them my searches," she says emphatically. "I told Sutton that. We can get a burner phone, and I'll look up some random stuff for the sake of the show, but my phone is off-limits."

"*Oh.* Something to hide?"

"Come on. Don't act like you'd let someone near yours."

I shrug. "I'm an open book."

She grins like she's caught me in a trap. "Give me your phone, then."

"Only if I get to see yours."

"That's *so* mature of you."

"That's called a fair trade. What would I gain by letting you see mine without getting something out of the deal?"

"Speaking of seeing my stuff," she says, pressing her lips together. "I assume we'll have to hold hands and touch a little. Keep your hands in respectable places. No touching my ass."

"I wouldn't dream of it." *Any more than I already have.* "If we kiss, no tongue. Try to control yourself."

She snorts. "I think I'll be able to manage."

"I hope so."

"So no dating anyone else while filming without the other's consent, no touchy-feely crap, and no tongue." She wrinkles her nose at me. "No showing up unannounced or spreading the word outside our friend circle that we're doing this with each other. Is that it?"

"That's all I have," I say, finishing my drink.

"Me, too." Her eyes shine despite the dim light hanging above our heads. "Then, if you don't mind, I need to go."

I sit back, taking her in one final time. "Have plans?"

"Something like that." She giggles, sliding her purse on her shoulder. "This all goes into effect on Thursday night. That means I have tonight and tomorrow night to"—she scoots to the end of the booth—"you know. Do whatever I want."

I cross my arms over my chest and study her. She's too happy—too compliant.

Georgia is just trying to rile me up. *She's not going anywhere but home.*

"Have fun," I say, smiling smugly. "Sitting at home on the couch all alone eating white chocolate and macadamia nut cookies."

"You'd love that, wouldn't you?"

"I don't particularly care," I say casually, knowing it's eating at her that I called her out. "I just know I'm right."

"Well, you're wrong. But you can think whatever makes you happy." She gets to her feet. "Thanks for not drinking my martini this time."

She makes a show of threading through the tables of the bar to the door. I can't take my eyes off her hips as they sway in those jeans. *Damn.*

They say the devil is in the details. I laugh. *Not tonight.*

Tonight, the devil is in denim. And the only way to beat the devil is to outwit her.

Despite years of animosity between us, I know if I focus my charm on this woman, I'll achieve what I need to win this challenge. *Because I'm on a mission.*

The ultimate victory over Georgia Hayes is to make her fall for me ... and admit it.

I truly am an asshole.

Chapter Eleven

Georgia

"What did you end up wearing?" Sutton asks, her voice ringing through my car speakers.

I flip on my turn signal and take the exit toward downtown Nashville.

"The peach-colored dress that I bought for Valentine's Day and didn't get to wear because I canceled on my date," I say. "Do you remember that dress?"

"Spark my memory. Half of your closet is peach-colored, and you cancel so many dates."

I remove my sunglasses and toss them onto the passenger seat. The sun hovers above the horizon, creating a spectacular wash of color across the sky. I couldn't get the full effect with my sunnies on, and while I might cancel dates, I won't miss a sunset if I can help it.

"There's a deep V-cut in the front, and gold and cream flowers kind of crocheted on the fabric," I say. "Flouncy skirt that hits just above the fingertips. Three-quarter-length sleeves. Super feminine and flirty."

"Ah, yes. I do remember that one. You look gorgeous in that. Good choice. Tell me you wore your nude heels that clasp around your ankles and gold jewelry."

I laugh. "Yes. It's like you know me or something."

"I know you well enough to know that the only thing you do know about fashion is what looks good on you. I wish I had that skill."

"You don't need that skill because everything looks good on you, Sutton."

"You're too sweet."

"Well, I'm feeling particularly sweet tonight since I had a whole spa day today and forwarded the bill to Myla." I sigh blissfully. "I feel like a million bucks."

Sutton laughs. "See? I totally hooked you up. You really have no reason to complain about this gig."

"*Oh no.* You don't get to act like you're doing me a favor here, bestie. I still have to put up with Ripley Brewer for the next few weeks. My complaint stands."

I follow the GPS through traffic, getting all green lights as I drive toward Ruma ... and Ripley.

A shot of adrenaline courses through me.

The pep talks I've been giving myself over the past two days have helped settle most of my anxiety. I've reminded myself that I handled Ripley well at The Swill on Tuesday and walked out of there with the upper hand, just like I planned. Thanks to my degree and work in broadcasting, I also have loads of filming experience. I've been in front of more cameras than I've been behind. Remembering that helps my nerves.

Besides, there's no reason that I can't have fun with this. What's not to love about going out a couple of times a week, essentially for free, when, quite frankly, you have nothing else to do and little discretionary money in the bank? Getting paid to help prove your best friend is brilliant is a great gig. And having the opportunity to flirt with a handsome asshole who knows I'm only pretending but has no choice but to keep his mouth shut and just smile back? That's gold.

"You're meeting Myla at the restaurant, right?" Sutton asks.

"Yes. We're meeting at the VIP entrance in the back. She called this afternoon and gave me the rundown but said she'd meet me there just in case I panicked or had last-minute questions."

"Are you getting close?"

"Actually, I'm pulling up right now."

Ruma looms in front of me on the right-hand side of the road. Crimson letters, lit up from the inside, spell out the name on the front of the brick building. The parking lot is packed, and a line extends along the front sidewalk. It's only slightly intimidating.

I drive to the back and spot Myla standing beside an oversized bald man next to a matte black door.

"I see Myla," I say.

Sutton cheers. "Okay. Go. Have fun! And, Georgia … thank you," she says, the final words softer. "I know I've said it a million times, and I must sound like a broken record, but I owe you, friend. Big time."

"You're welcome for the millionth time. And you don't owe me anything. We don't keep a scorecard in this friendship." I pull into a parking spot between two fancy sports cars. My little cracker box with a dented bumper looks very out of place. "Love you, Sutton."

"Love you. Call me on your way home."

"I will. Bye."

"Goodbye."

I end the call, turn off the ringer, and shove my phone into my purse.

My heart pounds as things get very, *very* real. I take a deep breath and give my teeth and nose a quick check for food and boogers—a fear I picked up from my mother—then open the door.

The balmy air is scented with spices as I step onto the asphalt. I lock the door behind me and navigate the cars worth more than some small countries. All the while, I remind myself that I have nothing to worry about.

This is going to be fun.

"*You look stunning*," Myla says, her red curls bouncing as she steps toward me. "I absolutely love that dress."

"Thank you." I stand a little taller, her words building my confidence. "I took way too long picking it out. I had it down between this and an icy-blue number I'm obsessed with. But I watched this woman on Social explain color wheels and how to dress for your season. Icy blue isn't in my preferred color palette, so now I have second thoughts every time I put it on."

Myla laughs. "I've seen those videos. Is it narcissistic to think I look the same in all of them? I'm not saying I look good in them. I'm just saying they all look the same."

"I had to get Sutton to tell me which one I am, so no judgment here."

Her warm grin is disarming. I appreciate it.

"Do you have any questions for me?" she asks, fastening an audio pack to the back of my dress. "We've already been inside and fitted your table and the surrounding area with cameras and microphones. They're all discreet, so you shouldn't notice them. Gary is on the other side of the door and will follow you as you *'meet'* Ripley. Be warned that the camera will roll as soon as you walk in."

"No pressure."

"No pressure." She winks. "A man named Adam will be standing at the host stand. He knows who you are and will usher you to the table. Ripley is already inside and waiting."

Of course, he is.

"Just remember that you and Ripley don't know each other," she says. "You're meeting here for the first time after being matched based on your search history. Aim for an easy conversation and take some time getting to know each other. You don't have to dig in too deep right off the bat."

I sense the apprehension in her tone. I can't blame her. Besides seeing our interaction last week, I'm sure Sutton filled her in on our typical exchanges. Someone had to explain.

"And avoid bloodshed, right?" I ask, hoping to make her relax.

Myla sighs in relief. "I'd love that. Although, if we skewed the concept, we might have a different show on our hands."

I laugh.

She steps back and looks me up and down. "You're a knockout, have confidence in spades, and you're funny. You're going to do great. Remember that we'll do a quick confessional after you're done this evening before you leave."

"Can't wait."

"I'm excited to see how it goes. Good luck, Georgia."

"Thanks." I take a deep breath and turn to the giant man at the door. "How are you this evening?"

He nods and opens the door. I have to stop myself from saying, *"I'm fine, thanks for asking,"* because he explicitly didn't ask.

"Here goes nothing," I mutter, entering the restaurant.

Thanks to years of working in broadcasting, my instincts kick in, and I focus my attention on Adam. Gary stands just out of my periphery with a camera catching my every move.

Breathe.

"Welcome to Ruma," Adam says, his posture perfect. "How are you this evening?"

"I'm great, thank you. How are you?" I ask, wondering if Baldy is still behind me. He should take notes.

"Very well." Adam smiles. "Please, follow me."

Shoulders back. Keep a pleasant look on your face. Don't start wondering if the back of your dress is hiked up your ass.

Adam leads me through an arched doorway.

Act natural.

We pass quietly through the restaurant, and I notice its beauty. Dark wood and brass hardware give the space a true elegance. Deep reds, warm golds, and rich browns and blacks create a cozy yet regal ambiance. Even the other patrons are beautiful.

It's no wonder Ruma gets so much press. It's a total vibe.

We turn a corner, my heels tapping against the hardwood floors, when my gaze lands on Ripley. My steps falter.

Holy shit.

He stands slowly when he sees me coming, unfolding his long, lean body from the table. His wide smile showcases his perfectly straight, white teeth. His baby-blue eyes are bright and clear, twinkling in the light. I'd think he was happy to see me if I didn't know better.

But, of course, I do know better.

A dark, well-tailored suit fits him like a glove. A crisp white shirt lays beneath his jacket with the top button undone. He's dapper and dashing—and I can't even say anything mean to knock him down a few pegs.

Lord, help me through this.

He has the wherewithal to act impressed with me as I approach him. "You must be Georgia."

I smile at him like I didn't loosely plot his demise last night. "I am. And you must be Ripley."

"It's a pleasure to finally meet you."

Oh, please. I bite my lip to keep from laughing as he presses an *almost kiss* to my cheek.

"I like this quiet version of you," he whispers, his breath brushing the shell of my ear before pulling away.

My body betrays me as goose bumps spread across my skin. It's the first time since the Senior Mixer that we've had contact without the threat of pain, and I wasn't prepared. If he notices, he doesn't make it known.

Ripley pulls my chair out for me. "You look beautiful tonight."

"Thank you," I say as I sit, wondering how badly that pained him. "Are you always this charming?"

He pushes my chair a smidgen closer to the table than necessary. "Always."

I stifle a laugh. *Sure, you are.*

"I think we should address the elephant in the room right from the beginning," he says, taking his seat.

My lips part to fire back a snarky response, but I quickly remember there are cameras.

"What would that be?" I ask.

"What do you search online the most often? Because I'm dying to know how we were matched."

My laughter is loud and immediate.

"I'm serious," he says, laughing, too. "Give me your top three. If we can find the overlap, it will give us a natural starting point."

My top three searched terms? Conspiracy theories, random medical ailments I have no business looking up, and deep dives into the backstories of strangers I encounter online.

If I say those things, it'll give him ammunition somehow to use against me later. But more importantly, I know our overlap doesn't exist because this is all for show. That doesn't mean I can't use it to learn a little about Mr. Brewer, though.

"Cleaning hacks, meal prep tips ... and porn," I say instead, watching his features closely for a reaction.

His eyes widen. "Porn?"

"Yup. That must be where we overlap."

The grin kissing his lips is one that I haven't seen before—not directed at me, anyway. It's suggestive in the dirtiest of ways. Butterflies flutter in my stomach as if they didn't get the memo that we don't react to Ripley ... or that he's acting and trying to make the audience believe he finds me attractive.

"I feel like I should say that porn is one of mine because that would be quite the overlap," he says, chuckling. "But it's not."

"Well, it's not mine either. I might as well admit that since they'll probably show you the list at some point." *Except you know as well as I do that there is no list.*

His brows lift in confusion. "What?"

"I was just trying to learn something about you." I shrug. "I don't look up porn. Well, it's not in my top three searches, anyway."

He tilts his head to the side, clearly amused, as the server steps to our table. After a quick introduction, Vernon takes our drink order and hands us menus before leaving us alone.

"So porn is out," he says, grinning cheekily. "Should we move on to meal prep?"

"My meal prep consists of making sure I have enough string cheese and cookie butter to get me through the week."

"Did you give up cookies?"

I laugh. "Never."

"I'm guessing you don't clean either."

"What would give you that idea?" I drop my attention to the menu and my eyes about bug out of my head. "*Whoa.*"

"What's wrong?"

"Nothing," I say, bringing my gaze to his. "I've just never eaten at a restaurant where one meal will be easily over one hundred dollars. Seems rather excessive."

"It's a little fancier than string cheese and cookie butter, huh?"

I laugh. "A bit."

Vernon returns with our drinks. "Are you ready to place your order, or do you need more time?"

I stare at the dinner options, none of which include cookie butter, and start to panic. The steaks have a location beneath them, which I don't understand. I'm fairly certain one of the appetizers is whale, and I'm not sure of the legality of that. There are duck tacos, which I didn't know was a thing, and so many variations of butter you can order on the side that I don't know where to start.

Where are the bacon cheeseburgers?

My palms begin to sweat.

"Would you like me to order for you?" Ripley asks softly.

My smile is wobbly as relief washes over me. Ordering food I'm not familiar with and food that's this expensive makes me self-conscious. I want to do it myself, but the longer I fumble with this decision, the goofier I'll look. That would be worse than letting him have this small victory by looking like a gentleman.

Surely, he'll choose something I like, right?

"That would be nice," I say. "Thank you."

He returns my smile and then turns to Vernon. "We'll have an artisanal cheese board as a starter. Georgia would like an iceberg wedge, please hold the tomato, and an eight-ounce filet cooked medium and an order of truffle fries. I'll have the wedge salad, roasted chicken with pistachio gremolata, and potato gratin."

"Excellent choices, sir," Vernon says. "I shall return."

He takes the menus and leaves.

"I'm not sure if you have a personal vendetta against tomatoes on salads, but I do, so thank you," I say, my face flushing.

He furrows his brow. "You never eat tomatoes."

"You can't know that about me," I say through a fake smile. "We just met. Remember?" *How do you know that anyway?*

"Fuck." He looks at Greg. "I ..."

Greg pops his head around the camera. "We'll edit it out. Keep going."

Ripley nods, and for once, I think he senses that he's a mere mortal. *Ha.*

"So no porn, meal prep, or cleaning hacks," he says, as if he's actually interested. "Tell me something about you—something real."

I think you're a pretty good actor. But you haven't seen anything yet.

"Let's see …" I try to think of something that will get a reaction. "Okay. I applied for a weatherwoman job last week."

Ripley knows I don't have a meteorology degree—but he can't say that, so his reaction is perfect. "*What?*"

"I'm really hoping I get it. I have a knack for predicting the weather."

He chuckles. "I'm glad to hear that although I think the weather is more of a science than a guessing game."

"Then we don't watch the same weather reports."

He shakes his head, holding back a comment. God knows what he'd say if there wasn't a camera in our faces. But there is. That means he has to behave.

I'm starting to like this. *Now, let's level it up.*

"I really think it's hard to believe you're single," I say, fluttering my lashes. "Why is a man like you on a reality show looking for a date?"

"Because there's a chance I'll meet a woman like you."

Oh, well played. I smile, acknowledging his game. "What are you looking for in a relationship?"

We pause as a plate of cheeses, nuts, and fruits and two small plates are placed between us.

He sits back, his features pensive. "Honestly? One of my brothers just got married and had a baby. Watching him with his wife and little boy has made me start thinking outside of myself."

"So you're looking to settle down?"

"Yeah. If I can find the right woman to build a family with, I'd love to be able to raise my children alongside my brothers."

I open my mouth to respond, but nothing comes out.

I'm not sure how I expected him to answer my question—or if I had a response in mind. But this reply wasn't on my radar. The worst part, the most confusing part, is that I don't know if he's being honest or just creating a good soundbite.

No, maybe the worst part is that I'm curious.

"What about you?" he asks. "What are you looking for in a relationship?"

That suddenly feels like a loaded question.

I take a drink to buy myself some time to shake out of the weird headspace I've inadvertently entered. I'm not sure whether to answer honestly, or if I should give him a bullshit response to maintain my privacy. His eyes sparkle as if he's being vulnerable with me, but I don't trust him.

He's still Ripley Brewer behind all that charm.

"I'm looking for a man who can complement my life," I say, setting my drink down. "I don't need to be saved and don't want to save anyone, either. It would just be nice to find someone honest who doesn't play games."

Our gazes lock. I search his pools of blue for any inkling that he understands what I'm saying.

And I come up empty-handed.

Why did I almost hope for something else?

Silly me.

Chapter Twelve

G eorgia

"Thank you for an amazing evening," Ripley says, his hand lightly covering the small of my back.

We exit Ruma side by side.

The sky is dark, and a cool breeze makes me shiver as we enter the parking lot. Most of the cars are gone, leaving my little ride alone with a security lamp shining like a spotlight on top of it. It makes me smile because I can relate—I don't really belong here, either.

"I had a great time," I say, facing him. "And thanks for ordering for me. You really are my hero tonight."

His lips twist to hide his smirk. *He knows that was for the audience.*

We spent the past three hours eating our meals and ordering dessert and coffee. We did what we were hired to do—ask ridiculous questions and receive bullshit answers. And I'm surprised to admit that we are both damn good actors. There were a few times I had to remind myself that we were pretending. That should bode well for Sutton.

"When can I see you again?" he asks, his voice smooth and steady.

The breeze picks up the ends of my hair, causing them to flutter around me.

I rack my brain trying to remember when we are supposed to meet again. Then I realize the producers can edit the video to say whatever they want.

"So there *is* the promise of a second date?" I ask, smiling up at him.

"Of course, there's a promise of a second date. I'd be out of my mind not to want to spend more time with you."

I wonder how many times these lines have worked on other women —those poor souls.

"I might have a night this weekend available," I say.

"Even if I didn't before, I do now." He takes a step closer. "Can I text you a time and date?"

"You better."

We exchange a slow smile, milking it for Greg, who stands off to the side with his camera angled at us.

My heart starts to pound as the world around us stops. I'm caught up in the waves in Ripley's eyes and the anticipation of what comes next.

Do we kiss? Do we shake hands and call it a night? Will someone call cut like they do on television?

I'm not prepared to kiss Ripley, and shaking hands feels very business-y. So I stare up at him like a woman who just had the best date of her life and really, *really* likes what she sees. The last part isn't all that hard.

Ripley begins to lower his mouth to mine when I take a step back.

"Cut," I say loudly, laughing to hide my nervousness.

He runs a hand over his jaw, smiling.

My heart thumps as Myla and Greg join us, and I wish I could run to my car and fly home. I need some space from all of this. I glance up at Ripley, who's still watching me. *And space from him.*

"You two did a phenomenal job," Myla says, clapping softly. "I watched the live feed and was so impressed with your chemistry. Have you two taken acting lessons?"

"It was much easier than I thought it would be," Ripley says.

I snort at his weak attempt at winning Myla over. "It turns out that it's not impossible to pretend to like Ripley."

He bristles at my side.

"You will film yourselves on your next date," Myla says. "Use the cameras we gave you on Monday, and you can even use your phones if you want to. Remember—the more material you give us, the better. We can edit things down but can't easily create new content. Just send us everything you have by noon the next day."

"We understand," I say, ignoring Ripley brushing against my shoulder.

"Great. Greg, can you film Ripley's confessional?" Myla asks, looking around. "Over by the pampas grass should be good. Do you have the questions to ask him?"

"I do." Greg nods at Ripley as he unstraps a camera from his back and hands it to Myla. "Follow me."

Ripley looks down at me as if he wants to say something, but instead, he turns away and follows Greg across the parking lot.

"If you put your back to the brick wall right there, we'll knock this confessional out," Myla says. "Don't forget to record one of these after your next date. I'll email you both a set of questions to use as a starting point."

"Great."

I get situated, and Myla sets up the camera on a mount.

"I'm going to ask you a series of questions," she says. "Be candid with your answers. If you start going down a tangent with something, feel free to follow it. There isn't a right or wrong answer here."

"Got it."

She touches the camera. "Here we go. First question. What was your first impression of Ripley when you entered the restaurant?"

I glance across the parking lot at Ripley and wonder what he's saying about me.

It doesn't matter. This isn't about him; whatever he says is a lie, anyway. This is about Sutton.

Oxygen fills my lungs, and I stand tall.

"My first impression of Ripley was that he's extremely good-looking. I had a hard time not wearing a goofy smile the whole night. It's one of those situations when you see a hot guy, and you think you'd play it super cool if you met them, but then you do meet them, and you're not cool at all. I just prayed the entire time that I didn't make a fool of myself."

"What kind of a first impression do you feel you made on Ripley?"

He watched me walk down the hallway carrying my books. His smile chased away the chill from my fear of starting a new school, so I'd say he liked me back then.

"I feel like we had an instant connection," I say, figuring that's what I should say. "Our conversation flowed easily, and he seemed interested in what I had to say."

Myla smiles. "You seemed a bit intimidated by the menu, and Ripley stepped in to save the day. How did that make you feel?"

A lump settles in my throat as I recall the moment in question.

"I was a little intimidated by the menu," I say. "When Ripley offered to order for me, I was initially shocked. But the shock wore off fast. It's such a sexy thing—to have the confidence to read a situation, step in and handle it. And then to handle it with class? It's very attractive." I laugh. "He also ordered a perfect meal for me, so that's a plus."

I glance over my shoulder to ensure Ripley isn't standing in the shadows to hear all this. While it's true, I don't want him to think I think he means any of it. That would be messy.

"How do you feel about a second date?" Myla asks.

"I'm very excited to see Ripley again. He checked off every box for me tonight, and I feel like there's still so much to learn about him. It's great to meet someone with whom you share an underlying nexus from the get-go. It's the golden ticket."

"Last but not least, do you have any indication what your overlapping online searches might be?"

"Not porn, apparently." I laugh, remembering the look on Ripley's face. "You know, I'm not sure yet. We had a great conversation tonight, but things were pretty superficial. I know I didn't tell him what my most searched-for terms are, and I don't think he would've told me his yet. It's such a personal thing that you do because no one is looking—only now, someone is looking."

Myla touches the camera again. "That's a wrap. And good job with the answers, by the way. They were the perfect responses for this first scene."

"I'm glad."

She takes my audio pack off my back and shoves it in a black bag at her feet. "That's it for me. We're done here."

"Awesome. I'll see you soon."

"Have a good night, Georgia."

I pace across the asphalt to my car, feeling Ripley's gaze heavy on my back. I don't turn to look at him because I'm not sure what that exchange should resemble. *Are we still in character when the cameras aren't rolling? Or are we back to normal?*

And was Myla serious about our chemistry?

I snort. Maybe I am a good actress, after all.

It's moments like these that I wish I could read Ripley better. He is so damn charming when he wants to be, and if I didn't know him better, I'd think we had a connection. *Sutton, you're welcome.*

But the truth is that I know not to trust him.

Still, I wonder what he thought of our "date."

"What does it really matter, Georgia?" I ask, climbing into the driver's seat. "That's one fake date down and a few more to go. You've got this."

I turn on the engine, put the car in drive, and leave the parking lot—and Ripley—behind.

Ripley

"Sorry about the delay," Greg says, shoving his glasses up his long nose. "I gave Myla the good camera. This one glitches from time to time."

"Not a problem, man. Don't worry about it."

I look over his shoulder, watching Georgia move across the parking lot to her car. No one is around her, and the area is well-lit. Still, I don't take my eyes off her until she's in her seat with the engine running.

Satisfaction hangs over the evening events. I achieved my goal of doing just enough but not too much, so she thinks about me until she sees me again.

Her predictability makes me grin. Georgia performed exactly how I knew she would. She dressed like a knockout, flirted her ass off, and would've had any man in the building eating out of the palm of her soft, little hand.

Except me.

"Are you ready?" Greg asks as a red light glows on the camera.

"I am."

"Great. First question is this—what was your first impression of Georgia as she entered the restaurant?"

Better keep this politically correct. I clear my throat. "Well, I don't know how you notice anything before you notice how beautiful she is. It took me a moment to get my bearings. And then she smiled at me and ... wow."

"What kind of a first impression do you feel you made on Georgia?"

I laugh. "She seemed interested in what I had to say and asked a lot of questions. We seemed to share a lot in common, which I didn't necessarily expect. I think she walked away from this evening thinking we have a potential connection."

"Is that how you are walking away this evening—feeling a potential connection brewing?" Greg asks.

"Yes. Absolutely. I'm really looking forward to seeing her again. Sometimes you just click with someone on a different level, and Georgia and I were definitely clicking tonight."

I grin, trying to hide it from the camera. We always click. *It's just usually more like the click of a gun than the click of a connection.*

Greg looks at a sheet of paper in his hand. "What's the one thing you hope viewers aren't noticing about you tonight?"

"Well ..." I laugh, looking into the camera. "I hope they didn't notice my shaky hands when I pulled out Georgia's chair. She's stunning in person, and it took me a moment to grasp it."

"You talked briefly about what search results might overlap. There was a bit of joking back and forth about that. Do you have any guess on what your common areas might be?"

I stifle a laugh as I think about her answer. *"Cleaning hacks, meal prep tips ... and porn."*

"It's too soon to tell," I say. "Although, I will say I'm walking away after our first date worried about her eating habits. We have to do better than string cheese and cookie butter."

Greg smiles at that, and it reminds me of the smile of relief on Georgia's face when I ordered for her. It had been so tempting to order something I knew she'd hate—fish or a duck—and watch her suffer through it. But for some unknown reason, I didn't. And the look of utter relief strangely reminded me of many years ago when she looked relieved to see me approaching her.

It was the same smile—her most genuine one.

The one I never get.

Greg drops the paper to his side. "Last, are you looking forward to date number two?"

I never in a million years thought I'd look forward to spending time with Georgia Hayes. But tonight, with our torches and pitchforks put away, it was fun. Sure, it was only fun because we weren't really us—just characterized versions of ourselves. But it was enjoyable, anyway.

"I am," I say, honestly. "She's the kind of woman who will keep you on your toes. I feel like things might get interesting, and I'm curious to see what happens between us."

Greg turns the camera off. "We're good to go. Thank you for showing up tonight with such professionalism. It's appreciated."

I shake his hand. "Thank you, Greg."

"If you hand me your audio pack, you can be on your way."

It's a bit tricky to get everything unwound and handed over to Greg, but I manage. We exchange goodbyes, and I wave to Myla as I head to my car.

Date one is in the books. Now to figure out how to amp things up for date number two.

Chapter Thirteen

G eorgia

"I don't know what Eloise will do about this," Mom says from inside the dressing room. "I don't even think she has his name."

I turn the page of my book and sigh.

Halcyon is one of the nicest boutiques in Nashville, and my mother has no business shopping here. But did that stop her from twisting my arm to accompany her on a try-on excursion of outfits she can't afford? No. No, it didn't. I could've put my foot down and stayed home, but that would've given me too much time to think.

And God knows I've thought it through a million times.

"I'm sure she'll figure it out," I say, forcing my mind away from my date with Ripley and back to the task at hand—saving my mother from spending money she doesn't have on clothes she doesn't need. "Don't fall in love with the black dress. You don't need it."

"You're so negative."

"I'm realistic. I saw the price tag."

"Let's not rule anything out until we see it on me."

I roll my eyes and curl up in the oversized orange chair in the corner. Then I go back to my book.

Halcyon's private fitting areas are divine. Each pod, as they call them, has a sitting area, dressing room, and a stocked refreshment center with fancy seltzer waters and various snacks. And it's quiet. If a personal shopping assistant didn't check on you every ten minutes, I might try to hang out here. It gives bougie library vibes without a kids' play center. It doesn't get much better than this.

"I told Eloise that burning was never good, but she's in her fifties. She should know that," Mom says.

"Sounds like she fucked around and found out."

"Georgia! Mind your mouth. We're in public."

I set my book on my lap and laugh. "You're talking about one of your friends contracting a burning sensation from a college-aged kid in Florida, and I can't say the word fuck?"

"Not in public." She groans. "This zipper is too tight."

"I told you to size up."

She gasps. "I'm not a size ten, Georgia Faith."

"It's just a number. Besides, every fabric and every designer are different. An eight isn't always an eight."

"If I were your size, maybe I would say that, too. But I'm not. Have a little empathy."

I sigh and go back to my book. Just as I get to the part I've been waiting for—when the hero realizes she's always been the one for him—the dressing room door flings open.

"Have you been listening to me?" Mom asks, fixing an earring.

"Honestly? No."

She runs her hands down the little black dress and turns to a full-length mirror. "I don't know why you brought a book, anyway."

"I'm trying to feel things, Mom."

She grins over her shoulder. "If you'd take my advice and start using men for what they're good for, you could feel a lot of things."

"Seriously, Mother?"

"Maybe you need to go to Charity Club with me. We can give you some pointers."

I snort. "With all due respect, I prefer my sexual encounters not to include burning sensations."

"That's just Eloise. Now come here and help me zip this thing up."

I stand and make my way to my mom.

"Did you see Josie Kipper died?" Mom asks, sucking in as I slide the zipper up her back.

"I did not."

"It was on Social this morning. I looked everywhere to see what she passed away from, but it didn't say." She exhales, and the zipper stretches but thankfully doesn't pop. "There should be a rule—if you die or get divorced and you're going to put it on Social, then you have to state the reason."

"That's ridiculous."

"It's true," she says, twisting and turning to see all angles of herself. "What do you think? Does it make my hips look big?"

"Your hips are fine. It makes your bank account look small. That's the problem."

She gives herself one final look before spinning to me. "The frugal gene is the only thing you got from your father."

Her golden eyes meet mine before she scampers back into the dressing room.

I turn toward the mirror, taking in my reflection. Everything I see—my auburn hair, the shape of my ass, and tanned skin—all came from my mother. But a lot I can't see came from her, too. I notice more of it all the time. And, truth be told, that scares the shit out of me.

Every day that passes, I wonder in the back of my mind if I'm destined to become my mother. Will I wind up alone, bitter at the world, and hating men? Will I amble through life without clear direction because I'm too scared to let anyone close? Will I ever find my dream?

That thought's been lingering heavily on me since last night. Something about the evening with Ripley brought it back to the surface. Maybe it's because he's so calm, cool, and collected. He has a career, a pathway, and enough confidence to carry him through any bump in the road. I might hate the good-looking fucker, but he does have his shit together.

It makes me want to have mine together, too.

It also makes me think of Ripley's response about relationships.

"One of my brothers just got married and had a baby. Watching him with his wife and little boy has made me start thinking outside of myself. If I can find the right woman to build a family with, I'd love to be able to raise my children alongside my brothers."

His siblings are all starting to settle down. I've overheard him talking about it when hanging out with our friend group. His best friend is getting married soon, and if Sutton has her way, they'll have kids soon after. *So was he serious when he told me he's looking for the right woman, or was that a part of the act?*

"Okay, you're right," Mom says, huffing through the door. "I'm not getting the black one." She holds up an emerald miniskirt she tried on hours ago. "This one is a winner, though, right?"

"Yes. That one is on clearance."

"Don't say *clearance*. It makes me feel cheap."

I roll my eyes, grab my book, and shove it into my bag before we exit our dressing pod.

"What about you?" Mom asks, fingering through a rack of halter tops. "Did you want to look for anything?"

"We've been here for three hours. If I did want to look for myself, the feeling would've passed."

She frowns. "We can do a quick shop for you, if you want. Check out these tops."

"Mom." I laugh. "No. I don't need anything, and I'm starving. Let's go."

"Now you're making me feel bad."

"Don't. I only came to ensure you don't forget who you are and start buying five-hundred-dollar little black dresses."

She sticks her tongue out and places the green skirt on the counter. I leave her to pay for her item and wander toward the front of the store.

Bright afternoon sunlight floods the boutique. I stand beside a mannequin with a hot-pink tube top and dig my phone out of my bag. One text alert awaits my attention.

My heart beats faster as I unlock the screen. I tell myself to stop it

THE INVITATION

and remind myself this is part of the contract. Still, seeing a text from Ripley—one that's not in the group chat—makes me nervous.

Which Ripley am I getting? Asshole Real Ripley or Fake Actor Ripley?

> Ripley: Wear something warm.

Huh? My fingers fly across the keys.

> Me: This winter?

> Ripley: On our date, smart-ass.

> Me: Why? What are we doing?

> Ripley: 🙄

> Me: Don't 🙄 me.

> Ripley: Every time we're together, I understand why you aren't dating someone a little more.

I smile, glancing up to make sure my mother isn't near. *You walked right into this one, buddy.*

> Me: Someone a little more ... what? A little more patient than you?
>
> Ripley: 😒 You know what I meant.
>
> Me: A little funnier than you?
>
> Ripley: 🙄
>
> Me: Ah, a little better at keeping up with me than you. Got it.
>
> Ripley: Whatever you say, Peaches.

I growl. "I hate when you call me that."

"Who?" Mom slings a bag over her shoulder and opens the door for me. "Who's calling you names? I'll fight them."

My phone vibrates with another text, but I shove it inside my bag. *No need to continue that conversation and ruin what's left of my day.*

"Mom, I have no doubt about that." I laugh at the irony. "Are we done shopping now?"

"I mean, I guess." We slide our sunglasses over our eyes and stroll down the sidewalk. "We could always grab an early dinner."

My mind wanders back to Ripley's text. *Wear something warm.* I have no idea what that means beyond the obvious, but why would I wear a jacket when it's still warm enough for shorts? Is he trying to set me up? Does he want me to look ridiculous?

"Georgia?" Mom asks.

"What? I'm sorry. I didn't hear what you said."

Her brows lift over the edge of her glasses. "You've been dazey all day."

"Not sure that *dazey* is a word."

"You know what I mean. Are you getting enough rest, honey?"

"I've sat on the couch all alone, eating white chocolate and macadamia nut cookies every night for the past two months," I say. *Just like Ripley said I was.* I grip my bag at my shoulder and squeeze it, pretending it's his throat.

"Maybe you should take a vacation day, and we can have a girls' day together. Brunch, then mani/pedis. Maybe the spa. We could catch a comedy show or something."

My steps slow as a ripple of annoyance snakes through me. *A vacation day? That would require a job, Mom.*

She doesn't know that I'm technically working for Canoodle Pictures, and she *definitely* doesn't know, and won't know, that I'm working with a Brewer. As far as my mother knows, I'm still unemployed.

Or as far as she *should* know because God knows if it doesn't affect her personally, it's not taking up space in her head.

She stops and waits for me to catch up. "What? Why did you slow down?"

"No reason."

She glances at my fingers. "Oh. You just had your nails done. Okay, we can do something different."

"Yeah, let's do something different." I force a swallow down my throat and start walking again. This conversation is headed toward employment, and it's better if I get ahead of it and spin it. "Did I tell you I'm working for Sutton?"

"No, you did not." She smiles, but it falters. "What happened to your job at the ... where were you working?"

"For the last time, I was laid off months ago. We've been over this."

"I'm sorry, sweetheart. I keep forgetting."

"Well, it's not hard to remember." I sigh in exasperation. "Anyway, because I was laid off from my last job and needed money, I took a position with Canoodle Productions. It'll last a few weeks, but it pays well, and the perks are great."

"What will you be doing?"

I race to devise a simple explanation and kick myself for not thinking this through before I brought it up. I don't want to lie to her —not that she'll remember any of this. But Nashville can feel like a small town, and one of her friends could see me somewhere with Ripley.

I would just have to hope they don't know who Ripley is ...

"Get this," I say. "I'm filming a pilot for a reality show."

"That's so exciting!"

My smile grows at her genuine response. "It is, kind of. I get to go on dates that Canoodle pays for and film it."

"With multiple men or just one?"

"Just one."

We get to my car, so I unlock the doors, and we climb in. Mom nearly hits me in the head with her bag as she tosses it in the back seat.

"What's he like?" she asks as I start the engine.

"Well ..."

I look over my shoulder and back out of the parking space. My face is warm when I face forward, so I blast the air-conditioning in the car to hopefully hide my flush.

"He's handsome," I say, using adjectives to describe Actor Ripley and not Real Ripley. "He's ... smart. Charming." I pause as I search for a word besides *fake*. "He seems very loyal."

"That's what I'm talking about. That's exactly what you should be doing in your life. Dating around. Having fun. Meeting men and enjoying them. I love this for you, Georgia."

"I'm really just helping Sutton out of a bind."

"I think this is the spark you need to get off your couch." She grabs the door handle like I'm about to wreck into the car in front of us. "I know you just dated ... dammit. What was his name?"

"Donovan."

"Yes, Donovan. He didn't put any sparkle, any pizzazz into your life. Maybe this new gig you have going on will do that for you."

"Yeah, maybe."

We drive quietly toward my mom's house. She plays on her phone, and I think about my lost pizzazz. I disagree with her in theory. I still feel pretty damn pizazzy. But I know what she means, and she's not totally wrong.

Last night, I felt a little more alive than I have in weeks. So maybe this is the spark I need to propel me forward. This might be the path to dreaming again.

The sound of Ripley's laughter streams through my ears. I can see his face, feel his hand on the small of my back, and his breath against my ear.

THE INVITATION

I shiver in my seat.
It might also be the path to a nightmare.
I guess time will tell.

Chapter Fourteen

Ripley

"I highly advise against that," I say, leaning back in my chair. "If you put Charleston straight into conditioning at that level, you may as well write him off for the rest of the season."

"He's in that bad of shape?" Coach Shaw shakes his head. "For fuck's sake, Ripley. I need a shortstop. Is there anything we can do to expedite getting him field-ready?"

"That's up to him. He must put the work in. We reviewed his personalized program this morning, and I explained how imperative this is to his recovery and reducing injuries going forward. But I mean ..."

"How much confidence do you have in him?"

I grin. "I give him a ten out of ten that he's going to go home tonight, eat a bunch of shit, and engage in inappropriate behavior."

Coach rolls his eyes.

"He gets a four-point-seven that he's going to walk in here tomorrow fully committed to his health and the Arrows program," I say.

THE INVITATION

"You know, when I got into coaching at this level, I didn't expect it to resemble chasing kittens around all damn day." He puts his hands on his knees and groans as he stands. "Yet here we fucking are."

I chuckle, watching his thoughts fly around his head like a cartoon character.

"I'm going to get with Landry about this roster," Coach says. "If he wants to make the playoffs, I gotta have a shortstop."

"Seems important to me."

He laughs, side-eyeing me. "Any chance I could get your ass in a pair of cleats?"

"Sure. I'll lace up for the right price, but I'm not sure that'll help your play-off objective."

His laugh grows louder as he heads for the door. "Thanks for your help. I can always count on you."

"You're welcome."

Coach's words echo through my mind as he steps into the hallway. I smile as I pick up my phone to check the texts chirping inside my desk for the past ten minutes.

"Good grief, you fuckers," I say, opening the family text thread.

> Bianca: Is it just me, or is Renn withholding baby Arlo pictures?
>
> Tate: I've gotten pics every day this week.
>
> Jason: Of Arlo, Tate.
>
> Tate: Oh. 😬
>
> Bianca: 😳
>
> Gannon: Are you not getting the pictures? Wow, B. That's rough.
>
> Bianca: You better be joking.

I laugh, imagining my sister's face all distorted and fire coming from her head. When she lived in Nashville, we were all borderline scared of her. She might be younger than all of us but Tate and short as hell, but she won't put up with anything—especially from us.

> Jason: Did you see the one where Blakely put Arlo in Renn's old jersey?
>
> Tate: Did I send you the one from last weekend when I was over there and caught him smiling at me?
>
> Gannon: Ah, yeah. That was a good one.
>
> Bianca: This isn't funny, guys.
>
> Bianca: I WANT TO SEE MY NEPHEW.
>
> Renn: I sent you ten pictures yesterday. What the hell are you talking about, B?
>
> Bianca: I wanted to ensure they weren't getting pictures I wasn't getting.
>
> Tate: Aw, is someone getting homesick?

My smile stretches from ear to ear as I read the messages from my brothers and sister.

> Bianca: I don't want to be excluded from anything just because I'm not there.
>
> Jason: That means you're homesick.
>
> Bianca: Does it?
>
> Renn: You know that holidays, birthday parties, kindergarten graduations, and rugby games will be much easier if you live here.
>
> Tate: And late-night milkshake runs.
>
> Renn: What?

> Tate: That's going to be our thing.
>
> Renn: Whose?
>
> Tate: Me and Arlo. I've decided.

I chuckle, scrolling to keep reading.

> Renn: You better talk to his mother before you do that.
>
> Jason: Our thing is going to be flying. He's going to want his pilot's license.
>
> Renn: Chill. Out.
>
> Jason: I can see it in his eyes. The kid was born for the sky.
>
> Renn: You guys are stressing me out.
>
> Bianca: CAN WE GET BACK TO ME, PLEASE?

Renn spams the chat with more baby pictures than most people take of their offspring.

I flip through the images, wondering if they ever let the kid go a minute without a camera in his face. I get it, though. Arlo is adorable. And, if I'm being honest, I do the same to Waffles.

When your baby's cute, your baby's cute.

"Knock, knock."

The words correspond to the sound of knuckles against the door. I look up and find the Arrows GM, Lincoln Landry, standing in the doorway.

"Look who it is," I say, getting to my feet. "The man. The myth. The legend."

He extends his hand and laughs. "I like the sound of legend."

"How are you?" I shake his hand. "It's good to see you."

"It's good to be here and finally be settled in. Mind if I take a seat?"

"Be my guest."

We sit across from each other. He looks the same as he did when he was a star centerfielder for the Arrows years ago—fit and strong. The coach should see if Landry wants to lace up and play. He's in better shape than half of the team.

"It's nice seeing you in purple and gold again," I say.

"It's nice being back in the fold. I was floored when Gannon called and asked me if I was interested in being the general manager. I hadn't given much thought to returning to baseball at this level, but as soon as I heard the idea, I knew I had to do it."

And the Arrows will be damn lucky because of it. He truly is a legend, both in the sport and as a human.

"How do you like the new facility? I've heard it's quite different from the old Memphis stadium."

"Oh, yeah. This is state of the art. I would've killed for these amenities when I played." He grins. "Still, the franchise is the franchise. It's like coming home."

"That's probably because I saw your kids running up and down the halls yesterday."

Lincoln laughs. "My kids would be here every day if I let them. And I'd let them if I weren't afraid of being fired—and even more afraid of their mother."

His affection for his wife is as clear as day, and I can't help but note it. I've met her, and she's a wonderful person. Lincoln is happy in the Arrows facility but seems even happier when he's with Danielle and their children.

The thought makes me pause, and a weird energy ripples through my chest.

I wonder what it would be like to have my own children running the halls?

"How is Danielle?" I ask.

"She's great. We met in Tennessee, so it's like coming home for her, too. I know she misses being in Savannah a lot. She's really close with my sisters, and we loved the kids being close to their cousins. But the flight is just over an hour, and with a Brewer Air jet at our disposal, thanks to my contract, they've been able to go back all the time."

"I'm glad it's working out for you all."

"Me, too. So how are you? I saw Coach in the hallway, and he said you suggested a new shortstop."

I lean back, propping one ankle on the other knee. "I didn't say it in those terms ... I don't think. But I don't have a lot of faith that Charleston's focus is on this team. His injuries are pretty severe, and while I've seen guys get through it and play excellent ball on the other side, it takes a lot of dedication. I'm not sure Charleston is the poster boy for that."

Lincoln sighs, his shoulders sinking. "I appreciate your insight. And to be honest, I feared as much. Some guys are born ballers, and some, most, are not. Can't say I met him and walked away thinking he was the future of the team."

"Just a tip I heard in the training facility the other day. Darryl Goggins might be pushing for a trade from the Rebels. He'd be a hell of an addition to our infield and our lineup."

"I think you're right, and if that's true, that's a damn good piece of intel." He stands. "I'm going to make some calls and see what's possible." He heads for the door. "Is there any way we can keep you here full-time instead of sharing you with the rugby and hockey teams?" He faces me. "You know your heart is here. Those rugby guys are animals, and the hockey guys are wimps. Baseball is where it's at."

I laugh. "Why don't you head over to the rink and let the hockey guys know that?"

"I'm good." He laughs, too. "I do appreciate you a lot, Ripley. You're an excellent example of professionalism and hard work for both the players and our staff. And considering your family owns this team ..." He grins. "If more franchises had owners like you, we'd have a harder time winning a championship this year."

Wow. My mouth opens to speak, but nothing comes out. I'm taken by surprise, but I also don't know what to say to that kind of praise.

"I'll talk to you later, Ripley."

"Yeah, thanks. Good to see you, Landry."

I wait until he's out of sight before I scrub my hands down my face. It's slightly embarrassing that his praise feels so good. But really, it's all I want to do in life—have a role, a place, a purpose. I've always felt like what I do is important to our athletes, and it's always given me great satisfaction to help others get and stay healthy. But no one has really appreciated it before. If they have, they've never said it.

I sit back in my chair and exhale deeply.

"Thanks for ordering for me. You really are my hero tonight."

My breath turns into a throaty chuckle as I ponder this wild situation with Georgia. *How in the hell did I wind up fake-dating the woman who hates me more than anyone in the world?*

I'm not her hero, and we both know that. She's playing her part just like I'm playing mine. But even though I know she's saying things for the hell of it—to make herself look good and to try to bother me—it's still amusing.

And it makes me curious.

She was nervous about placing her order last night. She's always hesitant about ordering from new places. When our friend group goes to a new restaurant or we're at a bar, she always waits for someone to order first. Then, more times than not, she copies whatever they say. I wondered what would happen when it was just me and her.

When I pulled her chair out, she paused as if she was surprised. And when I told her she was beautiful, which wasn't a lie, she basked in those words. And when I offered to order for her, she appreciated it.

My lips twitch.

Since our date, I've wondered what kind of guys she usually sees. *Are they taking care of her? Building her up? Making her feel safe?*

Not that I care, because I don't. It's just hypothetical. After all, she's the reason my life went sideways. *"I'm sorry, Mr. Brewer, but your scholarship offer has been rescinded."*

I force a swallow, ignoring the pit in my stomach.

"This isn't complicated," I tell myself. "It's very straightforward. She hates me. I hate her. We just have to get through these next few weeks."

I turn off my computer and stand.

Unscathed, hopefully.

Chapter Fifteen

Georgia

"Sorry to keep you waiting," I say, flashing Ripley a smile so sweet that it might give him a toothache—just in case.

I'm flustered from the traffic on the way to the skating rink, nervous about skating, and I'm not sure if I have cameras aimed at my face. I tried to get in character on the drive over, but an old man flipped me off while we were going over the bridge, and my character went from *girl falling in love* to *girl on the verge of road rage*.

I told Sutton I wasn't the kind of girl you put on television. She should've believed me.

Ripley shoves off the half-wall in front of the skating rink in a pair of black joggers and a gray hoodie. A black bag is slung over his shoulder.

"Are you recording this?" he asks.

"Do you see a camera?"

He narrows his eyes.

"Are you?" I ask.

"Nope."

My smile disappears. "Then, you know what, I'm not sorry for keeping you waiting. Shit happens. It's not my fault."

"Actually, it *is* your fault. If you had let me pick you up, I wouldn't have been standing here for the past twenty-seven minutes."

"Oh, did you learn to tell time?" I tease. "It's a little late in life, but I'm so proud of you."

"The irony of *the person who was late* mocking *the person who was on time* is rich."

"Whatever."

We stop at the entrance to the rink. People walk by and around us, moving through their day. I glance inside, a bubble of excitement rising in my stomach.

"When was the last time you skated?" Ripley asks.

"Actually, this will be my first time."

He stops fiddling with his bag and looks up, confused. "Seriously?"

"It's not like riding a bike. Not everyone ice-skates."

"Huh."

"What?" I ask, my brows tugging together. "What's that *huh* about?"

"I swore I remembered you said you were going skating our senior year at Christmastime. A bunch of us were going caroling for extra credit, and you couldn't go because you were going skating." He shrugs. "Guess I got my people mixed up."

My shoulders fall as I stare at him. *How the hell did he remember that? I didn't even remember that until now.*

"No, you're right," I say in disbelief, clutching the hoodie I brought as instructed. "It was me. I just didn't go."

He waits as if he knows there's a story, and he's giving me time to share it. Maybe he senses that I need a moment to process the hidden memory. But when it becomes clear I'm not delving into that particular holiday tale—ever, if I can help it—he clears his throat.

"Myla contacted the rink and had cameras configured before we got here," he says. "There won't be audio, though, until we turn on our audio packs. I have them in my bag."

"Got it. Remind me where we left off the other night," I say. "So we can keep the vibe nice and steady."

He flashes me a killer grin. "You thought I was the hottest guy you've ever seen and couldn't wait to see me again."

"And you were clearly smitten with me and practically begged to take me out one more time."

"You begged to go home with me, but I refused. I'm just not that kind of guy."

I gasp. "You like men?"

"*Right*." He shakes his head, amused. "Are you ready to do this?"

"As ready as I'll ever be."

He unceremoniously slings open the door to the rink, and as I step inside, a blast of cold air smacks me in the face.

The rink smells odd, kind of like frozen sweat.

"Do you know what's truly ironic?" I ask, sliding my hoodie over my body.

"Probably not."

"The devil just took me somewhere freezing. Who would've thought?"

He groans, ignoring my laughter, and leads me to a long bar extending along a wall. A blond man smiles at us, mostly me, from the other side of the counter. *Good grief.*

Ripley frowns, his eyes hardening as he introduces himself to the man and explains why we're here. Billy, as his name tag reads, provides a rundown of the next two hours that I have the luxury of spending with Ripley. *Not.* It's not lost on Ripley or me that Billy keeps watching me out of the corner of his eye. As the seconds tick by, and Billy seems more and more interested in talking to me than Ripley, my date starts to grow annoyed.

"We're on video," I whisper just loud enough for Ripley to hear.

Ripley's jaw pulses. He slides an arm casually around my waist, his gaze locked on Billy.

I gasp as Ripley's fingers sink deep enough into my side so I'm aware of the pressure through my two layers of clothes. It's a subtle yet intentional move, which isn't lost on me ... or Billy.

Billy reads between the thin lines, takes our skate sizes, and disappears through a doorway behind him.

I'm frozen in place, tucked against Ripley's solid frame and enveloped in the spicy air surrounding him. *My God.*

The only movement he makes is to peer down at me with an uneasy yet unapologetic look in his eyes.

I press a hand against Ripley's abs and swivel to face him. My throat is tight. My body hums. And, by the growing humor in his baby blues, I'm pretty sure he knows all of that.

"Was that necessary?" I ask, my heart pounding.

He grins mischievously. "If you hate it so much, step away from me."

His voice is low and smooth. It's a dare, a goad. It's a test to see who will win our battle of the wills. He's snapped into character quicker than I have.

Get yourself together.

Thankfully, Billy reappears with our skates before I have to respond. We thank him, take the skates, and silently move to a bench near the ice.

My head is spinning. I can't make sense of my reaction to his touch. I knew it would happen eventually, and I've been mentally preparing for it—practicing how cool I'd be when the time came. But it came out of nowhere, with absolutely no warning. His arm wrapped around the small of my back, his fingers splaying against my hip. I didn't have time to remind myself to brace for impact.

Dammit.

Ripley tosses a bag beside him and sits. I sit, too, leaving enough space between us so I can't use my skates as a weapon.

"I'm happy to sit and watch you," I say, placing my purse next to me. "You can have all the attention on you. We know how much you love that."

"You're skating."

"I'm not much of a skater," I say.

"You are today." He slips off his sneakers and starts putting his skates on. "We have to start filming at some point, so let me know when you want to be nice."

"To you? Never." I slip off my shoes. "It's so draining."

He laces up his last skate while I fumble with mine. "You signed the contract."

That I did.

I finish my skates and sit up. Ripley hands me an audio pack. We work quickly to attach them to our backs like the crew showed us at Canoodle.

"Smile at me," I say, straightening my hoodie.

He looks up, puzzled. "Why?"

"I want there to be photographic evidence that you think I'm funny."

"We can't lie to the people, Peaches," he says.

I laugh, pulling my hair back into a ponytail. "The fact that we're here is lying to the people. And if I don't punch you in the face for calling me Peaches, that'll also be disingenuous."

"Why do you hate it so much?"

I tap my skates against the ground. "You don't think I've lived with Georgia Peach jokes my entire life?"

He smirks, making a show of turning on his mic. "I was referring to your ass, not the state."

My jaw hangs open, much to his amusement.

"I brought you a pair of gloves," he says, handing them to me. "It's impossible to have fun with cold fingers."

"That's what she said."

He laughs and shakes his head. *Actor Ripley is back.* "You just never know what you're going to say."

"It's a part of my charm."

"Something like that. Are you ready to get on the ice?"

I glance out over the skating surface. "I'm nervous."

"You haven't skated before?"

I start to remind him that I just told him that, but then I remember that the studio audience won't know we went to high school together. Still, I see the question in his eyes—the curiosity about why I didn't go way back then. If I don't answer now, I'll look suspicious.

Besides, who cares? I can say it, and we can move on. It'll probably get edited out, anyway.

"I was supposed to one year," I say, putting on the gloves. "Dad had planned an entire outing for Christmas—a trip to a ski slope, ice-skating, a sleigh ride. I was so freaking excited and told everyone about it. As you know."

Pain hits my chest at the memory, making me wince.

Ripley shifts from one foot to the other as he listens.

"A couple of days before we were set to leave, he got the bill for my tuition at Waltham Prep, and he went crazy. He called me like it was my choice to go there and screamed at me for ten straight minutes while I sobbed." I inhale a long breath. "Needless to say, we didn't go on our trip. And I never heard from him again."

"Ever?"

"Ever."

My cheeks are pink, and I'm not sure if it's from the cold or the way he's looking at me. His concern is genuine, and it wallops me right in the chest.

Why am I so emotional today? I must be starting my period.

"If I know anything in life, I know all about asshole fathers," he says softly. "I'm sorry he did that to you. If he was capable of that, you are better off without him."

Tears fill my eyes, clouding my vision.

He's not wrong, and to make matters worse, he now knows about my mom and his dad, yet another way his father fucked his family.

I hope he realizes he's better off without his father being a part of his life, too.

"Dammit, Ripley. You aren't supposed to make me cry."

He chuckles.

"Say something mean," I say, wiping my cheeks. "Add a jab. Something."

He pulls me to my feet. "You'll probably fall out there, and I'll laugh at you. Does that help?"

I move to punch him, but my balance gets wonky, and I teeter on the thin blades of the skates. I yelp, grabbing his forearms and steadying myself.

"Don't forget we're on camera," he whispers in my ear. "Now, come on. Let's get out there and skate."

"I don't think I can do this." My movements are short and jerky as I step onto the ice. "I'm going to fall."

"I got you. I won't let anything happen to you."

His words light a cord that burns into my core. I want to believe him. I really, really do. *But Actor Ripley doesn't mean it. It's all for the show.* Real Ripley would probably let me fall ... and most definitely laugh at me.

Still, it's hard not to let his words make me feel good. It's nice to hear a man give you assurance. It's usually the other way around.

Which is partly why I might die alone.

"Try to keep your feet under your hips," he says, skating in front of me. He holds my hand and skates backward effortlessly, pulling me along slowly. "Do you feel your blade and how it touches the ice?"

"I can imagine how the ice will feel against my face when I fall."

He laughs. "I told you I won't let you fall. Have a little faith in me, won't you?"

"I haven't known you long enough to have that kind of faith in you."

"Is there a length of time you must know someone before you have faith in them?" he asks.

"Thirteen years."

"So specific," he says, pulling me around the ice. His eyes twinkle. "Doing some quick math, but I'm guessing that's about your senior year of high school."

"Junior year. My senior year was pretty shit."

His twinkle fades, and our speed slows. I start to wobble at the change of pace. Ripley helps me get my balance but follows through on his promise—I don't fall.

"Don't lock your knees," he says, his voice gentle. "Stay loose."

"No woman ever wants to be loose."

He smiles at me. "You're doing great."

"I'm holding on to you like a child."

"You know, there are a lot of women who would pay big money to get the chance to hold on to me for a couple of hours."

"I—*fuck!*" I lose my balance and begin to flail. "Ripley!"

He slides an arm around me and pulls me against him. I'm afraid I'll knock him over with my bullshit, but he doesn't budge. Not even an inch.

His body is warm against mine, delivering a level of safety and reliability that I didn't expect. That I didn't want.

That I *don't* want to like.

He stares into my eyes like there's something he wants to say. This is the moment on television where the audience *oohs* and *aahs*, sensing the actors' chemistry.

Well done, Ripley.

"Try letting yourself glide a little bit," he says after steadying me yet again. "Don't fight it so much."

"Okay—*ah*!" I yell, grabbing at him again as my knees start to go one way and my ass starts to go the opposite direction. "How do people do this and live?"

He snickers. "Most people are more coordinated than you."

"Hey!" I try to be annoyed but laugh—because he's right. "I think I'd like this if I could actually get moving. I'm just waddling here like a ninety-year-old woman needing a hip replacement." I pause. "Come to think of it, if I do get moving, I'll probably be a thirty-year-old woman needing a hip replacement."

"If you start to fall, squat like you're going to sit in a chair with your arms in front of you."

I look at him over my shoulder. "There's no way in hell I'm squatting on skates. But thanks for the tip."

"Just hold on to me and trust me. You can just glide along with me to feel the motion."

"Sounds like something you'd hear in a porno."

He laughs, his cheeks now pink, too. "You're the one with porn in your search history, so you tell me."

"Don't act like you don't look at porn."

"Don't act like you have to justify watching it by accusing me of the same. It's perfectly fine for you to watch whatever the hell you want to watch. How about that?"

I nod approvingly. "Okay, I like that take. You earn a bonus point."

I pull my attention away from him and to my skates. Then I look up. Our pace has picked up, and my skates are moving like a skater and not a toddler. "Look! I'm skating!"

We're moving smoothly across the rink as the cold breeze tickles my face. The sound of the blades scratching into the ice fills the air, and the sensation feels freeing.

It's everything I hoped it would be.

"Well, technically, you're skating and dragging me along, but semantics, right?" I ask, my legs starting to wobble. "My thighs are screaming right now. How is this so hard? It just creeps up on you."

"Are you ready to call it a day?"

"Yeah, at least for now. I'm afraid I'll wind up flat on my back if we go too much longer."

His smirk hits me right between the legs.

"Not like that." I roll my eyes. "I don't know how to stop in these things, by the way."

We skate to the bench, and Ripley brings us to a stop. He holds my hand while stepping off the ice and then faces me.

We're nearly chest to chest, still joined by our gloved fingers, and our breaths come out in little puffs. The rink is quiet, save for the hum of a machine doing something somewhere.

It's just us.

And I don't have anything snarky to say to disarm the situation.

Although I thought it was ridiculous, I've always understood that Ripley charmed women. But standing on the ice, my hands in his, and without the pressure of having to come up with something to keep my guard up, I get it on a different level than ever before.

There's something attractive about him that transcends his jawline and cheekbones. There's a reliability, a sturdiness—a masculine energy that makes me feel protected that's seductive ... or it would be if I let it.

The fact that I can see this, *feel this*, is terrifying. Life was easier when I looked at him and wanted to hit him in the face with a pie. Because now, after knowing this part of him exists, I'm afraid it might be harder to get back to where we once were.

We were there for a reason.

As if he can read my thoughts, his smile is soft yet timid. It's not the arrogant, self-absorbed man who drives me crazy. It's a man who might be reevaluating himself … and the woman he's with—just like he was hired to do.

It'll make damn good television.

Chapter Sixteen

Georgia

"I come bearing snacks," Ripley says, sitting beside me on the bench.

We took a few more laps around the rink until I couldn't feel my thighs anymore. I lambasted myself for choosing chicken nuggets in the gym parking lot and not the actual gym itself. I am not in skater-girl shape. Then he returned our skates.

"You know the way to this woman's heart." I blow on my hands through the gloves to try to warm them up. "I'm not sure I'm ever going to thaw."

He hands me a steaming cup of hot cocoa. "Try this. It might help."

"You get another bonus point. Maybe even two."

He chuckles. "You're easy to please."

"If you're ever in doubt, bring me chocolate in some form. It helps."

I hold the cup with both hands, trying to let the heat seep into my body. While I had a lot of fun skating and would love to try it again sometime, I don't think I could ever get past how cold it is on the ice. It's unnatural.

"The snack selection was sparse, so I got popcorn," he says. "It looks the freshest. Open up."

I open my mouth, and he feeds me a piece.

He's laid-back and relaxed, with his hair not perfect and his five o'clock shadow giving him a slight edge. I don't see him like this often—not even with our friends. *Maybe I don't want to see it...*

"I had to answer a call from my mother at the snack stand," he says, feeding me another piece of popcorn. "One of my brothers wasn't answering her calls, so she was doing a welfare check."

"That's adorable."

"You think?" He wrinkles his nose. "Maybe it just feels odd because she wasn't always like this. It's hard getting used to it when you're thirty."

"What was she like growing up?"

He pops a few kernels in his mouth and thinks. "She was busy. She had a lot of kids, so she was always running someone somewhere. There was a lot of charity work, too, and she traveled with my father a lot when we were younger. If we were home, we were usually with a nanny."

"Oh."

"Why do you say it like that?"

He places another piece of popcorn on my tongue, making my stomach flutter.

"I guess I had this vision of big family meals and holiday traditions," I say.

"Would've been nice."

"Are you close to your mother now?"

He nods. "We're closer than before. Although my brother Renn just had a baby, so now he's the star of the show."

I laugh at the look on his face. "Babies usually draw all the attention for a while."

"Yeah, well, he's a cute little shit. So I get it."

"Do you want a big family?" I ask before sipping my cocoa. "Or has having a bunch of siblings been enough for you?"

He pauses to think.

We're sitting quietly side by side on the cold bench, our breaths billowing in front of us, and there's a strange calmness between us—an

THE INVITATION

almost cocoon of sorts. If I think about it too much, I'll panic. So, I don't.

I know none of this is *actually* happening. I'm rational. But the way he's opening up about some things, and the look in his eye has me momentarily forgetting that this is for Canoodle.

My stomach twists at the realization that I'm slowly starting to slip into a gray area. That must stop.

It would behoove me to focus on why we're here and not get sucked into the pretend world we're intentionally creating. While he's probably telling some truths here, he'd never show me a hint of vulnerability. He's showing me what he needs to show me for the show, and probably to make me start to question things between us.

Because he's a sadist.

"If I have a family someday, I do probably want a large one if my wife is on board," he says, staring across the ice. "But the big difference is that I want to be involved. I want to be there. I want to have big meals and holiday traditions like you mentioned. On Saturdays, we go to soccer practice or ballet lessons—whatever the kids are into." He looks at me. "I want to be everything my father wasn't."

My heart swells in my chest. I had no idea that Ripley was so deep or so thoughtful. That he's thought this through is such a green flag.

"I think that's a nice dream," I say.

He throws a piece of popcorn at me, hitting me in the nose. "What about you? Do you want a big family?"

I grimace before taking another long sip of my drink.

"What?" he asks.

I study him and the genuine curiosity on his face. He's been pretty honest with me today, so this can't be too much of a trap. Besides, I need to play my part as much as he's playing his. I promised Sutton I'd do my best to make this a success.

"I'm not really sure what I want, to be honest." I sigh. "I love the idea of having a family. But I'm kind of ..."

"Kind of what, Georgia?"

"Kind of not sure what to say. I'm scared to think about it because then I might want it, and if I want it and don't get it, that'll hurt. Or what if I do get it, and then it all falls apart, and I turn into my mother?"

Thank God this is a pilot, and she'll never see this. I wouldn't want to hurt her feelings.

He folds his hands between his knees. "I understand that, actually."

"Really?"

"I mean, I wouldn't say I'm scared."

"God forbid."

"But I'm nervous that I don't quite have what it takes to be a good dad."

His words fall through the air like dead weight, landing on the ice and slipping away. Regret shifts across his face, and I wonder if he regrets telling me that. If so, that makes me sad—mostly because I suspect he hasn't really shared this with anyone before, and now he's clamming up on me.

"Are you ready to go?" he asks.

"Sure."

He gets to his feet and picks up his bag, so I hurry to stand and gather my things, too. We remove our audio packs, and he shoves them hastily into his bag. I'm not sure what caused the sudden change in him, but I scramble to keep up.

We make our way to the exit and step onto the sidewalk. The freedom from the cameras is a relief as the warm air heats my bones. Ripley walks me to my car without saying a word, and I give him space, thinking he'll eventually talk. But he doesn't.

I should let it go. I should let this be his problem elsewhere. Why should I care if he doesn't want to talk to me?

And I don't care, really. But ...

We stop at my car, I toss my things in the back seat, and then I take off his gloves.

"Can I ask you something?" I ask, hesitating. I'm not sure which Ripley I'm going to get, nor do I know if he'll still be interested in talking to me like he was a moment ago. But I know I can't go home without trying ... both for my curiosity and his well-being.

"Sure."

I lean my back against my car. "Why would you think you don't have what it takes to be a good dad? I mean, I might hate you ..." I grin at him. "But that's a personal decision. You seem like a pretty decent guy to the rest of the world."

He shrugs like it's no big deal. That's how I know it's a big deal.

A shadow crosses his face as he licks his lips. "Someone told me once that I don't have a lot of value as a person. And while I know that's bullshit, it lingers in the back of my brain."

"Who told you that?" I ask, instantly angry.

"My father."

I touch my lips to keep from gasping. My wide eyes gawk at him. I want to reach out and pull him into me and hug the embarrassment off his handsome face. But I don't. I hold back. For both of our goods.

"Ripley, fuck that guy," I say instead. "I mean it."

He laughs sadly. "It's okay."

"No, it's not. Who says that to someone, let alone their child?"

"It's okay."

"Give me his prison address, and I'll write him really mean letters," I say, wanting to do something.

"Georgia, *it's okay*." He smiles. "Really."

It's not okay. Not even a little. "What would cause someone to be such a complete bastard?"

"We always butted heads. I guess I just didn't accept his bullshit. Like, by the age of six, when he'd come home yelling at everyone, I'd call him out on it. He hated that. Who was I to challenge the great Reid Brewer?"

I bite my lip as he continues.

"I wanted to box, so he made me play soccer. I wanted to be a chef for a while, and he called me a pussy." He takes a breath. "I lost my scholarship, and he broke my nose. It's the only thing I'd ever done that made him proud of me, and I lost it."

"He broke your nose?" I yelp.

"Yeah."

"And no one hit him back?"

"You don't always win violence with violence, Peaches."

"I want to fight him. I'd have to train a while first, but I want to at least get a couple of shots off on him."

Ripley shakes his head, his chest bouncing with a suppressed chuckle.

Our gazes hold each other tight, and I couldn't look away if I wanted to. My heart pounds so hard I wonder if he can hear it. The energy between us crackles—I can hear it—and I'm drawn to him in a way I've never been before.

"It's getting late. Do you want to film our confessionals at home?" he asks, his voice low.

As the sun goes down behind him, creating a beautiful backdrop, his skin glows from the golden hour, and I wish I had a camera to capture the moment.

"That sounds good," I say. "I'll send mine to Myla tonight. Our next date is supposed to be an adventure, and I'm not very adventurous, so I don't know what you want to do with that."

"I think you were very adventurous today."

I blush. "Thank you. I tried. And thank you for remembering that I wanted to skate way back then. That's ... slightly stalkerish, but sort of sweet."

He grins. "You're welcome. And I'll pick the adventure if you want me to."

"Please. But nothing with ice. I think I'll be cold for a month."

"No ice. Got you."

"Then I guess I should get going," I say, shifting my weight.

Even as I say I should leave, I don't actually want to. None of this is real, but it's ... fun. When the cameras are rolling, it's fun to see the other side of him. And without the cameras in the parking lot, it's nice to have a real conversation without snark and gossip. It's nice to talk about something substantial. It's nice to feel seen.

Especially by someone as handsome as Ripley.

His hair ruffles in the breeze as he slips his hands in his pockets. He rocks back on his heel as if he's dragging his feet, too.

Something in his eyes soothes me, and something in his manner lures me to him like a magnet. I crave the feeling of his arms around me again.

My body hums with anticipation as he takes a hesitant step closer.

His nearness sends my heart into a freefall. I'm heavy, and warm, and hear my pulse strumming in my ears as his gaze drops to my mouth.

He's going to kiss me.

He wraps his fingers around mine and pulls me toward him. His touch is caressing and possessive, and the combination makes my knees quiver.

I force a swallow and lift on my toes just as a car horn blares beside us, breaking the moment.

Ripley stands upright, and I fall back against the car. I drag a lungful of air into my body and try to quell the scream in my head.

I almost kissed Ripley Brewer. What am I thinking?

"I need to go," I say, fumbling at the door handle. "Let me know about the adventure, okay?"

He runs a hand through his hair. "Yeah. Drive safe."

I climb inside, tossing the gloves onto the seat beside me. Once the door is closed, I melt into the seat. *What in the hell just happened?*

He steps back and watches me pull out of the parking lot. I don't look back because I couldn't read him if I tried.

I do look across the console, however. And at the gloves on the passenger seat.

The *purple* gloves that Ripley brought for me to wear.

My throat squeezes as I turn my attention back to the road.

Chapter Seventeen

Ripley

"I just got back from my second date with Georgia," I say, a towel around my shoulders as I film my confessional. "I think it went really well. We met at the ice-skating rink, and she seemed really happy to see me, which was great."

"Then, you know what, I'm not sorry for keeping you waiting. Shit happens. It's not my fault."

I chuckle, drying my damp hair with the towel. "I took her skating because sports are a big part of my life, and I wanted to see how she responded. She did great."

But I knew she would. Because Georgia Hayes doesn't back down from a challenge.

Ever.

She's courageous on top of everything else although I'd never tell her that. That was even further proven when she told me about her dad.

"A couple of days before we were set to leave, he got the bill for my tuition at Waltham Prep, and he went crazy. He called me like it was my

choice to go there and screamed at me for ten straight minutes while I sobbed. Needless to say, we didn't go on our trip. And I never heard from him again."

What a fuck.

I shake my head, then pull the paper over and scan the questions Myla sent over.

"I was feeling pretty confident going into this date," I say. "We seemed to hit it off at Ruma, and I was excited to spend more time with her. I was also really excited to interact with her in a more relaxed environment—just to see how we connected without a restaurant full of people." I smile to myself. "It was fantastic."

My mind slips to the end of the date, a place I've tried not to focus on too much. Instantly, my heart pounds.

I didn't mean to share so much of my personal life with her. It just came out. And I never dreamed she would share anything personal with me, either. *She makes a point not to do that most of the time.*

But there we sat, talking about our dipshit fathers and how they're both fuckups. We listened to each other. Encouraged each other.

Supported each other.

My throat is tight, so I shut the phone off.

I know this entire exercise is for Sutton. Georgia has made it clear she doesn't really want to do this with me. *So why does it feel like that might not be true?*

And why do I hope that maybe it's not?

My fingers comb through my hair as I heave a breath in frustration.

"If we took you out of the equation, life would carry on."

My hands fall to my sides. My stomach knots into a tight ball.

I've never been a part of Georgia's life, and she's carried on just fine without me. She saw what a fuckup I can be years ago and made the right decision to freeze me out of her world.

She's not wrong. My goal was—*is?*—to make her fall for me for the hell of it because I'm an asshole.

Who am I to even consider that her motivations might be different? I know better.

I've always known better.

And I need to remember that. No matter what.

Chapter Eighteen

Georgia

The bathroom mirror is foggy from my afternoon bath, so I grab a hand towel and wipe off the glass to see my reflection.

My hair is twisted up in a towel, pulled away from my face, and there's a rosiness to my cheeks. My lips are slightly swollen from the hot water. I look like I've been kissed.

I press my fingertips to my lips as butterflies take flight in my stomach—and I think about almost kissing him. Again.

"What is happening?" I whisper.

I've had so many thoughts rolling through my mind since my second date with Ripley. *How is he so funny, thoughtful—sweet—when I know him to be the opposite?*

The purple gloves. Taking me skating because I mentioned it over a decade ago. His promise not to let me fall.

This is the same man who would rather spit nails than speak to me most days.

What's the difference now? The cameras?

The cameras weren't in the parking lot.

"This is a mindfuck of exponential proportion," I say, heading into my bedroom.

I get dressed quickly, my thoughts still with the blue-eyed monster.

If this were the real Ripley, would things be different between us? Would it change anything? Would it erase the hurt he's caused me in the past?

"Two fake dates don't change the behavior of a man for the last twelve years," I say aloud. "Especially when it's two fake dates with his actions being tracked by people outside of our friend group."

My stomach drops.

I don't know what I want. I'm not sure which result I want to be the answer. *Do I want him to be the asshole he's always been? Or do I want there to be more to him than a rich prick who thinks he's better than me?*

I flop on the bed and stare at the ceiling, memories from a decade ago floating through my mind.

"You know he doesn't really like you, right?" The blonde giggles, blowing a big pink bubble in my face. "There was a bet. He won. They're all in the refreshment room laughing about you right now."

"And he's probably at home laughing at me right now, too," I say on a sigh.

"Hey!" Sutton's voice drifts through my townhouse. "Where are you?"

"Bed," I shout back.

She bops around the corner. "Still?"

"Hey, unemployment has its perks."

"You're technically employed by me." She sits on the edge of the bed. "Well, the company I work for, but whatever."

I sit up, my body feeling heavy. "What are you doing here in the middle of the day?"

"Just checking on you." Her smile is as bright as the strand of pearls around her neck. "Myla said the footage she's gotten so far from your two dates is perfect, by the way. You haven't really texted me much, so I thought you might need a face-to-face bestie sesh."

I smile at her.

"So how's it going?" she asks.

I get up, wishing I could get out of this conversation. There's no way to pull it off. If I try to change the subject away from Ripley, it'll send a red flag shooting to the sky. I'm always happy and free to talk shit about him.

"We talked on the phone last night," I say. "You already know. It's going fine."

"I know you said that. But I wanted to see your face when you said it."

My hand stalls over my dresser. "Why?"

"A couple of reasons," she says. "One, Myla said the two of you are, in her words, *absolute fire* together."

I find a pair of random earrings on the dresser and put them in my ears.

"Myla said it's such a natural back-and-forth that editing is going to be so much easier than she feared," Sutton says.

Really? "Did you tell her it's because we can't stand each other?"

"I did. She found that interesting. And the second reason I wanted to see your face is because you haven't exactly called me screaming about him. That, my friend, is a bit suspicious."

My body stiffens. "Yeah, well, he behaves because a camera is in front of him. He's professional. I'll say that about him."

Except that he nearly kissed me … twice.

Flames spiral through me as I think about the first time he nearly kissed me at Ruma. The flames burn hotter as I remember his face just before he lowered his mouth toward mine at the rink. There was no camera then, and his gaze was without the promise of mischief.

I'd give anything for this feeling to be real—to feel this alive. I haven't felt anything about anyone in such a long time. Even with Donovan, things felt blah. I didn't even realize it until I compared it to what I'm feeling now.

Talking about my father isn't something I do for fun, and I never share stories about him that make me feel sad. I don't even discuss those things with Mom—she doesn't even know the skating story. So why did I share it with the man who can't stand to be around me most of the time?

Is it because I was anxious and I talk too much when I'm nervous? Did

I tell him those things because I know once this is over, I'll never have to talk to him—about anything—again? Or was it because once we were on the ice, I felt safe?

I dreamed last night, remembering things I used to want to do. Things I wanted to see ... places I wanted to go. I woke up happy and inspired.

I woke up feeling like me.

"Are you okay?" Sutton asks.

Her words make me jump. "Me? Yeah. I was just thinking about whether I had any snacks to offer you."

She laughs, standing. "It's you, Georgia. Of course, you have snacks somewhere."

"Let's see what I have."

She follows me into the kitchen, regaling me with tales of work that bleed into wedding planning. Then she transitions into potential honeymoon spots. She talks so fast that I can't get a word in edgewise.

I pour us each a glass of sweet tea while she finishes her monologue.

"Oh," she says, stopping only to take a sip. "Tate came over last night with Carys."

"Hey, now. Don't get cute on me. I'm the best friend."

She laughs. "I know. Settle down." She takes another drink, her red lipstick imprinting on the glass. "Anyway, Jeremiah and Tate went to pick up food, and Carys and I stayed back and talked. That poor girl ..." She laughs again, shaking her head.

"What about her?"

"She's getting trashed by men left and right. Her stories have made me chuckle all day. I told her she's too nice for the men she's trying to date, and that she either has to toughen up or find a new type."

I open my computer and unlock it. "What's her type?"

"Tate, but older and edgier."

"Why doesn't she just date Tate and put a leather jacket on him? He'll be older in a few years."

Sutton rummages around my pantry and pulls out a box of cookies. "She'll never date Tate. And I don't think Tate would ever date her. They're literally the same person, except one has a dick. I think if I brought up fucking Tate, Carys might puke."

"Okay, probably not a love connection then."

"Definitely not."

I open my email, and my heart starts to race. A message from an hour ago sits at the top of my inbox.

"I'm so glad I'm not dating anymore," Sutton says. "I like this era of picking out furniture and wedding invites way better than—"

"Sutton!" My hand clamps over my mouth as I read the rest of the message. "I got a job."

"You did?"

I read the email aloud to her, bouncing on my feet like a child. "Sincerely, Todd Downing, Downing Enterprises."

I squeal, jumping into Sutton's arms and hugging her.

"This is amazing," she says, pulling away. Her face is lit up like Christmas as she peruses the attachments to the email. "That offer is phenomenal, Georgia. The benefits alone would have me saying yes, even if I wasn't getting that salary."

"I know." I glance over my shoulder. *Yup, the email is real.* "I'm just … shocked. *But so happy.*"

"And I'm so happy for you. I knew you'd get something as soon as the universe found a job worthy of you."

I blush.

"I'm coming back tonight with cake. We're celebrating," she says. "But right now, you need to accept that offer, and I need to get back to work. Don't make plans for tonight. I'll be here around six."

"I'll be here."

"Love you. See you then."

"Bye," I say, watching her walk out the door.

The email is maximized on the screen, each word easily visible. I read through it again, just to be sure. It's almost too good to be true.

Dear Ms. Hayes,

THE INVITATION

We are pleased to formally offer you the position of Media Relations Specialist. Our offer includes a salary and benefits package detailed in the attachment to this email. Your expected start date is two weeks from the date of receipt of your signed contract (also attached). Please respond within ten business days.

In the meantime, please feel free to contact me via email or phone should you have any questions.

We look forward to having you on our team.

Best regards,
Todd Downing
Downing Enterprises

I hit reply, but my phone rings in my bedroom. I jog there to get it, and after finding it on my nightstand, I pick it up.

There's a text on the screen. From Ripley.

My breathing is shallow as I sit on the edge of the bed.

> Ripley: Saturday. Noon. Work for you?

I stare at the words. Five words. Short and simple.
My brows tug together as I try to read his tone.
Is he mad? Busy? Irritated?
Or just being a dick?

> Me: Okay.

His response is almost immediate.

> Ripley: Love the excitement.

My fingers fly over the keys.

> Me: I was trying to be succinct.

> Ripley: I noticed. Why change your behavior now?

> Me: Very funny. 🙄

> Me: You sent five words, so I was trying not to take up your time in case you were busy.

> Ripley: Don't you want to know what we're doing on Saturday at noon? 😉

I laugh, sighing in relief.

> Me: Nope. If I would've realized we were skating, I might not have gone. It's probably better that I don't know.

> Ripley: Did you enjoy skating, though?

I bite my lip, attempting to read between the lines. *Does he actually mean skating? Or does he mean the date as a whole? Or is he asking how I feel about almost kissing him?*

My cheeks burn as I decide what to say.

THE INVITATION

> Me: I didn't fall, so that's a plus.

> Ripley: So, you didn't like it?

> Me: I didn't say that. At all.

> Ripley: That's what it sounds like.

> Me: You can't read tone.

"Even though I've been trying to do it for the entirety of this conversation," I say.

I get to my feet, too much energy flowing through me to sit, and sort out my response. I don't want him to think I don't appreciate him going to the trouble of putting the skating thing together or that I don't remember how thoughtful he was about how he selected that location.

If he makes fun of me for being nice, I'll deck him.

My stomach tightens as I type.

> Me: To be honest, I had a REALLY great time. I never would've done it if it weren't for you. I think it helped jostle me out of a funk that I've been trying to snap out of for a while.

> Me: It was also very sweet of you to have remembered that I wanted to go skating. Thank you. I hope you had fun, too.

> Ripley: You're welcome.

I sigh.

> Me: So YOU didn't like it?

> Ripley: You can't read tone.

My lips twist in annoyance although it's borderline funny.

> Ripley: I'm glad we went, too. It was fun. It would've been more fun if you'd fallen, and I could've laughed at you. But you surprised us both by staying on your skates and picking up the concept really fast.

> Me: Would you really have let me fall?

His response comes right away.

> Ripley: No.

I pace through the house. His response was immediate. No hesitation.

My heart tugs in my chest. "Why do you have to be so damn confusing?"

> Me: Ever thought of going into acting? Because you're pretty great at it.

> Ripley: I learned from the best.

> Me: Who?

> Ripley: You.

I bite my lip and stare at the words like they'll suddenly make sense. I can't figure out if he means that he thinks *I'm* acting—which I am, but also, I'm not.

THE INVITATION

I don't know where to go from here, and the tension gathers in the back of my neck.

> Me: I got a job today, by the way. I start in two weeks. It might interfere with some of our filming, but I'm not sure. I'll let you know.

> Ripley: Congrats. That's great, Peaches.

> Me: Thanks.

> Ripley: I'll see you Saturday. Wear sneakers and sunscreen.

> Me: Will do. See you then.

I wait for him to respond, but he doesn't.
Wear sneakers and sunscreen.
I sigh.
The devil just might be taking me to hell.
I hope I don't get burned.

Chapter Nineteen

Ripley

This was a mistake.

I flip off the camera as a crack of thunder breaks through the air.

"Will you please hurry up? Just a little?" I ask, sitting on a large boulder.

"Hey! You can't sit if I can't sit." Georgia stops in the middle of the trail with her hands on the curve of her hips. "If you're sitting, I'm sitting."

"If you sit, we'll never get to the top of the hill."

"Oh, like that would be a tragedy."

I roll my eyes. "You picked this trail. I gave you three choices. This is the one you wanted."

"It has an adorable name—Sugarplum Trail. That's very misleading."

"Except I told you it was harder than the others."

"Yeah, but you didn't warn me that this one was so ..." She looks around at the dense brush, large trees, and rocks jutting out of the path. "Trail-y."

I look at the sky and sigh. *This woman.*

"Can't we just go back?" she asks, jutting her bottom lip out. "Please?"

"We currently have no usable footage. Do you want to quit now?"

"How is that possible? We've been doing this *for an hour.*"

I take my backpack off and set it on the ground beside me.

This trail should've taken us an hour at most. I thought we'd do a little hiking, get video at the top for Myla, and then have a picnic down by the stream near where we parked the car. Instead, we're two-thirds up, and I'm not sure we'll ever make it the rest of the way.

"Let's see ..." I pretend to think. "How is it possible we've not gotten any film? Well, you drank all of your water in the first twenty minutes and started complaining."

"It's hot out here."

"Then you had to stop and pee—twice."

"Because of the water."

I sigh. "You've complained about the pollen count, the number of rocks on the pathway, and that you think you pulled a muscle in your leg."

"And the heat, the bugs, and that I have to walk all the way back down. What's your point?"

"Good news. I can fix one of those problems."

"Which one?"

"I'll throw you over the cliff if we ever get to the top."

She gasps, then bends down, picks up a rock, and tosses it at me. Naturally, it doesn't come anywhere close to hitting me.

"You missed," I say, grinning.

"I can't believe this is how you date women."

"This isn't how I date women. This is how I date *you.*"

She growls, making me laugh louder. She then trudges toward me, kicking dust up as she moves.

Her antics today should've been expected. I've known Georgia for over ten years, and I've never seen her do many outdoor activities—or any, actually. But our date challenge was an adventure, and I thought a simple beginner-level hike would be something we could do together while capturing a bunch of great footage for the show. It would also give us time to talk—something I never thought I'd want to do with her willingly and on purpose but was looking forward to ... in a way.

Instead, I got a solid ten minutes of decent banter and a great view of Georgia's juicy ass as she stumbled up the mountain. The rest of it is us bickering back and forth.

We managed to capture the "hellos" in the parking lot before we headed off, and then did what Georgia called "pre-confessionals" at the trailhead for fun. She thought it made it feel more like a date for the viewer. I didn't disagree.

But that's it. That's the extent of what this day has delivered, which sucks because Georgia seemed to be genuinely excited about this at the start of the day. Now she's ... not.

The truly unexpected part of the whole thing, however, is that I find her grumpiness hot as fuck. Her jabs don't feel as sharp as usual. They come across as more self-protective than anything, which I understand. That's forgivable. That puts it through a whole new lens. It makes her snark less bitchy and more ... witty. *Weird.*

"If it rains, I'm really going to be pissed," Georgia says, marching past me.

I lug my backpack on and follow her.

"The forecast said no rain," I say. "You'll have to survive without being mad about that. I'm sure you can find something else to pout about."

"I'm not pouting, Ripley. I'm just expressing my displeasure." She whines, slowing her already sluggish pace. "I think I'm getting a blister."

"I have bandages in my pack. I'll give you one if you make it to the top."

She narrows her eyes. "Give me one now, and I won't complain until we get to the top."

"You're not supposed to negotiate with terrorists."

Her eyes shine as she looks up at me. She has a streak of dirt across her cheek, and I want to laugh, but she'll think I'm laughing at her. In reality, I just think she's adorable.

And that's my biggest new problem with Georgia. I find her grating one minute, sexy the next, and adorable after that. I can't make sense of her.

Or, rather, I can't make sense of what I think about her.

It was much easier before *The Invitation*. I hated her. She hated me. Life was grand. But now we've spent alone time together while on our very best behavior, and I don't think I quite hate her anymore.

In fact, I wonder if I ever really hated her at all.

Maybe what I hated was that she hated me.

"Fine," I say, absorbing the plea in her eyes. "Sit."

"Yay!" She plops down on a fallen tree and slides off her shoe and sock. She wiggles her purple-painted toenails. "Oh, my gosh, this feels good."

My cock twitches. *No. Don't even go there.*

"What do you have in that bag?" she asks as I rummage through it. "You're like a grown-up Dora the Explorer with your backpack."

I glare at her. That doesn't stop her from whispering, "Backpack, hooray!" under her breath.

We might not make it off this mountain.

I ignore her and find my bandages and petroleum jelly, then I pull out an antibacterial wipe and clean my hands. She watches me curiously.

"I think it's going to rain," she says as another clap of thunder breaks through the sky.

"Give me your foot," I say, crouching in front of her.

She stares at me. "My foot is sweaty."

I hold out my hand, matching her stare. She doesn't blink. I don't budge.

"Seriously, look at the clouds," she says, tilting her head toward the sky. "They look angry."

"Not as angry as I'm going to be if you don't give me your foot."

"Fine." She extends her foot to me and winces. "Do you have a plan if it rains?"

"It's not going to rain, Georgia. I know you applied for a meteorology job, but that doesn't make you an actual meteorologist."

"Rude."

I lift her foot and inspect her heel. It's bright red and starting to blister. I carefully apply a coat of petroleum jelly and cover it with a bandage.

When I look up, she's watching me with a softness in her eyes that makes my breath stall in my chest.

"There you go," I say, my voice low. I clear my throat. "Put your sock and shoe back on, and we'll head down the hill."

"What are we going to do about footage?"

The sky rumbles overhead. "We can get it another day, or you can swing by my house with me."

She gets back to her feet. "To your house? Why?"

"Waffles is scared of storms."

Her lips twist into a smile. "Your dog?"

"Yeah."

She catches up and walks alongside me. The wind picks up, and the air cools. Treetops sway back and forth in a menacing movement. And I hate to admit it, but I can smell the dirt in the air.

There *is* a storm coming.

"Where did you get Waffles?" she asks.

"I was downtown one day for something, who knows what now, and a guy was sitting on a bench with a cardboard box with three puppies." I smile sadly. "Two of them were healthy-looking dogs. A couple had found them just a few minutes before me and were haggling with the man about taking them. He wanted something like fifty dollars each for them, and the couple wanted to give him fifty total."

"What about the other puppy?"

"Well, the other puppy was about half the size of the others. Still, he was biting their tails and trying to dominate them, and he was so damn cute. I heard the guy say that the puppy was the smallest of the litter, and the mother didn't really seem to care much for him. I picked him up, and he bit the tip of my finger and growled at me." I chuckle. "And I kind of fell in love with him right there."

She smiles up at me. "So you took him home."

"I did. He's my buddy. And he hates storms—*shit!*"

Water pours from the sky in buckets. The wind rocks the trees, causing them to sway back and forth so hard they appear to bend. Lightning strikes across the sky, cracking in the distance, and Georgia shrieks and looks at me for instructions.

"Don't run," I shout over the commotion. "The ground will be slippery."

She shrieks again. "What do we do?"

"There was a ranger cabin a few minutes back. Let's go there."

"Okay!"

We start down the trail that's already slick from the rain. Georgia's feet slide out from beneath her, and I catch her before she falls on her ass. Mud splashes up the backs of our legs, and water soaks our clothes.

"I told you it was going to rain," she yells. "Don't you have an umbrella in that backpack of yours?"

"No."

"Figures."

We slide partially down a small hill, holding hands as we go. Droplets stream down my face, making it hard to see, so I run my hands over my head to push my soaked hair out of my face.

"Careful," I warn. "Don't grab those branches to keep you steady. They'll snap off."

"Ugh." She looks at me with melted mascara around her eyes. "Will you carry me?"

I laugh. "No, I will not carry you. I'm barely not wiping out on my own." I shake my head, blowing water off my lips. "Why are you like this?"

"Because I'm a Taurus!" she shouts. "I love creature comforts and solitude. This is neither of those."

"Oh, sure. Blame it on astrology."

She shoots me a dirty look, which is impressive considering the situation. "Take your Scorpio tendencies elsewhere. This is not the time."

I'm a Scorpio? "There's the cabin. To your left."

"Thank God."

We step across a washout on the trail and hop to the other side. An unkempt pathway leads to a porch that has seen better days, but we climb the rickety stairs. Georgia shivers at my side.

The sky lights up with flashes of lightning that seem to last forever.

"That rain is so freaking cold." She trembles. "What if we can't get in? We're going to die out here in the wilderness, all alone and hungry?"

I try my best not to laugh, but a small snort escapes before I can stop it. I get another dirty look in return.

"They usually leave these places unlocked in case of emergencies," I say. "I promise you won't die."

"Is this an emergency?"

"Did you or did you not just express a fear of dying in the wilderness?" I ask, teasing her.

"I mean, that might've been *a tad* dramatic."

I look down at her and grin. "Do you want to try to make it back to the car?"

"No."

"Then it's an emergency."

A tree snaps behind us as a flash of lightning brightens the sky. The sound of the wood hitting the ground roars through the forest.

I open the screen door, which creaks as it swings free, then I try the handle on the innermost entrance. Thankfully, it, too, opens with ease.

"After you," I say, motioning for her to enter.

"If we get arrested for this, I'm blaming you."

I smile. "I'd expect nothing less."

She goes in first, and I follow.

Chapter Twenty

Georgia

The rain patters against the roof. As soon as Ripley closes the door, the sound intensifies. It's harder. Denser. It's hail.

He flips on the lights.

"Right on time," Ripley says, knocking water droplets off his hair.

I roll my eyes. "You say that like you planned it."

"I accept your gratitude for me finding you a warm, dry, safe place to stay during a thunderstorm. You're so welcome."

"And I accept your apology for not listening to me when I predicted this exact situation."

He side-eyes me, heading toward the table. "So you get credit for the cabin?"

"Okay, fine. This situation minus the cabin. But the fact not to be overlooked here is that we wouldn't have needed the cabin had we not decided to hike a mountain on a day it was clearly going to storm."

He grumbles something I can't hear—lucky for him.

The cabin is small but clean, with a gray sofa beneath a window. A wooden table sits along a wall. A large fireplace made of stone is in the center of the structure, and a kitchen with the basics—a simple, stainless sink, dorm-sized refrigerator, and a cooktop—is tucked behind it. It's slightly musty but not bad.

I cross my arms over my chest, shivering. "This place is kind of cute."

"It's better than getting pelted with ice out there."

"True."

I peek into two rooms on the far side of the cabin. One is a bedroom big enough for a bed and a single nightstand. The other is a bathroom with the tiniest shower I've ever seen, a toilet, and a sink.

Ripley slings his backpack onto the table.

"We just wait it out in here?" I ask. "I didn't even bring a book."

He pulls his phone out and holds it high into the air. "There's a tornado warning for this area right now. We're supposed to take cover, so, yeah, we wait it out here."

The wind picks up, howling through the trees, and the windows rattle. When a tree falls just outside the cabin, the force of the crash makes me jump.

Ripley comes around the corner from the bathroom with two towels, handing me one.

"Here," he says. "Get dried off."

I force a smile at him. "Thanks."

I start with my hair. Ripley tosses his towel over a chair and picks his phone back up again. He walks to the window, staring at the screen.

"What's wrong?" I ask.

"I have spotty reception, but I'm trying to get a text to Tate to go through in case he can swing by my house and pick up Waffles."

My chill is pushed away by the warmth that floods my veins.

I've been with men—with people—in similar situations before. They worry their car will be destroyed in a storm. That no one will know where they are. They panic about how to get to safety, or how they'll pay for damages, or that they'll miss a meeting.

Ripley is worried about his puppy. I cannot deal with this information.

"There," he says, pausing a few moments before putting the phone back on the table. "Tate's going to get him."

I stare at him, confused.

"What?" He lifts his brows and picks up his towel.

"If we were recording right now, I'd tell you that I think it's freaking adorable how much you love your dog. It's really endearing—and unexpected." I shrug. "But since we're not filming, and I don't have to pretend to be nice, I'll say it's weird seeing you think of someone outside yourself."

He fights a grin. "Yeah, well, you need to be more worried about the fact that you have a soaked white T-shirt on than how much I love my dog."

My attention drops to my chest. Sure enough, I'm giving him a show. *Again.*

"Good thing you've already seen them once, I guess," I say.

He rummages through his bag again and pulls out a long-sleeved shirt.

"Was one of your top search terms *'Things to put in a backpack'*?" I ask.

He tosses the shirt at me. "You're welcome."

"What else do you have in there?"

"Jerky. Nuts. Water."

I wrinkle my nose. "Any candy bars? Mints? Gum?"

He wrinkles his nose back at me. "No. No junk food."

Red flag. "How long do you think we're going to be stranded here?" I ask.

"The tornado warning is until four o'clock, but Tate said the storm is supposed to stick around all night."

"All night? Are you kidding me? Did you even look at the weather this morning?"

"Did you?"

"*I* didn't plan the date."

He strips himself of his shirt, displaying his bare chest and rock-hard abdomen in plain sight.

My God.

"Well, *I did* plan the date," he says, "but I don't claim to be a pseudo-meteorologist, either. The sky looked clear when we left."

I should say something, but I'm apparently unable to come up with a quick retort and stare at his thick shoulders and the way they slope from his neck to his arms at the same time.

He kicks off his shoes and socks. "We should grab some content here. How often do you get trapped in a cabin on a date?"

My mind immediately goes to X-rated content, and my cheeks heat.

Ripley drops his shorts to the floor. *That doesn't help.* He stands in front of me wearing a pair of black boxer briefs—and nothing else.

The storm rages on outside the cabin, and a small storm begins to stir inside me, too.

His muscled thighs stretch the fabric around them. The ratio from his shoulders to his waist is perfection. Lines are cut into his groin, directing attention to the bulge in his briefs, and I try to throttle the dizzying current racing through me.

"What?" he asks, smirking. "Do I have something on me?"

He runs his hands over his chest as if inspecting himself for a blemish. My gaze follows the movement, moving from his pecs to his shoulders and then down to his waistband.

His eyes hold a maddening touch of arrogance, which is enough to snap me out of my daze.

Two can play this game, pal.

"Yeah, you had a bit of drool on your stomach, but you got it," I say, meeting his smirk with one of my own. I grab the edge of my shirt and slowly drag it over my head.

The fabric is cold and heavy as it lifts, and the air meeting my damp skin causes a flurry of goose bumps. But my insides are smoldering. I barely even notice.

My heart pounds as I remove my shoes and socks. Bending over, I give him a full view of my cleavage. I know what I'm doing, yet I don't have a clue. I'm playing a perilous game that I can't stop.

Ripley's eyes rake boldly over my body. His Adam's apple bobs just before he licks his lips. I'm uncertain if the wetness on his skin is from the rain or sweat.

His attention, *his arousal*, is flattering. The power from knowing a man this virile is attracted to me is heady. And the intensity of the flame licking my core is almost unbearable.

I'm only human.

But we've been here before...

My stomach twists into a tight knot as a cyclone of memories comes rushing back.

I've stood in front of him in my bra and felt his desire for me one other time. I've basked in the glow of being Ripley's chosen girl. I trusted him, bamboozled by his good looks and dazzling charm, and I got crushed.

Because I made the mistake of thinking his intentions were real.

A full-body shiver hits me with full force.

Suddenly, everything is clear.

This really is just a game to him.

The sweet words, gentle touches, the fucking purple gloves—it was all a side quest in his effort to help out Jonah. He was using me as entertainment. And I fell for it.

In fact, if I hadn't just come to that realization, I could have fallen for him.

My breath stalls in my throat.

Oh my God.

"What's wrong?" he asks, a shadow dusting his features.

I laugh out of anger, mostly at myself. *I knew better than to do this. How did I let this happen?*

"Okay. All right. You win," I say, pulling the long-sleeved shirt he gave me over my head. I don't want to be enveloped by his clothes or his cologne, but I also don't want hypothermia.

"I win? What are you talking about?"

My mind races through the past few weeks. Ordering for me at Ruma. The promise of not letting me fall. The texts. The almost kisses.

You fucking asshole.

Fear mixes with embarrassment and swirls with anger inside me, creating a nasty cocktail threatening to explode.

"What's going on, Georgia?"

"I hate to admit this, but you might've gotten one over on me," I say, glaring at him. "Do you want to know where you went too far?"

His brows pull together. "I have no idea what you're talking about."

I laugh at his faux ignorance. "It was the almost kiss in the parking lot. And even that almost worked. The purple fucking gloves were a great addition—well fucking done, and I drove away thinking—*hey, maybe he means it this time.*" I glare at him. "Like an idiot. Because there were no cameras there, Ripley. That wasn't for the show. *That was for you.*"

The color slowly drains from his face. "You almost kissed me, too."

"Maybe. Maybe for a split second, I did. Maybe for a moment, I had the courage to hope that you weren't the rich prick who fucked with my feelings at a time when I was the most vulnerable, and you weren't using this stupid show that I never should've done to do it all over again—*oof.*"

He takes my hand and jerks me to him, capturing my mouth with his. His lips crash against mine. His fingers cup my cheeks, holding me still. It sends the pit of my stomach spiraling.

He kisses me with a savage intensity as if he's been waiting on this moment for a lifetime.

I melt, succumbing to the moment, my body sagging against his. I want to fight it, to shove him away, but find myself responding to his touch without thought. It's a challenge and a reward all at once.

"*Ripley.*" I breathe his name as he pulls away, my eyes fluttering open. "What the hell was that?"

"That was something I should've done a long fucking time ago."

"*What?*"

I stumble backward, nearly tripping over his backpack.

Nothing makes sense. The world is fuzzy. I'm weak, confused, *and desperate for more.*

His breaths are ragged, and his eyes are wild as he searches me for an answer to an unknown question.

"I tell you how mad I am at you," I say, my heart pounding, "and you answer that by kissing me? What is wrong with you?"

"*You.* You're what's wrong with me. You're what's always been wrong with me."

"Oh, so now you're blaming me for all the problems in your life? How fair."

He laughs angrily. "Don't you get it, Georgia?"

I take another step back. "Oh, I get it, Ripley. But don't even try to use this kiss as something new to hold over my head."

"Hold over your head? *What are you talking about?*"

"I'm talking about how the last time you kissed me, you did it to win a childish, immature bet with your little friends."

His features harden.

"And how everyone at Waltham laughed at me because I, the new girl, fell for you hook, line, and sinker."

"Georgia ..."

Now I'm just pissed.

I step toward him, fire coming out of the top of my head as I relive one of the worst nights of my life.

"You came up to me on the bleachers and asked me to dance," I say, glaring at him. "You'd made eye contact with me all week at school, and I thought there's a nice guy. *Wrong.*"

I stop a few feet in front of him, sliding his shirtsleeves up my arms like I'm about to fight.

"We danced, and you were so sweet," I say, "asking me about how I liked school, and where I was from, and what I liked to do. Then that jock spilled a cup of punch on my shirt, soaking it through. Do you remember that?"

He rubs his forehead.

"We go to the little nook off the cafeteria because you insist that I wear your button-up until my mom comes to get me," I say, getting madder by the minute. "I take my shirt off and ..."

"I kissed you. Dammit." He groans. "Georgia, listen ..."

"No, *you listen*. That little stunt hung over my head my entire senior year. The girls that came over to tell me that it was all a bet by the jocks, and you won—"

"*What?*"

"—don't *what* me. I heard you all talking in the restroom. I had to go through what should've been my happiest school year known as the slut because you apparently let everyone think we did a lot more than kiss while I put on your shirt."

"I would never do that."

"Bullshit," I say, firing right back at him. "Then I had to go home with no one to talk to, deal with my mother's complete breakdown over her love life, and a father who didn't want anything to do with me because, apparently, I wasn't worth the energy of a relationship."

Ripley's face falls as my bottom lip trembles.

"I've gotten over it," I say. "I don't care what you or anyone thinks of me. You can hate me. That's fine. But the fact that you would do this to me all over again ..."

"Will you listen to me? *Please*?"

"No."

I turn to march into the kitchen because it's the farthest I can currently get from him in nothing but his shirt, but he grabs my arm and whirls me around to face him. His eyes are wild. His features somber. Yet he holds on to me gently—just tight enough to beg me to stay.

"Did I know there was a bet that night?" He holds his breath. "Yes. I did."

"You asshole."

"But I wasn't a part of it. I overheard my friends talking about it—who could be the first guy at Waltham to kiss the gorgeous new girl?"

"Congratulations."

He narrows his eyes. "I'd watched you from the second you walked into that school. I couldn't take my fucking eyes off you. You were the prettiest girl I'd ever seen, and I tried to talk to you a hundred times but chickened out."

Right.

"Why would a girl like you talk to a guy like me?" he asks.

Is he serious right now?

He steps toward me hesitantly, as if he thinks I might bolt for the door. "Listen, Georgia, I kissed you that night because I wanted to—because I wanted to kiss you more than I'd ever wanted to kiss anyone in my life. And there was no way I was letting one of those assholes who wouldn't give a shit about you make a joke out of you."

"So you did it yourself?"

"I danced with you to warn you but couldn't figure out how to say it. And then your shirt was soiled, and I thought it was the perfect time to talk to you without everyone around. But then your shirt came off, and you looked at me and ..." He runs a hand through his hair. "I didn't do that to win a bet. And, as a matter of fucking fact, that whole incident is what cost me my college scholarship."

My jaw hangs open. "What are you talking about?"

"A few months later, Shawn Tonley made a comment about you, and ... it devolved from there. We got into a fight, and the cops got called. I got suspended and lost my scholarship."

My eyes widen, and I cover my mouth with my hand. *Oh my gosh.*

"He ran his mouth because he knew I couldn't do anything," Ripley says. "The college I was going to had a strict behavior clause in the offer. Shawn knew that."

"Then why didn't you just let him talk shit?"

A softness drifts across Ripley's face. "Because it was about you."

I gasp a breath, my mind spinning. *That's why he got suspended? That's why he lost his scholarship?*

That's why his father broke his nose?

Because of me?

I take him in, hoping I can find something that makes me think he's lying to me—but there's nothing. He's more unguarded, more vulnerable, than I've ever seen him. There's no joke, no smirk, no mischief in his eyes. *No hatred.*

He's telling me the truth.

That one event caused this terrible snowball effect that tore apart my self-confidence and derailed his future.

God.

"Why didn't you tell me?" I ask.

He shrugs. "Because I didn't know you didn't know. I thought you just decided I was a jerk, or a bother, and went on your way."

"Someone told me once that I don't have a lot of value as a person. And while I know that's bullshit, it lingers in the back of my brain."

Oh, Ripley.

"I don't know what to say," I say, stumbling over the words as I try to process the bomb that's been dropped in my lap.

"Yeah. Me either."

"I'm sorry. I—"

"Doesn't matter. What's done is done. I've done enough things to piss you off over the years to warrant you hating me."

I groan. "And I've certainly done enough over the years to warrant you hating me." *Not to mention being the reason your own father punched you in the face.*

Thunder booms, rocking the cabin.

"Where does this leave us?" he asks, nibbling his bottom lip.

I know what he's asking—*how do we go forward? Do we forgive each other? Talk it out?*

Does this change anything at all?

He's right in that we have done a lot of mean things to each other over the years. We have made it difficult for the other. There's not been an interaction that passed without us getting under each other's skin.

But we're also always together—in the same room, at the same parties, on the same television show ...

If I had known the truth over the years, things would've been different for us. And if he'd realized that I didn't know what really happened—if his father hadn't fucked up his confidence—things would've been different for us, too.

Fuck you, Reid Brewer.

I'm starting to realize that my perception of Ripley has only been decided from behind very hurt and anger-filled glasses. *And that anger has manifested such bitterness ... and could have been avoided.*

Ripley has always been a loyal friend to his friends and an amazing brother to his siblings. Tate adores him. I've seen it, but my perception has been skewed.

"I'd watched you from the second you walked in that school. I couldn't take my fucking eyes off you. You were the prettiest girl I'd ever seen, and I tried to talk to you a hundred times but chickened out."

He wanted a very different relationship with me. Truthfully, I would've died to have one with him before the mixer. And the fact that we were robbed of that—because it very much feels like a robbery at this point—and it affected the next decade of our lives feels devastating.

I study his pools of blue and the stress in my body fades away.

"Doesn't matter. What's done is done." He's right. We can't fix it. We can't erase the stupid things we've done and said to each other over the

years. But we can refuse to allow the trauma from our fathers and childish mistakes steal anything else from us. We can see each other for who we are now.

And, right now, there's a very handsome man standing in front of me who just might be the only man in my life to ever do anything to protect me. He had my back in rooms I wasn't in.

How wild is that?

I don't have all the answers, and I don't know where we go from here. But I do know the answer to his question.

"Where does that leave us?" I ask, grinning. "You better get over here and kiss me again."

Chapter Twenty-One

Georgia

The air shifts, growing hotter by the moment.

Ripley's long-sleeved shirt is suddenly too warm against my skin. The cabin is too small. The look in Ripley's eyes is so scorching, so electric that I might combust from it alone.

Now that I'm free from having to hate him, I want him so badly it hurts.

"You want to be kissed, huh?" he asks as a bolt of lightning illuminates the cabin. "I don't know ..."

"What do you mean *you don't know*?"

He acts like he's weighing his options. "We're just getting on the right track. After all these years, we might be able to be friends."

"We might not, too. Choose carefully."

The corner of his mouth tilts to the ceiling. "And if I kiss you, that might screw it up."

"And if you don't, I might screw *you* up."

He laughs, his face free of the usual stress lines that appear when he's around me. If I ever thought he was handsome before, I was wrong because seeing him like this—like a weight has been lifted from his shoulders—is simply spectacular.

My thighs clench in a futile attempt to stop the aching between my legs.

"Well, I don't want to be screwed up, do I?" he asks, stalking toward me.

"I hope not. You've come so far in such a short amount of time."

The words are barely spoken before Ripley's mouth finds mine.

His arm slips behind the small of my back, dragging me into his body. I throw my arms around his neck and palm the back of his head, pulling his face closer to mine, then I moan as I feel the hardness of his cock against my belly.

Wow.

The cabin spins as his tongue traces along my bottom lip. Shivers race down my spine as his free hand palms my ass. He parts my lips with his tongue before sweeping it across mine, sending shock waves through my entire body.

A decade's worth of pent-up sexual tension hits a boiling point.

I need him.

Now.

"What do you want, Peaches?" He kisses across my jaw and down the side of my neck. "*Tell me what you want.*"

I tilt my head back and he places a kiss in the hollow of my throat.

"What do you think I want?" I ask, the sound raspy.

His chuckle vibrates against my cheek. "Knowing you? Probably carbs."

"Asshole." I laugh, pausing when he nips my bottom lip between his teeth. "*Ah!*"

He takes a step back, smiling mischievously.

I pant, my body pulsing from his touch ... and craving more. Needing more. *Dying for more.*

"Are you stopping now?" I ask.

"Look, this has been one of the most unbelievable days of my life, and I'm not about to ruin it by assuming I know what you want. You'll have to tell me."

"What are my options?"

He licks his lips, grinning. "Option A: we get dressed and wait for the rain to stop."

"Okay. Option B?"

"Option B is we get *undressed* and wait for the rain to stop."

"*Option B.*"

"That's an excellent choice. But that option has sub-options."

I throw my hands up. "Can you just pick one that includes you inside me? That's the one I want."

He laughs, his eyes twinkling. "Ah, there you are. I wondered how long it would take."

"Sadly, it took less time than it did for you to get me naked." I grab the bottom of his shirt and rip it over my head, throwing it at him. "There. I did it for you."

His gaze lazily drags down my body, taking in every inch not covered by my bra and panties.

"My God, Georgia. You are fucking stunning."

My cheeks flush. "You've seen me in a bikini before. It's not any different."

His eyes find mine again. "It is different. I couldn't touch you then."

"Will you touch me now?"

He drops to his knees in front of me and peers up at me through his thick lashes. His fingers loop the strip of fabric at my hips. Then he pulls them slowly down my legs, letting his knuckles drag against my skin behind them.

I force a swallow, stepping out of my panties, and he flicks them toward his backpack.

The sight of Ripley kneeling before me is almost more than I can handle. It's something I never expected. I never dreamed this would happen, and I know I'll wonder if it was real when I wake up in the morning ... and every morning after that.

He grips my thighs, squeezing tightly until it borders on pain. He motions for me to spread them, so I do.

Goose bumps dot my skin as his fingers drag up the insides of my legs, through the moisture coating them, until they reach the apex.

THE INVITATION

I gasp softly while my heart pounds so hard it's the only thing I can hear.

"You have no idea how long I've waited for this," he says, drawing a finger through my slit. I tremble at the touch. "You are *so* wet."

"Well, you've been walking around here for the past half an hour with a hard cock. What do you expect?"

He grins. "Do you want my cock? Is that what you're saying?"

"I'm saying—*shit*." I bite my lip as he strums his thumb over my swollen clit. I buck my hips toward him. "Never mind. I don't know what I was saying."

He laughs, plunging his finger into me. "I never knew it was this easy to shut you up."

"Now you know." I moan as he adds another finger and strokes them in and out of me. "*God, that feels good.*"

"Take your bra off. Let me see your tits from this position."

I whimper as his fingers twist before resuming their slow and steady pace.

I unhook my bra, letting the straps fall down my arms. Ripley's gaze is pinned on my chest as he leisurely works my pussy. I've never felt so desired. It's intoxicating.

It's addicting.

His strokes grow faster and deeper, working me into a frenzy. I grind against his hand. My desperation for relief is nearly unbearable.

The front of my bra falls into my hands, letting my breasts hang free. A slow, shit-eating smile covers Ripley's lips as he brings a hand to my chest.

"These are fucking perfect," he says, palming one of the heavy globes.

I flex against him again.

"Do you want to come, Peaches?"

"Yes," I hiss, straddling the edge of an orgasm.

He drops his hand to my hip ... and his face to my mound.

"*Oh my God*," I mutter, my mind blowing into a million pieces. My hands fly into his hair, pulling him tighter to me as I moan.

He fucks my pussy with his fingers relentlessly, and the sounds of my arousal ring through the air. He traces a figure eight against my clit, and my breathing gets heavier. Harder. More desperate.

"Put your foot on that chair," he says before blowing against my clit and making me tremble.

I do as instructed—I'm in *no* position to argue—and as soon as my foot is in position and his tongue touches me, I scream in delight.

A hand on my breast. Two, maybe three fingers inside me. His tongue licking back and forth over my sensitive nub.

The intensity is too much. The pressure almost painful. The sight of Ripley's mouth on my pussy, his eyes trained on mine, is the icing on the cake.

"Don't stop," I warn him, my voice wobbling through the orgasm.

I pull his hair, drawing him into me, nearly smothering him—but I don't care. He devours me like I'm his last meal on earth.

I ride out the climax on his face, milking it for every last shot of pleasure. My mind hosts a fireworks display that's a burst of every color of the rainbow. My breasts bounce as I endure the heat of the moment and try not to shatter.

As my sounds lessen and my shakes calm, Ripley slows and softens his touches.

I slump against the wall, my mind putting itself back together much faster than my body.

Holy shit. I just came on Ripley Brewer's face.

He stands, a smile splitting his cheeks, and presses a long, hard kiss to my lips. I taste myself on his tongue and feel the lingering wetness from my body on his face. When he pulls back, he's still grinning.

"That was worth the wait." He winks at me, heading to his backpack.

My head spins. "That's not all, right?"

"Why?" He grabs the shirt he wore today and wipes his face off. "Did you want something else?"

He can't be serious. "Yeah. Your cock."

He chuckles as he digs through his bag. "Oh, you're going to get my cock, Peaches. But I need a condom first."

"Tell me you have one."

"I think I do."

Is he freaking kidding me?

I sit on the coffee table in front of the sofa. Ripley watches me out of the corner of his eye, amused.

"If you don't have a condom, you're fucking me anyway," I say. "I had a physical after I broke up with Donovan, and I'm healthy."

"I'm healthy too, but that's not the problem."

"Then what is?"

He rocks back on his heels and turns to me. "Do you really want to know?"

"I don't know. Are you going to ruin this moment and tell me you have some terminal disease?"

His laugh is loud. "If I had a terminal disease, do you think we would've gotten this far? For fuck's sake, Georgia."

"Look, I need fucked, okay? I'm horny as hell. Help me help you."

He shakes his head. "Fine. The problem is that if I fuck you without a condom, I don't trust myself to pull out."

"Why? Do you think I'll be that tight, and it'll feel that good? Or do you have a breeding kink?"

I say it as a joke—to get an eye roll. To make him laugh. But that's not what happens at all.

Ripley's eyes darken, and he licks his lips. "Something about thinking about putting a baby inside you is remarkably hot."

I still, shocked by his admission. I'm more shocked that I'm not freaked out by it. I'm shocked even more that I agree. It *is* kind of hot.

"*Condom*," I say emphatically, leaving no room for discussion. I can't lose my mind completely in the sex haze. That would be a big regret later.

He retrieves a foil pack from his bag and stands. "I wasn't going to do it without one anyway. No matter how much you begged."

"We're both lucky we don't have to put that to the test."

He grins, sheathing himself with the condom. "How do you want this?"

"Honestly? I want it hard and fast. I'm too amped to enjoy it slow. I'll just run my mouth, and we'll both be mad."

"At least you know yourself. Get on your hands and knees."

I look around the room. "Where?"

He points at the coffee table. "It's the perfect height."

"Fine by me."

I get situated with my ass in the air. The rough, wooden tabletop digs into my knees and palms while thunder rumbles through the dark sky outside.

A hand cracks against my ass, making me yelp. The sound isn't fully formed before Ripley slides his swollen cock through my slit. I gasp, arching my back, unprepared to fully take him in.

"Do you still want it hard?" he asks through what I imagine is gritted teeth. "You're so tight, Peaches."

His fingertips trace my spine lightly, dancing in a straight line from the nape of my neck to the crack of my ass.

Being filled by him while feeling him caress me so sweetly awakens feelings in my chest that I can't quite rectify. That I can't name. That I'm afraid to even try to label.

"Fuck me, Ripley. Hard."

I squeeze my eyes shut as he slides out and then slams into me. Once. Twice. Thrice.

Over and over, he gives me exactly what I asked for.

A fucking.

There's no tenderness, no kindness—nothing to get sappy or tripped up about. He fucks me until my arms go weak and my legs threaten not to hold me up anymore. And just as I reach the point where I can't hold back anymore, where I shout my pleasure into the air, he presses into me and moans my name.

I bite my lip as I'm flooded with an orgasm bigger and stronger than the first.

He grips my hips so hard that the skin burns beneath them, and then I feel him swell inside me. He grunts, his whole body shaking as he loses himself alongside me.

My arms buckle. He scoops an arm under my stomach, and I think he presses a kiss to my shoulder. I close my eyes, relishing in the moment just in case I never experience it again.

He pulls out and then helps me to my feet. When I turn around, he's removing the condom.

A blast of anxiety riddles me because I'm unsure what happens now.

But when his gaze meets mine, and a soft smile graces his lips, my nerves melt away.

"Shower?" he asks.

I grin. "One at a time because that thing is tiny."

"Thank God that's the first time I'm hearing that today."

I snort, shaking my head at the mischief on his face. Suddenly, I think everything just might be okay.

Somehow.

Chapter Twenty-Two
Georgia

"Should we leave rent or a tip when we leave?" I ask, coming out of the bathroom. "And by we, I mean you. I have no money—here or elsewhere."

Ripley's sitting on the sofa, repacking his backpack. He grins, nodding toward the table. A letter and a business card have been placed in the center.

> Hello,
> We used this cabin for shelter during a storm. Please contact me at the number on the business card, and I will pay for any cleaning fees or inconveniences.
> Thank you,
> Ripley Brewer

"Aren't you afraid someone is going to get ahold of this and extort you?" I ask.

He laughs. "Extort me for what?"

"I don't know. The possibilities are endless. Don't you watch television?"

"Ironically, no."

"Not to freak you out or anything, but they could burn this place down and then charge you with arson," I say. "They could break everything in here and say you did it and demand you refurnish the place. They could kill someone, drop the dead body here, and say you're the prime suspect."

"First of all, who is this *they* you're talking about?"

"Whoever owns this place."

"Second," he says, as if he wasn't expecting an answer to the first question, "someone would have to be very diabolical to burn their own cabin down just to blame it on me."

"It happens."

He nods like I'm the diabolical one. "Third, DNA would clear me on murder, so I'm not worried about that. And if they say I broke everything, I'll pay for it and move on. Or I'll have my attorneys fight them. Either way, the karma of not leaving a note is worse than taking my chances."

I roll my eyes. "You have such a rich person's perspective on stuff."

"Well, probably. But am I wrong?"

"I mean, no. Not technically." I wander to the window and peer out. "It's just interesting how you think about things that other people don't." I face him. "I'd be terrified to leave my contact information just laying out for the public. What if the wrong person found it and tracked me down?"

His features darken.

"What if I walk out my front door one day and there's a man with a handlebar mustache in a beat-up white van with tinted windows sitting across the street?"

"So specific."

"Little girls grow up painting pictures of who the 'bad guy' might be," I say. "That was mine. His name was Gilbert. He smelled like cigarettes and wore sunglasses."

Ripley cocks his head to the side. "I have so many questions."

"The point is that as a female and as a person who couldn't just hire an attorney to defend myself in court, I'd never leave my information like that. Maybe I'd call in after I got home or something. But that?" I point at the letter. "That's a risk I'm not willing to take."

His brows tug together as if he's never once contemplated something like this. It blows my mind. *How has he made it thirty years without considering these types of things?*

He scoots over on the couch. "Why don't you sit with me until the rain stops?"

"Oh, do you want to cuddle? Heads-up, I'm not much of a cuddler."

"Why doesn't that surprise me?"

"You're a smart man ... sometimes."

I sit beside him, leaning against his side and drawing my knees up to my chest. He wraps an arm around me and rests the side of his head against mine.

I wait for the weirdness to settle in, for the moment when we realize that we might not hate each other anymore, but we also aren't friends. Now that we've had sex, things are forever changed. And no heart-to-hearts, no arguments, no truths will ever fix it.

But nothing happens. *Huh.*

"What are you thinking?" he asks softly.

"That we didn't film at all today."

"That's not what you were thinking," he says, chuckling.

"How do you know?"

"I just know."

I take a long breath and wonder if I should broach this topic. It makes me nervous to go there, but we'll have to do it sooner or later. And he did bring it up, which is a green flag.

"I'm wondering when things get uncomfortable," I say.

"Why do they have to get uncomfortable?"

He strokes my arm gently, his even breathing lulling me into a trance. I forget he's asked me a question. Instead, I close my eyes and let his presence bleed into me and make me feel protected in a way I can't remember feeling before.

"I don't want you to feel pressured by this," he says hesitantly.

"By what?"

"When we walked up this mountain, you felt one way about me. Now that we've had sex, I don't want you to think there's pressure there."

Oh. "So you're saying that as far as you're concerned, what happens in the cabin stays in the cabin?"

"That's not what I said."

"Then what did you say?"

I hold my breath and wait for his explanation.

I don't want to jump to conclusions although I guess I already did. I suppose I just don't want to assume that this was anything more to him than a fuck. Because I don't know what it was, and I'm afraid to think about it too much.

My chest tightens at the silence.

"You know, I believe you didn't plan this," I say, leaning off him. "I don't think you expected this to happen any more than I did."

He places a hand on my shoulder and gently guides me back into him.

My heart races.

"But I don't want you to feel like you're somehow ... I don't know. I guess I don't want you to feel like I have any expectations going forward. You have a life, and I'm just—"

"*Hey.*"

I stop talking and sit perfectly still.

He sighs. "I'm going to be very honest with you, okay?"

I nod.

"And no matter what I say, I don't expect you to reciprocate those feelings," he says. "I actually doubt you will. But I've spent over ten years keeping them to myself, and even if you laugh in my face, I think it's time to get it out in the open."

What the hell is he going to say?

I stare at the wall across the room, listening to my blood rush through my ears. Ripley draws small circles on my arm as he presumably figures out what to say.

I have no idea what that's going to be, and the anticipation is killing me. I would swivel around and tell him how I feel if I knew what that was—or, if more honestly, I wasn't afraid to speak first. The last thing I want to hear is that I don't fit in his world like this.

Why would he want it to be anything more after I've already screwed up his life? And how do I act like he didn't lose his scholarship over me? And his dad didn't hit him in the face over it?

Surely, he still has some disdain for me in his heart, and I can't blame him.

"What I told you earlier is true," he says, his voice a few octaves above a whisper. "I was smitten with you the day I saw you. I felt this connection to you the moment I saw you walking down the hall—like I was your protector. Like you were mine to protect."

Tears fill my eyes. No one has ever said anything like that to me before.

"I—"

"Please let me finish." He presses a kiss to the top of my head. "I couldn't stand you hating me, but I was too prideful to ask why. It was easier to spar back with you. That way, I still got to be in your world, in your life, even if it wasn't with you."

He presses another kiss on my head.

"I'm sitting here right now hoping that it rains forever," he says. "Because if we walk out of here and I never get to experience this again, I want as many memories with you as I can get."

My gosh. I sniffle back the tears, his words hitting me in the heart.

"I don't know what I want," he says. "It seems crazy to even start talking about things long-term when I don't even know if you want to see me again. But if I have my way, I'd really like the opportunity to try to make up for the years we've wasted being mad over goofy things."

I sit up, pulling away from his grip, and turn to him. I straddle him so I can see into his eyes.

"I hate being emotional," I say, laughing as tears stream down my face. "It makes me feel weak."

He brushes the tears away with the pads of his thumbs. "It doesn't make you weak. It makes you human."

"Well, it feels really stupid that we've gone our whole lives without realizing the truth," I say. "And I feel absolutely shitty for hating you when you were protecting me the whole time. I'm a terrible person."

"No, you're not." He kisses me softly, smiling. "I didn't think a girl like you would be interested in me, so I let you think the worst. It was easier having you hate me without knowing me than having you hate me after you did."

"You seriously break my heart when you say things like that."

He shrugs.

I stare into his blue eyes and see my reflection in them. They're clear and honest and fill me with a peace that I've been searching for my whole life. *Who would've thought I would find it here?*

"Honestly, I don't know what I want either. I think we both need a little time to clear our heads and be sure about things." I groan. "And I need to deal with my mother."

The thought of telling her about Ripley makes my stomach hurl. She's not going to take it well. At all.

"I would never want to come between you and your mom," he says, brushing my hair out of my face. "Family's everything to me. You know that."

I nod. "All of that being said, today has been pretty eye-opening, and I've already decided what I want our next date to be."

He smiles. "What's that?"

"I want to meet Waffles. And we probably need to do it soon since we didn't get any footage today."

His head falls back, and he laughs. "I much prefer the footage that's in my head from today than I would have the footage we would've captured on top of the mountain."

"Yeah, well, same."

I thread our fingers together and hold our joined hands between us. "So what do you say?" I ask. "Can I meet Waffles?"

"You can absolutely meet Waffles. He'll like you. You have a lot in common."

"Really?"

"You're both adorable."

I kiss him.

"And a little mean."

I laugh but kiss him again.

"It's impossible to stop both of you once you get going although he does listen a bit better than you," he says, laughing as I gasp. "And you're both very food motivated."

I smack him, making him laugh harder.

"I'm going to get a dog just like you and name him Pancakes," I say, grinning at Ripley's amusement.

"Oh really? What's he going to be like?"

"Very handsome." I run my fingers through his hair. "Loyal, almost to a fault."

Ripley's smile softens.

"He'll be cocky to hide the fact that he has insecurities—which I won't hold against him," I say. "And I think we'll have the potential to share a very loving, fun, and probably argumentative at the time, but it'll be okay because that's who we are relationship."

Ripley wraps his arms around my waist. I pull his head against my chest and hold him tight. It feels so ... right.

"The rain has stopped," I say, noticing the sun peeking through the clouds.

He pulls back and looks up at me. "So we're friends now?"

"No. We're friends with benefits."

"I better be the only friend getting those benefits."

I smile, kissing him again. "I have a feeling there will be lots and lots of benefits in this friendship, Mr. Brewer."

He thrusts his hardened cock against me. "How about one more round of benefits before we leave?"

"We might as well since you're basically giving them your bank information—*ah!*"

I giggle as he pulls my face to his and makes me forget about the world. About everything but him.

Chapter Twenty-Three

Ripley

"Thanks for bringing him home, Tate," I say, watching Waffles chase a bug around my backyard.

The storm didn't hit my neighborhood as hard as it hit the mountain. Some branches were scattered around the pool, and an umbrella flew down the hill and into the neighbor's yard. But it was nothing compared to the logs Georgia and I had to traverse to get down the trail and to my car.

Note to self: Limit outdoor adventures with Peaches.

I had to carry her on my back the last quarter mile thanks to the blister, the heat, and the mud puddles that splashed on her legs and made them itchy. She complained and chastised me for not checking the weather during pretty much the entire descent. But instead of finding it grating, I'd just look at her, and she'd give me a little smile. Then I didn't care so much.

"He just laid on the couch and watched the door." Tate shakes his head. "I think he thought I dog-napped him at first. He barked at me until he realized I was taking him for a ride, then he was all too happy to jump in the car. You need to review stranger danger with him. One cute poodle or a pepperoni stick, and he's toast."

"You two talk about that dog like he's a person," Gannon says.

"Take this for what it is, Gannon, but *that dog* has more people skills than you," I say.

Tate laughs, picking up a wet tennis ball and throwing it across the yard. Waffles sees it bounce and chases it, stopping it before it hits the fence. The ball never had a chance.

"Why does he hop?" Gannon asks, confused. "He gets going and hops sideways."

"He was a kangaroo in a past life," Tate says.

Gannon rolls his eyes. "I think your dog is broken, Ripley."

"And I think you might be broken if you keep up the shit talk about my puppy."

Tate laughs, swinging his attention to Gannon. He loves this kind of bickering. *Baby of the family energy.*

"All right, enough about the dog," Gannon says. "I came here to discuss a couple of things."

"What's up?" I ask.

My brothers and I sit at a table by the pool. The air is muggy from all the rain and my clothes stick to me. My mind goes immediately to the lack of clothes with Georgia a few hours ago.

Dropping her off at her house was difficult. It felt unfair to have to say goodbye to her already. I tried to talk her into coming home with me, but she was insistent on giving us both room to think before we went all in.

I hate to tell her, but I'm already so far in that I can't see above water.

When it came to Georgia Hayes, only a few days ago, I believed I was only capable of assholish behavior. But somehow, through honesty—finally—an enormous burden has been lifted.

Sex with her has been mind-blowing, hot, and intimate all at once. *Even better than I expected.* But it was her confessions of how she saw me, albeit through the description of a fictional dog, that showed me I was not only an asshole in her eyes.

That gave me hope that we could be ... more. Maybe everything.

"Do you remember Bobby Downing?" Gannon asks.

"Fuck him," Tate says immediately.

Just hearing the name makes my stomach curl. "How could we forget?"

Bobby Downing, an acquaintance of our father, tried to make life hell for us after Dad's arrest. He claimed he was promised a portion of the Arrows franchise for helping Dad secure the purchase. It was bullshit, unethical, and it cost us a few million dollars in attorneys' fees to fight him in court. But we did, and we won. There is no love lost between us now.

"I got a tip today that he has been contacting our investors—the ones he helped secure for the Arrows purchase," Gannon says. "I'm not certain what's being said, but he's up to something. I notified our attorneys today and called Nick to see if he can dig anything up."

"Good ole Nick," Tate says. "The best private investigator in all the land."

Gannon folds his hands on the table. "The second thing I wanted to talk to you about is that Jason apparently thinks it's hilarious to have Callum assigned to my security team."

Tate and I can't help it. We laugh. *Hard*.

Gannon isn't entertained, which makes it that much funnier.

Landry Security is in charge of our family's security operations. Jason is the liaison and coordinates it all since he has a background in all things espionage. We all have guards at the entrances of our homes, as well as security systems. Renn has an extra guard at his house, thanks to being a public figure and having a baby at home, and Mom has a detail with her at all times. She hates it, but we insist. The only exception to the rule is Bianca, and that's because she's married to Foxx Carmichael. He's a walking army on his own. If he can't protect her, no one can.

Out of all the security guards that rotate in and out of our lives, Callum is the one we dislike the most. We've all taken turns with him and couldn't wait for his round to be done. He's cocky, abrasive, and so full of himself that he might just pop.

If he's oil, then Gannon's water, and we've all waited with bated breath for Gannon to have to deal with him. It looks like now's the time.

"I need to grab the popcorn." Tate snickers.

"It's not funny," Gannon says, glaring at us. "I hate that motherfucker."

"Join the club," I say.

"I told Jason to get him off my detail, and he did that thing he does where he acknowledges what you say and acts like he's on your side, but you know he's not going to do shit."

"Ah, I know that look well," Tate says. "I get it for just about everything I say."

"I'm not sure what I can do to help you with this one, Gan," I say. "I don't want Callum here."

"He's not working with me again," Tate says. "I just got rid of him."

Gannon groans. "Fine. I'll just call Ford Landry myself. Fuck Jason."

Tate and I exchange a grin. *Fuck Jason? This should be fun.*

I glance around the yard for my puppy, only to find him in the pool and chasing a floating tennis ball.

"Get out of there." I give him a look that tells him he's disobeyed me, and I'm not pleased.

He looks at me and then charges toward the ball like he either doesn't understand or doesn't care.

"Come on, Waffles," I say, sterner this time. "Don't make me get in there to get you."

He paddles twice in a circle and heads back for the steps.

"Hey, Ripley," Tate says. "Carys wants to go to a concert this weekend, and she has four tickets. Her new boyfriend won't go with her—surprise fucking surprise—so she wondered if you and I wanted to go with her and one of her friends. Could be fun."

"Are you fucking her yet?" Gannon asks.

"Who?" Tate asks him.

"Carys."

"Hell no," Tate says. "Not happening."

"She's a hot little thing," Gannon says. "What's wrong with her?"

Tate wrinkles his nose. "I know too much about her. I've heard too many stories that I can't unhear. Besides, she's into the kind of guy who will stomp all over her heart. I'm too nice for her."

"Maybe she should give Gannon a shot," I joke. "He'll break her heart. She'll love it."

Gannon smirks.

"I couldn't handle that drama," Tate says. "And you couldn't either —either one of you."

"While that sounds like an absolute barrel of fun, I can't go with you," I say. "Sorry."

I don't know if it's the way I say it, the tone I use, or just that Tate can read me better than almost anyone. But he looks at me with a curious, skeptical look that makes it clear he knows something is going on. That it's not just me not wanting to deal with Carys's friends.

That something else is at play.

I know it'll come out that things have substantially changed with Georgia and me sooner or later, but I don't really know how to explain it without it seeming like we got trapped in a cabin and fucked. Because that's not what it was. At all. And I don't want to cheapen the story by miscommunicating it and painting it in the wrong light.

"What?" Tate asks.

"Nothing," I say.

"Liar. What's going on?" Tate asks, studying me.

I smile. "Tate, *nothing is going on.*"

Tate leans toward Gannon and points at me. "See that little grin? That cocky wobble? That means fuckery is afoot."

"Really? What kind of fuckery?" Gannon asks.

"I don't know."

Gannon glances at me, then back at Tate. "I have no idea why you think you know this."

"It's called context clues, Gannon." Tate sighs. "How can you be the oldest kid out of six and run a multi-million-dollar operation and not know how to read people?"

"It's simple. I hate people. I don't care what they think or what they feel. I'm going to do what I want, and they can take it or leave it. Doesn't matter to me. Their opinion isn't going to change a damn thing, so why would I waste my time trying to decipher their opinions?"

I grin. "Suddenly, so much makes sense about you, Gan."

He rolls his eyes.

"Don't change the subject," Tate says, resting his elbows on the table and leaning forward. He's like a bloodhound on a trail. "Start talking."

"*There's nothing to talk about.*"

Gannon settles in. "If I cared, which I do not, I'd start by considering what he's been working on, who he's been dealing with. Where has he been in the last twenty-four hours—"

"Gannon, you're a fucking genius!" Tate exclaims, bolting upright.

Oh, fuck. Here we go ...

"Tate, before you get too carried away—"

"Do you know who he's been spending time with?" Tate asks our brother. "And who he was with today in the storm?"

"Tate ..." I warn.

"Let me check my notes and see who he was scheduled to be with today," Gannon deadpans. "Come on, Tate. I have no fucking idea who he was with. Do you not listen to anything I say?"

"No." Tate turns crisply to me and gives me a shit-eating grin. "*Georgia.*"

Waffles barks in the distance.

Her name is a sentence, a concept—an answer. I can't dispute it. I don't want to. But I do need to rein him in before he gets on the phone like an old spinster and tells the world.

"Let me explain," I say.

"Yeah. Please do." Tate turns to Gannon. "I've been waiting for this for years."

Gannon is puzzled. "Should I know Georgia?"

"No," Tate says. "She went to school with us and is best friends with Jeremiah's fiancée, Sutton."

"Okay." Gannon nods. "I remember her. I met them ... somewhere recently."

"Yes. We played golf against Jeremiah in the cancer charity tournament last weekend."

He nods. "Right."

"Anyway," Tate says, forever the gossip, "Georgia and Ripley fight like cats and dogs."

Gannon smirks.

"They once had an argument in the comment section of one of my Social posts. Totally stole all the attention from me," Tate says, sticking me with a quick glare.

"The horror." Gannon shakes his head. "So you and Georgia have a contentious relationship. Got it. Now what happened so I can move on with my life?"

They both look at me expectantly.

How do I say this correctly? Carefully? How do I put something into words that I don't fully understand myself just yet?

"You fucked her," Gannon says without a hint of emotion.

"It's not like that."

"What?" Tate's jaw drops. "*You fucked her?*"

My temple throbs as I pin him to his seat with a look. "I did *not* fuck her."

He leans back. *Smart move.*

"We were trapped in a cabin during the storm," I say. "It gave us time to talk."

"And fuck," Gannon says.

"Gan, I don't want to fight you, but I will."

He smirks, the son of a bitch.

"We cleared the air about a lot of things," I say. "It turns out we just needed some time to get on the same page."

"So you got on the same page?" Tate asks carefully.

"Yes." I fire a look at Gannon not to interject. "We rehashed a lot of things, got to the bottom of a number of events and misunderstandings, and—"

"And you fucked." Gannon shrugs. "We know where this is going, Ripley."

"You know what? This is why I don't invite you over much, Gannon. You're an asshole."

He grins. "Fine. Shoot the truth teller."

"So the two of you are … what?" Tate asks. "Friends now?"

"With benefits, clearly," Gannon says.

"Gannon, I swear to God I'm going to kill you," I say.

He holds his hands in front of him as if he's deferring to me—which we both know he's not.

I get up from the table and walk to the pool. I snag Waffles's ball out of the water and toss it across the yard. The sight of him chasing it with his tongue waggling out of the side of his mouth calms me down a little.

"I don't know what we are," I say. "We're taking some time to process it." I take a deep breath. "I know where I stand."

"You love her," Tate says simply. "You always have. We all know it."

My head whips to him, my mouth hanging slack.

He laughs. "We talk about it all the time, wondering if you two will patch things up or if you'll screw up and marry someone else."

My heart pounds as I watch him smile, seemingly happy that this has transpired.

Does he really think that? Do our friends? Why didn't anyone say anything?

And hell, if she married someone else ... *Fuck. Fuck no.*

"So is this a done deal as soon as you 'process it'?" Tate asks.

I take the ball from Waffles and throw it again.

"There's only one little hiccup that concerns me," I say. "Georgia hasn't mentioned it specifically, but I think she's worried about it, too."

"What is it?" Gannon asks.

I take my seat again. "It turns out that Dad had an affair with her mom."

"When?" Anger paints Tate's face. "Recently?"

"No, I'm not sure, but it was when we were in high school."

Gannon shakes his head. "Just when you think you can't hate Dad more ..."

"Apparently, her mother hates all things Brewer," I say.

"You can win her over." Tate nods. "Bust out that charm, and she'll be eating out of the palm of your hand."

"You could fuck Georgia and her mom," Gannon says.

I ignore him and keep my focus on Tate. "That's my hope. I think Georgia is trying to figure out how to get around that. Her mom is the only family she has." I bite my lip. "I couldn't get in the middle of that, you know?"

"No, I don't know." Gannon stands up and stretches his arms over head. "If her mom had a problem, that would be it—her problem. You can't carry around everyone else's problems, Rip."

"This is why no one likes you," Tate tells him.

Gannon smiles. "And that keeps life simpler." He winks at us. "I gotta get going. Good talk. If you need any more life advice, *do not* let me know."

"See ya," Tate says, giving me a look.

"Later," I call after him.

Tate waits for Gannon to disappear inside the house before speaking again.

"I truly hope this works out for you," he says. "You and Georgia? I think it makes sense in a very hurricane-meets-a-tornado kind of way."

"Me, too."

I hope. God, I hope. Because I know I can't go back to trying to keep my distance and try to hate her.

Not when I think I might love her.

Chapter Twenty-Four

Georgia

Sutton stares at me with her mouth agape.

"Say something," I say.

"*Holy shit.*" The words stir her out of the fog my admission just cast around her. She shakes her head. "You and Ripley?"

I wince. "You think it's a bad idea?"

She laughs, the surprise on her face melting into excitement. "A bad idea? Are you kidding me? *Finally.*"

"Finally?"

"Georgia, it's about damn time. We were all waiting for this to happen. Granted, it took much longer than anyone anticipated."

I don't know what to say. *Is she serious right now?*

I refill our wineglasses—mine to the tip-top—and breathe deeply.

My expectations for telling Sutton about Ripley and me were all over the place. She knows our past, so I expected her to think it was a terrible idea. I also worried what she'd think because of *The Invitation*. I also wondered what she'd think about the one part that worries me the most—my mother.

She lifts her glass to mine and clinks them together. "To new beginnings."

"To new beginnings."

"And lots of sex."

I laugh before taking a sip of wine.

The alcohol, my third glass in a short period of time, fills my blood with an appreciated warmth. The nasty edges of my anxiety have been rounded off. I can finally think clearer, but that might be the wine talking.

When Ripley dropped me off this evening, I was on a high. I walked through the door, but I may as well have been floating on clouds. I was aware that I hadn't processed the ugly parts of this reality, and I was willing—*I needed*—to just enjoy the moment before I had to recognize the obstacles in front of us.

But now that time is here, and I don't know what to do.

"So what happens now?" Sutton asks, twirling her engagement ring around her finger. "Are you officially a thing?"

I smile at my friend. *Of course, she didn't worry about herself first. She's such an amazing person.*

"Before we get into all of that, let's talk about what this may or may not do to *The Invitation*," I say.

"I'll handle that. It might make things easier, actually, because we can stage more scenes. You'll be cooperative."

I gasp. "I've always been cooperative."

"You know what I mean." She grins. "Now, let's get back to the important part—where do you stand with Ripley?"

I take another drink before I respond. "I told him that we need to take some time to think about things."

She furrows her brow.

"This is just all really fast," I say.

"No, it's not. It's taken too many years to make this happen."

I laugh. "True. But what if he gets home, takes a shower, and realizes that he really just wanted to have sex with me, and I don't really have the potential for being a part of his future?"

My insides twist at the thought of Ripley not wanting to see me again. It's almost funny. Twenty-four hours ago, the idea of being a part of Ripley's life would've seemed deplorable. Now, not being in it seems unbelievable.

"I'm not saying that to mean I think we're getting married or something," I say. "I just mean that I don't want to get my hopes up."

She smiles sadly. "I know where this is coming from."

"No, you don't." *Except, she does.*

"You're the one that said you wanted to put your hopes into actionable items," she says. "This, my friend, is actionable."

Maybe.

"Did you ever set intentions for your life like I told you to?" she asks.

"No."

"I figured, so I set them for you."

"Can you do that?" I laugh.

She shrugs. "I don't know for certain. But I did it anyway and this is happening for you. You got a job. *Ripley*. My intentions for your life are coming true."

"You manifested Ripley for me?"

"Eh, no. Not necessarily. Kind of." She winces. "I manifested a great guy—someone loyal, honest, funny, handsome, kind, protective, and hardworking."

So, yeah, you did manifest him.

I flop back on the sofa and think about all the new things I know about Ripley. All the ways he's cared silently for me over the years. The way he loves his puppy. How he hides his pain under a charming smile and doesn't expect anyone to see beyond it.

The sad part about that is that I'm not sure that many do see beyond his exterior.

But now, I do. *Thank God for that.*

"So you're now giving him time to decide he's not into you?" Sutton asks. "That's the most Georgia thing I've ever heard."

I roll my eyes.

"But you're into him, right?" she asks curiously.

"Yeah. I'm into him." I get to my feet and pace my living room. "I can't explain this, and it's going to sound ... ridiculous, probably. But I finally feel like I can go forward now. There's a way forward for me that makes sense. I've been just paddling along, directionless, you know? Now there's this peace, I guess. Like I don't have any decisions to make." I look at her and smile. "It's like I can rest now."

Her smile stretches from ear to ear. "I'm so happy for you."

"I'm happy for me, too." My smile fades. "I just have to figure out how to tell my mom."

Sutton and I exchange a look, and I sit back down.

I stare at the dark television screen and sigh. "I don't know how to tell her."

"I know this is a thorny topic for her."

"You think?" I snort. "It's the only thing she's ever asked of me. *Do not date a Brewer.*" I lie back against the cushions, my heart sinking. "She's never going to go for this."

Sutton rests her hand on my thigh. "You don't know that."

"Oh, I kind of do. And she's literally the only family I have. I don't want to lose that, do you know what I mean?"

"She's your mom, Georgia. She loves you more than anything in the world. Sure, she might've had a bad experience with Ripley's dad, and she might've talked shit about it. But when it comes down to her daughter being happy with a really good man, she'll be supportive."

I look at her. "Do you even know Felicity Hayes?"

She smiles sadly.

"I wish I could compartmentalize my life," I say. "Deal with my mom in this box, and the rest of my life in another one."

"That's called having boundaries, and yes, you should do that."

I frown, knowing she's right.

I have such a hard time drawing boundaries with Mom. At the moment of my life when I should've been doing that—creating the framework for our relationship as adults—she was going through the most traumatic part of her life. She lost my dad, then lost Reid Brewer, and then whatever else she's gone through quietly. And instead of putting up boundaries, I became her therapist.

When she was depressed in bed, I brought her ice cream. I paid the bills. I did her laundry, washed her sheets, and let her cry on my shoulder while trying to motivate her to keep going.

Everyone needs a friend sometimes, and I was hers. We've just never gotten past that.

My phone rings and I snatch it up, hoping it's Ripley. Instead, it's Mom's name that flashes on the screen.

"It's like we beckoned her," I say, gathering my willpower before I answer. "Hey, Mom."

"You are never going to guess what happened to me today," she says, her voice loud and full of emotion.

Here we go ...

I pull the phone away from my ear and place her on speakerphone. "You're right. I'll never guess."

Sutton takes a long swig of her wine.

"Eloise and I had dinner last weekend," she says, talking a mile a minute. "And we were gossiping, as you do."

Sutton makes a face, contesting that point.

"And I might've told her something that Barbara told me," Mom says. "Barb didn't say it in confidence, exactly. I'm sure she didn't want the world to know she was sleeping with her son's best friend. But I don't see it as an awful thing, so I casually mentioned it to Eloise thinking she'd keep it between us."

"Right."

"And that bitch went behind my back and told Louisa and of course Louisa ran straight to Barbara and told her what she knew." She pauses to take a breath. "Barbara knew I told because I was the only person she said anything to. Now I'm the bad guy."

I sigh. "Well, Mom, you did betray her confidence."

"I told a mutual friend. *Eloise betrayed me, Georgia*. Now, none of my friends will talk to me, and there's an event next weekend and they're freezing me out." She starts to cry. "What am I going to do now?"

"Learn a lesson," Sutton whispers. "That would be a good starting point."

"Mom, calm down."

"How? How can I calm down? I've lost everyone in my life besides you. That backstabbing Louisa has just stolen my entire social life. I can't make new friends. I'm too old. Been there, done that and it sucked the first time around. I don't want to make new friends—I like the ones I have. Had. Whatever."

She breaks down into a fit of sobs. Her words are slurred, mixing with the tears, and I can't make sense of anything she's saying.

"Why don't you take a bath and relax and give this some time to settle?" I suggest. "Everything looks better after a bath."

"I'm beside myself. How could they do this to me?"

I wince. "Yeah, that's rough."

She sniffles. "Okay. I feel a bit better, I guess. I'm going to make some calls and see if I can salvage any of this."

"Good luck."

"I'll keep you posted."

"I'll be waiting."

"Love you, sweetheart. Bye."

"Good—" Click! The line is dead. "Bye."

Between the wine and my mother, my head feels like it's spinning.

Sutton takes our glasses and the bottle back to the kitchen. "You've had enough. I'm going to put this away, and then I need to get home to Jeremiah."

"Okay." I rest my head against the cushion and close my eyes, letting the warmth wash away my mom's drama. I can't deal with it right now, and I can't let her ruin my day. "Love you, Sutton."

"I love you, too."

There's a long pause that makes me open my eyes. She's standing in the doorway with her keys on her finger.

"I say this with all due respect," she says. "But Felicity Hayes lives for Felicity Hayes. You need to live for Georgia Hayes. Follow me?"

I nod. "I follow you."

"Good. I'm going now. Call me if you need me."

"Bye, friend."

"Bye, friend."

The door closes softly behind her.

I try to sit still and enjoy the question, but it doesn't work. I try to sort through my hazy brain and figure out how to tell my mom that I just might be in love with Ripley Brewer. That doesn't work, either. So

I do the only other thing I can think of—the only one I really want to do.

I pick up my phone and find his name.

> Me: Hey.
>
> Ripley: Hey.
>
> Me: I know we said we weren't really telling anyone yet, but I told Sutton.
>
> Ripley: What did you tell her, exactly?
>
> Me: 😊
>
> Ripley: I told Tate and Gannon the same thing.

I laugh out loud as happiness floods me again.

> Me: When do I get to meet Waffles?
>
> Ripley: I wanted you here right now. You were the one saying we needed to take things slow.
>
> Me: I changed my mind.
>
> Ripley: I can be there in thirty minutes.
>
> Me: I'll be ready.

Is this the right decision? I don't know. I hope so. Because it's the only one that feels right.

Chapter Twenty-Five

Georgia

"You live here? Holy shit." I climb out of the car, not waiting for a response, and look around. "I'm ... speechless."

Ripley leans against his car, smiling smugly.

His house, a place I've intentionally never visited, is absolutely breathtaking. It sits on top of a hill overlooking a never-ending valley. The deep gray exterior is brightened by tons of windows that probably offer an amazing view even from inside.

"So you like it?" he asks.

"What's not to like?"

He chuckles. "We're off to a good start then."

The wine I consumed earlier has started to dissipate. Ripley getting stuck in traffic and taking over an hour to get to my house helped. I'm still warm and blissfully happy, but I don't think that has anything to do with the wine.

"Would you like to come inside?" he asks.

"Shouldn't that be my line?"

He laughs, motioning for me to join him on the sidewalk leading to the house. He takes my hand in his, locking our fingers together, and ushers me into his home.

Immediately, a small Jack Russell terrier flies down a white stone hallway and launches himself at Ripley. He scoops him up, carrying him like a football.

"Waffles, I'd like you to meet someone," he says, petting his back.

The puppy tilts his head back and forth as if he doesn't understand who I am.

"This is Georgia," Ripley says.

Waffles barks. It's followed by a whine as he tries to jump from Ripley to me.

"Hey, Waffles," I say, holding my hand out so he can sniff me.

He does a couple of sniffs, then he licks my palm.

"He's a cutie," I say, taking in his sweet face. "I see why you're obsessed with him."

"Obsessed?"

"Yeah. You were literally stuck in a cabin with me in a soaked white T-shirt and you were trying to call your brother to pick up your puppy. That's obsessed. It's sweet and a huge green flag, but it's still obsessed."

He places the dog on the ground and then grabs me by the hips. He yanks me into him, penetrating me with his heated gaze.

"Wanna talk about obsessed?" He grins. "I'm obsessed with you."

Waffles barks at our feet.

I laugh. "You're making him jealous."

"Oh, I am not. He knows he's my boy." He bites his lip before a shy smile graces his lips. "And you're my girl."

Waffles growls, biting my shoelace and pulling it. He jerks it and twists his head back and forth like he's trying to kill it.

"Hey," I say, bending to his level.

He crouches to the ground, my shoelace still in his mouth.

"You're really strong," I say, playing to his pride. "Look at how ferocious you are."

All of a sudden, he stands, drops the shoelace, and leaps from where he's crouched right into my lap. I catch him but lose my balance. Thankfully, Ripley catches me before I fall flat on my back.

Waffles puts his paws on my chest and licks my face.

"We're still working on manners." Ripley sighs.

"It's okay." I set the puppy on the floor. "Do you have a ball? Go get your ball."

He whizzes down the hallway as if he understands what I'm saying. *What a smartie.*

I get to my feet with Ripley's arm around my waist. I slip off my shoes, and then let him take me by the hand.

He shows me his immaculate chef's kitchen with—as I suspected—an amazing view. From the window, I check out the pool and outdoor barbecue area that looks to be straight from a magazine. We pass through a dining room big enough to throw a party with a small army, an office, and a game room. Then we make our way up the stairs, Waffles leading the pack with his ball in his mouth.

Ripley's home isn't at all what I'd pictured in my mind when I imagined where he'd live. It's clean and bright with lots of natural light. The decor is minimal and tasteful. There are pictures of his family—none of his father—and baskets of Waffles's toys in almost every room.

Talk about a spoiled dog.

Talk about a swoon-worthy owner.

Ripley's home is quiet and comfortable, yet lived in.

It's the epitome of my dream home.

The thought makes me smile.

"Tate uses that room when he stays here," Ripley says, pointing at a closed door on our left. "He used to hang out here a lot—not as much anymore. But instead of driving when it's late and he's had a few drinks, it's easier for him just to crash at my house."

"Smart."

Ripley pulls me closer to him. "Those two doors are guest rooms. Every bedroom has a bathroom." We make our way down the hall. "There are three bedrooms in the basement, too."

"You have more square footage in bathrooms than I do in my entire townhouse."

He grins. "I don't really know what to say to that."

"You don't have to say anything. I was just commenting."

Waffles runs ahead of us and scratches on the door at the end. He hops in a circle when we don't get there fast enough.

Ripley then opens the door to the primary suite. "This is my room."

I step inside a small sitting area with a midnight-blue sofa, two fluffy chairs, and a small table. An arched doorway leads into a larger room—Ripley's bedroom.

A king-sized, four-poster bed is covered with a fluffy white comforter, and there are more pillows than I can count lining the headboard. A fireplace takes up much of the way across from the bed, and a television screen hangs from the ceiling just above it.

"Nice room," I say, peeking into the bathroom. "Did you design this?"

He leans against the doorway while I inspect the clawfoot bathtub situated inside an expansive shower with showerheads that befuddle me. There are two sinks. Brass hardware. In the corner is a sauna next to a linen closet.

"I had a hand in the design," he says. "There were things I wanted to be sure made it into the final product, but I didn't obsess about every little detail. Stuff can be changed."

"True."

"So what do you think? Do you like it?"

"It's not bad." I try not to smile and fail miserably. "I just saw you living in a cave somewhere with bats and lots of fire."

He grabs me by the waist and pulls me in for a kiss. I melt into him, giving him free rein to kiss me as hard, soft, and as long as he wants.

"I love having you here," he says, resting his forehead against mine.

"I love being here. I thought it might feel weird."

He pulls away. "Why?"

"You know, with the bats and all ..."

He smacks my ass, making me yelp. The contact sends a zing of pleasure shooting through me, snaking through my body until it lands deep in my core.

Something shifts between us. His eyes darken as he licks his lips, and my insides clench at the thought of having him again.

"Do you have plans?" I ask him.

"We were going to film, but ..."

I grab the waistband of his joggers, letting my fingers drift across his hips. I look him in the eyes and grin. "You better not film this."

His eyes flare as he waits with anticipation of my next move. I want him inside me so badly. But first, I want to taste him.

I push his pants over his hips so they bunch at his feet. He fists his cock, already so hard for me, and smiles.

"Now, what are you going to do?" he asks.

I drop to my knees, catching a glimpse of Waffles in the doorway and noting we're going to have to do something about privacy. I grip Ripley's cock with one hand, sliding my fingers up and down his shaft. He groans, widening his stance.

I kiss the head of his cock as I stroke his balls with my free hand. He hisses a breath, threading his fingers through my hair, and flexes toward my mouth.

"This would make one hell of a video," he says, shivering as I drag my flattened tongue from the root to the tip.

"Maybe one day."

He chuckles. "Really? You're going to let me film us fucking?"

My tongue swirls over the tip, collecting the precum gathered there for me. "You never know." I flick my tongue across the underside of his cock. "It might be hot."

I keep my gaze pinned to his as I lick up to the head again. I suck the tip into my mouth, earning a hissing sound in return.

"Does that feel good?" I ask.

"You know it fucking does."

I know it does. Watching him react to me, to the things I'm doing to him, makes me feel like a goddess. He's warring with himself, struggling not to fall apart—struggling not to take control. And that leaves me feeling powerful.

"I love watching you while I suck your cock," I say before taking him into my mouth. He rocks his hips, encouraging me to take him deeper, and his fingers tug on my hair until the follicles burn.

It's a cacophony of sensations—enough to bring me to the edge of an orgasm without being touched.

The saltiness of his precum. The heat of his body. The smooth rigidity of his cock in my hand.

The look of pure desire in his eyes when he looks down at me.

"I'm never videoing this," he says, guiding himself deeper down my throat. "This is just for me. No one gets to see you like this but me."

I roll him around my mouth, letting my spit trickle down his length. Every sound coming from him causes me to get wetter. The thought of him splitting me open again makes me moan.

I take him deeper, pumping my fist—letting him guide me with his hands. He lifts his hips into my mouth, urging me to go faster, harder, until I feel his balls tighten.

My eyes water as he stops, and he refuses to let me move. His eyes squeeze shut as he pulls out of my mouth carefully.

"Dammit," he says, heaving a breath. "You almost made me come."

I wipe my mouth with the back of my hand. "That was the point. Thanks for stealing that from me."

"*Oh, no*. You're going to get it. I promise."

"Can I have it now? Or is that too much to ask?"

He laughs, pulling me to my feet. "I'm glad to see you didn't lose your moxie."

"Me? Never."

He kicks off his pants, takes my hand, and pulls me into his bedroom. Then he sits on the edge of the bed, leaving me standing in front of him.

"Can I ask a favor of you?" he asks.

I shrug. "Maybe. I can't guarantee anything."

He shakes his head, amused.

"Will this favor expedite you fucking me?" I ask.

"Yes, it will."

"Then the odds are in your favor, champ."

His eyes sparkle. "I want to sit here and watch you undress for me."

I blink once. Then twice.

"Not in any sort of specific way," he says. "Don't look at me like I just asked you to strip for me or something."

"You asked me to undress, which is the very definition of strip."

"You know what I mean."

I study him. "Why?"

He takes my hand and presses a simple kiss to my palm. The sweet, basic gesture hits me right in the heart. He doesn't know it, but he could ask me to do anything right now, and I'd do it.

Except anal. I'm not doing that.

"I just want to appreciate you," he says softly. "I didn't get to do this before."

How do I say no to that? I grin, pulling the hem of my shirt slowly over my head.

"You're very smooth at taking your charm and twisting it to fit your needs," I say, tossing my shirt at him.

He snatches it out of the air and places it on the bed beside him.

His gaze is riveted to my face, then slides slowly—seductively—down my body. I'm examined as if he's memorizing my curves and valleys. It's as if he's taking a photograph with his eyes. *It's incredibly empowering.*

I remove my shorts, dropping them onto the floor, then I'm standing before him in my bra and panties.

My heart jolts as he looks me over with smoldering eyes. Perspiration sprinkles my skin. Anticipation licks at my core.

I hook my fingers at my hips and push my panties down my legs. The bed creaks as he shifts his weight, but he doesn't say a word. I hold the fabric to my side and drop it to the floor.

He swallows hard, his throat bobbing with the force.

I remove my bra, letting my breasts topple from the cups. He licks his lips, his attention trained on my nipples.

My body aches for his touch. I have to fight the overwhelming urge to be close to him, on him, around him. Instead, I stand in the nude, feeling the warm air hitting spots usually covered, and let him have what he wants—an unobstructed view of me.

I can't imagine doing this with anyone else. I can't even imagine standing in front of Ripley like this. But in the moment, it doesn't feel wrong. I'm not even self-conscious.

He makes me feel that beautiful.

I move to him, unable to control my needs any longer.

He runs his hands over me—my stomach, up my chest, over my shoulders. He follows the shape of my ass around my hips and down to my thighs. His fingers slide between my legs and through my slit.

I gasp as his lips find my breasts and he teases them with soft licks and nips. I hold his head, pulling it closer to me, and spread my legs for him.

"That's my girl," he whispers.

One finger slides into me and then two. He works them lazily in and out as if we have all the time in the world.

"Everything about you is perfect." He palms my chest, playing with my nipple. "How did I ever resist you?"

I moan, rocking against his hand. I'm in desperate need of relief.

I need to fucking come.

"Well, you were kind of a dick," I say, my eyes shut. All I can focus on is the way his fingers twist and pull, strumming me—bringing me closer to sweet relief.

He laughs, flicking my bud with his finger. "Thank God I have you now."

The words zing straight to my heart and my eyes fly open. He's looking at me, a shy grin on his face, as his thumb finds my clit.

Fire bolts through me, stealing any words. The intensity of the orgasm erases any response I had planned.

"Ripley!" I shout, earning a whine from Waffles somewhere in the distance. "I can't take it. *Fuck.*"

I reach for his hand to stop the onslaught, the force of the orgasm too strong. My teeth grind together. My head threatens to blow.

"Don't stop me," he whispers, slowing his fingers. "Let me make you feel good. Let me watch you fall apart."

"*I can't ...*" My eyes squeeze shut as I become disconnected from my body.

"Yes, you can. You're so gorgeous coming on my hand. Ride it, Peaches."

He slowly brings me down from the highest high I've ever experienced. I sag against his shoulder as he removes his fingers from me.

"That was amazing," I say, heaving breaths.

"It's yours any time you want it." He kisses my chest. "But right now, my cock is about ready to explode."

I push away and then take his hand and pull him to his feet. Then I crawl on the bed and lie down.

He stands still, frozen in place, with a curious look on his face.

"What?" I ask. "You're not going to get all weird on me, are you?"

He smiles. "I just can't believe this is real."

I let my knees fall to the sides, giving him a view of my pussy. "Can you come to terms with it while you're deep inside me? Because I really want to feel your cock."

He laughs, peeling off his shirt. "You're going to be the death of me."

"Are you complaining?"

He jumps on the bed, covering my body with his. He presses a kiss to my lips and then grins.

"Condom?" he asks.

"Is there anything I need to know about your medical history?"

"No. And I have a report dated last month if you'd like to review it."

I lift my hips. "What I'd like is for you to put your cock inside—*oh fuck*."

I don't get to say another word. He fucks them right out of me.

Chapter Twenty-Six

Georgia

I curl up on a chair in Ripley's living room with Waffles on my lap. The T-shirt I found in Ripley's closet swamps me, since I don't know where most of my clothes from last night wound up, but I couldn't risk coming downstairs naked.

Does he have visitors that barge in? One of his brothers? A housekeeper? Cameras?

I have no idea.

The sun peeks up over the horizon, splattering the sky with the softest, prettiest oranges and pinks. It's a beautiful sunrise after an amazing night.

So why did I wake up feeling nervous?

Because it's going too well.

Detaching myself from Ripley was hard, but being alone with my thoughts was harder. I'm my own worst enemy sometimes, as ironic as that is. My fear is *my problem*, and he certainly hasn't given me a reason to question him since our soul-baring conversation where we shared our truths.

Still, fear is real, and my insecurities don't help anything.

I turn on my phone camera and look at myself. My lips are swollen, my eyes are tired, and my hair's a mess. I look like I've been fucked. But I need to record a confessional because I didn't do it after our filming session last night—a date consisting of playing with Waffles.

I actually think the footage might be the best we've done yet.

"Waffles, buddy, I wish I had a filter because I look like shit."

He doesn't even open his eyes.

"Typical man."

I take a deep breath and hope I remember the kind of questions Myla wants us to answer. Then I open the video app and press record.

"Hey," I say softly, holding the phone up to get my best angle. "It's morning. I wound up staying overnight last night. I know, I know. Don't judge me. He can be very persuasive."

I scratch Waffles's head just behind his ears.

"This was a curveball that I didn't see coming," I admit. "Things have been obviously going well between us, but I'm not the kind of girl who stays all night with a guy this quickly." I chuckle. "That's what all the girls say, though, right?"

I blow out a breath, knowing Myla can edit my blips out. *Thank God.*

"Do you know what the most surprising thing about this whole process is? It's realizing what your insecurities really are. I've met this guy and he's absolutely amazing. He hasn't given me a reason to think that his intentions aren't true. Yet here I sit this morning while he's in bed, wondering if this is realistic. Like, is this one of those things that's great right now but I'm goofy to think it'll really pan out?"

Waffles snores, making me grin.

"That's really unfair, you know? To both Ripley and to me. But how do you have the courage to hope for things? Hell, I barely hope for clean socks in the mornings. Hoping that a love connection might be real? *Terrifying.*"

I gaze out the window, taking in the beauty of Mother Nature.

"I guess that's all for me this morning."

I turn the camera off and go back to bed.

Chapter Twenty-Seven

Georgia

"Okay," Ripley says, taking a look around the kitchen. "I have all the cameras set up."

"This will work much better than our half-assed film job last night. Although, I do think that footage is gold."

He pulls me to him, kissing the top of my head. "It was fun. Waffles did steal the show though."

True.

"I filmed a confessional this morning," I say.

"You did? When?"

"I came downstairs for a while and let Waffles out to pee. The sunrise was gorgeous, so I sat for a while and watched it."

He smiles against my cheek before letting me go.

"That's okay, isn't it?" I ask.

"Of course, it's okay. Don't be silly." I reach for one of the cameras we positioned around the kitchen. "I'll turn this one on. You get the other two."

"Got it."

"And remember. You can't just fondle me and kiss me the whole time," I say, laughing. *Myla is going to have to cut so much out of last night's footage.*

Ripley groans as he presses record on the camera by the sink and the one in the corner. I turn on the camera by the pantry.

"We're rolling," I say.

"Act natural."

I snort, shaking my head. "Are you sure these pancakes are going to taste normal?" I peer at the ingredients list. "They look weird."

"You won't know the difference."

I watch him walk shirtless in front of me. *My God, his body is perfection.* "It says there's like one hundred grams of protein in this mix."

"It's an easy, healthy swap from the normal brands."

"I don't think I need this much protein in a day."

He smirks. "Probably not after the amount I've been giving you."

I pick up a hand towel and throw it at him. He ducks, laughing at his own joke.

The ingredient list on the back of the box calls for a ton of eggs and a bit of milk. I gather the things from the refrigerator and take them back to the counter.

Ripley fries bacon on the stovetop, whistling while he works. It's the cutest thing in the world to watch. This tall, strong man whistling a tune from an eighties kids' show. *Who would've thought?*

My anxiety has decreased as the morning has worn on. Everything feels worse at night. As soon as we woke up and climbed into a hot bath together, I remembered why I felt so happy yesterday.

Because I trust him.

"I think this batter needs a little sugar," I say.

"No, it doesn't."

"Look at it." I lift a spoonful of the brown, slightly lumpy mixture. "It smells ... not sweet."

"It'll be fine. Trust me. This is what I do all day."

"Yeah, well, I eat sweet stuff all day, and my taste buds are conditioned to it. You can't just take me off the good stuff cold turkey."

He mutters something I can't hear, which is probably a good thing.

I go through his pantry, looking for his sugar container. I spy it on the second shelf. Standing on my tippy-toes, I pull it down.

"Found it," I say, placing it on the counter. "You can't hide it from me."

A coy grin plays on his lips. "I wouldn't want to."

"Good, because I think ... Ripley!"

His grin grows into a full smile.

I pull out a white chocolate macadamia nut cookie. The jar is full of them.

My heart squeezes. *He remembered.* I laugh. *Of course, he did. This man is something else.*

"How?" I demand, smiling at him.

"How what?"

"How did you get these cookies here? Clearly, you don't keep them around because there's not a fun food in here. When did you get them?"

He flips over the bacon, his arm muscles flexing. "I got them delivered after I got home from the cabin."

What? "Why?"

"Because I knew you'd be here at some point, and I'll be damned if I ever let that cookie jar run dry."

I drop the cookie jar onto the counter and fling myself at him. He chuckles, putting the spatula down, and picking me up.

He sets me on the counter away from the stove, and I wrap my legs around his waist.

He kisses my nose. "What's wrong? I see it on your face."

I bury my head in his neck. "I hope you're real."

"What?" He laughs, pulling me back so he can meet my gaze. "What do you mean?"

"It's just that this is all so great. *You're so great.* And just a couple of days ago, I was sure you were playing with me, trying to get me to fall for you, for shits and giggles."

His face darkens.

"And now I think maybe you're not. I want to hope you're not. But ..."

He picks up my hand and places a kiss on my palm. "Honestly? I *was* trying to get you to fall for me."

My insides still.

"I told myself it was to put you in your place because that made me feel better, you know? I could justify that," he says, running a finger down my cheek. "But really, it was because I wanted you to want me. I was just scared as hell that you wouldn't and that would hurt even more."

I lock my heels around his back.

"But, Peaches, I swear to you—I swear on Waffles—that this is all real. I understand that you're scared or have reservations. That's not a problem. I can fix that. I can be here. I can prove to you that I mean all the things I say. And if I have to wait another decade to get you to understand, then I guess it'll really suck now that I've had you." He kisses me simply, sweetly. "But I'll wait until you're sure."

I scoot to the edge of the counter and drape my arms over his shoulders. Then I look at the camera in the corner. Myla won't be able to keep these references to our past relationship. But she definitely has to lose this.

"Myla, you're going to need to cut it here," I say, laughing at Ripley nibbling on the side of my neck.

He picks me up and carries me out of the room. We're upstairs when the smoke alarm goes off, reminding us of the bacon.

Chapter Twenty-Eight

R^{ipley}

"Well, ladies and gentlemen," I say into my phone. "She's the one. And that's the update."

I end the video and leave the bathroom.

Chapter Twenty-Nine

Georgia

Ripley's hand rests on my thigh as he drives me back home. Every now and then, he gives my leg a little squeeze, almost as if he's quietly confirming I'm still here.

"It feels wrong to take you home," Ripley says.

I rest my head on the window. "I know. It feels wrong to go home."

"So don't."

I trace a muscle along his forearm and wish I didn't have to.

"This is new," he says, glancing at me out of the corner of his eye. "But is it, really? It's not like we met at a bar and went home together. I've known you for years."

"And we've hung out for years, even if we stayed on opposite sides of the room."

"Biggest mistake of my life," he says, pressing his fingertips into my thigh.

I've thought about this a lot—all night while Ripley slept with a death grip on me. I've wasted so many years holding on to perceived infractions against me. And by refusing to let go of those things, I've kept myself in a holding pattern. My dreams died. I couldn't progress or continue with my life because I'd blocked my blessings.

My blessings were designed to come through Ripley.

I believe that with all of my heart, even if it scares me shitless.

I don't know what I'll do if this doesn't work because he already has my heart. I don't want to admit that out loud, and I'm not sure if I even want to admit it to myself in a *let's act on this* way. But that doesn't change the facts.

I'm fucked—in more ways than one.

A little voice in my head still warns me that his intentions might be cruel, and he might leave when things get inconvenient. And both things are possible. But I'm choosing not to let that small voice overpower logic ... or my heart. I've done that my whole life. Look where it's gotten me.

"I need to find a way to talk to my mother about this," I say, my heart growing heavy.

"She really hates my whole family that badly?"

"Unfortunately, yes. I think it was a perfect storm of things that hit her hard. My dad left her pretty much overnight. One of her closest friends was married to Dad's best friend, so Mom lost her in the divorce, too. Then your dad really broke her heart." I sigh sadly. "I think she put all of her hopes into a future with him—believed the things he said and really thought it was her happy ending, only to get crushed a second time on the heels of the first."

She's never been the same since.

Ripley frowns.

"She's a very ..." I bite my lip, trying to find a way to describe my mother without being disrespectful and sounding harsh. "She has main character energy. She is the star of her—everyone's—show in her mind. You can argue with her and try to explain that her self-image doesn't translate into other people's worlds, and she wouldn't understand. That concept doesn't exist with her."

He glances at me with many questions on his mind.

"Even if she's dramatic and her feelings are extreme ... even if we don't understand them all the time, it doesn't invalidate them."

"I understand. But do you really think she'd want to keep you from being with someone just because their dad fucked her over?"

"Simply put? Yes. I do. I know that will happen."

"That sounds selfish as hell."

I sit up and sigh again. "She is selfish. She doesn't understand boundaries. She has flaws like everyone else. But she's a good person, Ripley. Even though she frustrates me to the edges of the earth most days, I love her with all of my heart."

He squeezes me again.

"She's the only family I have," I say. "I haven't spoken to my father since the night I was telling you about when he called me over my tuition."

Ripley's jaw sets and he stares at the road ahead.

"My mother sort of raised herself, and then my father took over parenting her when they married, really, and now ... I guess it's me in that role." My heart sinks at the realization. "I know she's going to throw a fit when she finds out about us. I hope not, but I know she will. But if I can sit her down with a bottle of wine and catch her on a good day, I might be able to smooth it over enough not to worry about it anymore."

"It's whatever you want. Whatever you need. You know that I'll never come between you and your mother. Family is the most important thing in the world to me."

"I know."

He looks over his shoulder at me. "And you. You are quickly becoming number one on that list."

A wave of emotion cascades over me, crashing in soft, beautiful splashes in my heart and soul.

I've avoided hoping for much in my life because hope never pans out. It's a setup to being burned. It's akin to the universe laughing at you. *Here, see this thing? Want it so you can never have it.*

But maybe that's my experience because I've always hoped for the wrong thing.

Maybe hope only works when you hope for the right thing.

Admitting that I'm considering, maybe even dreaming of, a future with Ripley scares the bejesus out of me. My stomach churns, and my fight-or-flight reflex kicks in. But for the first time, flight feels like a scarier option than fight. Because if I fight, I have a chance to win. If I fly away, I leave him behind. And I can't think of a worse scenario than that.

"Do you know why this is so easy?" I ask.

He hums, turning back to the road.

"It's easy because this is the way it's supposed to be."

"You're damn right it is."

He turns onto my street and rolls through my middle-class neighborhood in his fancy car. People turn to look, little kids wave, and it's an experience that I don't know how to handle.

"When can I see you again?" he asks.

"I start my new job next week. It was supposed to be two weeks out, but I accepted their offer, and they emailed me back asking if I could start sooner. So I need to get a few things to the dry cleaner and clean my house. Stuff like that."

"You didn't answer my question."

"Oh." I laugh. "I was assuming I could see you tonight."

"Thank God. And then you can tell me more about this amazing job."

His relief makes me smile. "You bet."

We turn onto my driveway, and Ripley puts the car in park. I lean over the console to kiss him and gasp.

Oh no. Please, no.

I fall back into my seat, fumbling with my seat belt.

"What? What is it?" Ripley asks, his brows pulled together. "You're scaring the shit out of me."

I force a swallow and try not to cry. *This is not how this was supposed to happen.*

"My mother's sitting on the steps," I say, my voice eerily calm.

"And why would she be sitting on the steps?"

"Because I won't give her a key. She just shows up when she wants to hang out or talk, which is fine, except ... it's not."

He takes a deep breath. "What do you want to do?"

I glance at the porch. My mother stands and makes her way slowly to the car. It's as if she senses something is wrong.

My heart races. My brain screams that this is the time to choose flight, but I know I can't do that. *Not to Ripley*. It's too late to try to hide it now. All I can do is be thankful Ripley has some context before all hell hits the fan.

"I have no idea what she's going to do or say," I say quickly. "Please, please don't judge me for whatever happens."

"Of course not."

"Let's just say hello and pray she doesn't completely lose her shit." *Even though I know she will.*

I open the door, and Ripley opens his moments later. I hear his shut right after mine.

"Georgia?" Mom asks, holding a frozen pizza and a bottle of wine in her hands. "What's going on?" She turns to Ripley. "Who is this?"

She looks Ripley up and down. It's harmless, at first. But upon her second pass, a cold shield slides over her face.

Fuck.

"Remember how I told you I was working with Sutton?" I ask, my voice too bright. "Well, it's for a fake-dating show called *The Invitation*. We're shooting the pilot. This is my ... counterpart."

She lifts her chin at Ripley. "Hello. I'm Felicity Hayes. And you are ..."

"Ripley Brewer, ma'am. It's a pleasure to meet you."

The pizza box slides from my mother's hand and hits the ground. Her face goes from shock to absolute fury in a half a second. She glares at him before turning to me.

"*How dare you?*" she says, her voice stone cold.

"Mom, listen—"

"Ripley *Brewer*?" She spins back around to him. "Who is your father?"

He swallows. "Reid Brewer, unfortunately."

"Really?" She turns back around. "Really, Georgia? Are you fucking kidding me?"

Hurt colors her face, and that punishes my heart. I don't want to hurt her, but I don't want her choices to hurt me, either.

"Ma'am," Ripley says. "I—"

"Don't *ma'am* me," Mom sneers. "I have no idea how you weaseled your way into my daughter's life, but you can see yourself right out."

"Mother!"

"I know what kind of people you are, and I don't want you anywhere close to my child. Do you hear me?" she asks.

Ripley's jaw tenses, and I know he's pissed. He's ready to fight. But the way the blues in his eyes change to a dark, almost gray color tells me that her words are hurting him, too.

He's no more his father than I am my mother.

"That's not fair, Mom," I say, tears filling my eyes. "Don't talk to him like that."

"I can't believe you'd do this to me, especially when you know what a rotten week this has been for me! I've lost my friends. Now I've lost you."

"Ms. Hayes—"

"No." She glares at him, shaking the wine bottle in his direction.

I've never seen her like this. I've never seen her this unhinged. *Never this close to losing it.*

I don't know what to do. *Do I calm my mother down and try to be rational? Do I take Ripley's side and tell Mom to stop it?* I don't know.

"Just leave," Mom shouts, her voice cracking. "Get in your car and go. You're just another boy in her life who will be forgotten in a week. Just because your last name is Brewer doesn't mean you're special! Someone like you would never be good enough for my daughter!"

Ripley pales. I know she just hit a direct wound, and he has to be reeling from it right now. My heart shatters for him, but I need to show him I'm on his side.

That I believe in him.

That she's fucking wrong.

"You don't have the right to say terrible things to him," I yell back. "You can't talk to him this way. You don't even know him."

"And I apparently don't know my own daughter, either. You're betraying me just like your father. *Just like his father!* Just like my friends."

"Get over yourself! I'm not betraying you!"

"The hell you aren't."

"And don't you dare compare him to his father," I say, my voice shaking with fury.

My neighbor to the right sticks his head out the door before ducking back inside.

Great. We're the neighborhood Maury Povich Show *now.*

Tears flow down my cheeks. Ripley reaches for me, but my mother jumps between us.

"If you see my daughter again, you'll be taking her away from her mother," Mom says, crying, too. "Because I won't stick around to watch you hurt her. I won't watch you take her away from me."

Ripley looks at me. He doesn't look like the confident, slightly arrogant, self-assured man I know. He's sad, frustrated, and slightly broken ... just like me.

"Can I call you later?" I ask him softly.

"If you call him, I'll never speak to you again," Mom says, throwing down the gauntlet. "I won't stand for it. I won't have you running around with him when I know exactly what he'll do to you."

"Mom, that's not fair."

She shrugs as if she doesn't care if it's fair or not. And that's probably true. She doesn't.

Ripley nods at my mother as if he can't help but show some sort of respect—because he's such a good man—then he turns to me.

The pain in his eyes stabs me in the heart. Tears stream down my face, clouding my vision. But I know I see a shine of tears fog his gorgeous blue eyes, too.

He bows his head as if he can't look at me, then gets into his car and drives off into the afternoon sun.

"I raised you better than this, Georgia Faith."

I wipe my face, sniffling back snot. I don't even care. "You raised me not to trust anyone. You taught me that the odds of being happy weren't great. Because you had bad experiences with men, you taught me I should be wary of them, too."

Her hand shakes around the wine bottle.

"I know you love me and were just trying to help protect me, Mom. But you just pushed away a great fucking guy because *you* are scared. How fair is that?"

"You don't want him. You just think you do. You'll be fine after a couple of weeks."

I laugh angrily, taking a moment to pull myself together before I speak. "I know Ripley and I will be fine. It's you and me that I'm not sure about."

"What does that mean?"

I throw up my hands, exasperated. "I am thirty years old. *Thirty!*" I yell it entirely too loud, but I don't care. "I don't want to be mean to you, but you've left me no choice."

Mom takes a step back.

"I am an adult—a grown-ass woman capable of making my own choices. As a matter of fucking fact, I have a great life because of my choices. I have a job—which you don't know about because you haven't asked. It never occurs to you to think about anyone other than yourself."

"That's not true," she says, her bottom lip quivering.

But I don't care. I don't care that she's sad. I don't care that she's upset. I don't give a flying fuck that I'm about to hurt her feelings because she doesn't care about mine.

"Look at your life," I say, refusing to back down. "You don't have a boyfriend. You don't have a job, aside from a part-time gig at a consignment store. You don't have friends now—and that's your fault, by the way."

She gasps.

"You come to me for everything and *give me nothing*," I say, boring holes into her. "I'm not talking about money. I'm talking about support. Camaraderie. Friendship. Motherly advice."

"You're lying."

"Am I?" I ask, my voice squeaking. "What's my favorite color? Food? Movie? Cookie? I'll wait."

She stares at me.

"Exactly. But do you know who knows? Ripley has a jar of my favorite cookies in his house just in case I might swing by. He bought me purple gloves when we went ice-skating because he knows it's my favorite color. He knew I wasn't adventurous when it comes to food, and when we went to this really ritzy place, and I panicked, he ordered food I liked for me. *And you just ran him off!*"

I hold my temples, feeling a migraine coming on.

"I'm tired, Mom. I'm exhausted, and I can't do this anymore. I've felt happier and more alive the last couple of days than I ever have, and you just ruined that for me." I lift my gaze to hers. "It's like you want me to be as miserable as you are."

Tears fall down her cheeks, and I can't find it in me to care.

I leave her with her pizza and wine and storm into my house. The image of Ripley's face—the pain of being compared to and judged for being the son of the monster Reid Brewer—rips my heart in two pieces.

Ripley has protected me throughout my life. Now is the time I protect him.

Even if it kills me.

With the door locked behind me, I sob.

Chapter Thirty

Ripley

Waffles nudges my leg with his nose.

"I know, buddy," I say, downing another shot of tequila. "Give me a second."

He barks as if that's not good enough.

"That's the theme of the day," I say.

I sit at the island, hunched over. The cameras are still sitting where we left them this morning. The pan of burnt turkey bacon is on the stove. A single white chocolate macadamia nut cookie is on the counter, and I want to fucking cry.

My insides ache with a hollowness, a sickness that extends deep into my soul. I feel like I've been punched in the gut repeatedly and left to die.

Felicity's words echo alongside my father's in my head. It occurs to me why they would've been attracted to each other. They're both horrible people who like to manipulate those around them to get what they want.

If karma was real, they would've ended up together.

"Fucking hell," I say, slumping against the counter. "This is bullshit. All of it."

What's really bullshit? Is it that our parents are selfish assholes, or is it that I'm afraid Georgia might believe the things both of our parents said about me?

My phone rings and I jump, knocking my glass down the island as I reach for the call. But my heart drops when I see it's not Georgia.

"Hey," I say, pulling my glass back.

"Sutton just got off the phone with Georgia. Are you okay?" Jeremiah asks.

"I'm drinking tequila."

"Shit." He takes a deep, frustrated breath. "Want me to come over?"

"Nope. Sure don't."

"Hey, Ripley. It's Sutton."

"Hey," I say.

"What can I do for you?" she asks.

I take another shot for good measure. "Is she okay?"

"She will be."

"Her mother is a piece of fucking work. You should've heard the shit she was saying—and I don't even care about the stuff she said about me. You should've heard the way she spoke to Georgia."

Sutton sighs. "I know. This has been a long time coming. But this relationship is important to Georgia, even if it's unhealthy."

"So what do I do? If anyone else in the world had talked to her like that, I would've stepped in and ended it." My stomach curls, threatening to launch the tequila across the kitchen. "But it's her mom, and she's been very clear that she wants to preserve that relationship. So what do I do? I feel like I failed her today."

I hold my head, disgusted with myself.

Maybe my dad was right. Maybe I am good for nothing.

"You did the right thing," Jeremiah says. "Tensions were high. The right thing was to leave and let Georgia handle it. She was safe, and if she needed you, she would've called."

And she didn't call.

Fuck. I hang my head.

"She's really embarrassed about the things her mother said to you," Sutton says. "I know she feels awful."

"It's not her fault. I'm sure her piece-of-work mother will blame her for it, considering it seems like she blames her for everything."

"You have no idea," Sutton says, groaning.

Her mother's words echo through my head.

"I can't believe you'd do this to me, especially when you know what a rotten week this has been for me!"

"You're betraying me just like your father."

Georgia said she was selfish, but *holy shit*.

If this is the only family Georgia has, then I understand why she's reluctant to terminate their relationship, no matter how terrible it might be. But this isn't healthy. This isn't good.

Who does Georgia go to when she's sick? Hurt? When she needs support?

Who takes care of her? Protects her? Is her shield from the world?

It doesn't look like she has one. It appears she's out there, fending for herself, and *I can't handle that*.

"Dammit," I groan into the air, pounding my fist against the countertop. "I can't take this shit. What should I do? Do I call her? Go over there? Text her? What?"

"Why don't you give her some space tonight?" Sutton suggests. "She's trying to do what's right for everyone involved. Let's give her a bit of time to get her head together."

"I don't like that plan."

Jeremiah chuckles. "I bet you don't, man, but Sutton's going over there in a little bit."

"And I'll tell her I talked to you," she says.

"And if you need anything—if she needs me—you'll call me, right?" I ask.

"You're my first call," Sutton says. "This is going to be all right. I promise."

I look down at Waffles, his little chin resting on my foot, and smile weakly.

Just last night, Georgia and I were outside, taking Waffles for a walk and throwing him the ball. Ordering him jackets online for the upcoming fall—something that was a little extra for even me—but Georgia insisted.

And now, we're here.

It was so much easier when she hated me for something I'd done instead of possibly seeing me in the same way they did.

"Keep me updated," I say.

"Call me if you need me," Jeremiah says. "I'll be home all night. Keep away from the tequila tonight, just in case."

I push the bottle away from me. "Okay. Talk to you later."

"Bye," they say and hang up.

I hold my head in my hands and replay every conversation I've ever had with Georgia—until one conversation sticks out.

"Donovan started talking about me moving in with him, and I fought against it. It was too soon and, I don't know, I didn't really feel like we were at that point. That made him mad. Shortly after, he stopped buying cookies."

I swipe my phone up and find her name in my text list.

My heart pounding, I type out a simple text that I hope she understands.

Me: 🍪

A few seconds later, her reply comes through.

🍑 Georgia: 🍪 🍺 💚

It's not enough, but at least it's something until I can talk to her. She knows I'm not going anywhere.

Because I will talk to her.

I've waited my entire adult life for her. I can wait a bit longer.

THE INVITATION

The sound of my phone shakes me out of my sleep. I grasp wildly at my bedside table until I find it as I sit up.

> 🍑 Georgia: Hey, just checking on you.

> Me: It's so good to hear from you. How are you?

I stare at the screen until it goes black. My heart turns a dark shade with it.

> 🍑 Georgia: I'm actually terrible. I am so sorry for what happened today. I've tried to call you and text you a hundred times, but I just don't know what to say.

"Thank God."

> Me: You don't have to say anything. You don't have to apologize or explain. I just want to know that you're okay.

> 🍑 Georgia: Mom said some really awful things to both of us today, and I'm so sorry you had to hear them. I can brush them off because I know she'll come around. But you didn't deserve any of that.

> Me: And you think you did?

"You've got to be kidding me, Peaches."

I stare at the screen, waiting for her reply—one that takes far too long.

> 🍑 Georgia: I have to figure this out. It's time I place some boundaries with her and demand more respect. But I fear that's going to be a process at best, impossible at worst. But until I know, I can't have you being subjected to her word vomit.

> Me: I'm a big boy.

> 🍑 Georgia: Don't I know it? 🩶 I just need some time, okay? You've protected me for so long, and I need to protect you, too.

> Me: I don't need protecting. I need to be there for you.

> 🍑 Georgia: If you get involved, it'll make it messier. And I can't focus on my new job—which I start tomorrow now, by the way—you, and Mom. Even though it's not what I want when we've just found each other, I just need a bit of space. Please.

> Me: You can have all the space you want as long as you know this is where you'll end up.

> Georgia: Soon.

> Me: 🍪

> Georgia: 🍪

It takes a long time to fall back asleep. But when I do, I sleep a bit more peacefully.

Chapter Thirty-One

Georgia

I collapse onto the sofa with barely enough energy to even hold the phone up to record my confessional. I'm not sure why I'm recording it in the first place. Maybe it's a habit.

Or maybe it's because this feels like a continuation of my relationship with Ripley, and I don't want to give that up.

"Hey," I say, faking a smile. "This is kind of a strange update, but it's what I have to work with, so it's what you're getting."

Why am I doing this?

"I started a new job today," I say. "I actually loved it although you can't tell by my facial expressions. I haven't been up at five in the morning in a long time—well, not for work, anyway."

My mind goes back to waking up next to Ripley. I force it out of my mind.

"It's challenging and exciting, and I think I'm going to be a good fit there," I say. "In other news, I haven't heard from Ripley today."

My heart sinks.

"I could've called or texted him," I say. "But in my defense, I was super busy, and it's been a long day. I'm sure he had to work today, too. But the more time goes on, the more I think he's probably second-guessing everything. And I can't blame him ..."

Ripley

"You know what? This sucks," I say to the camera while I prepare dinner.

I don't know why I'm bothering. I have no appetite.

"I sent her a good morning text today," I say. "She sent me one back. That's better than yesterday when we didn't speak at all. I know she started her new job yesterday, and I hope it went well. It's killing me that I don't know. But she asked for time, so I'm giving her that. But motherfucker if it's not hard."

Waffles pops the cabinet open where I keep his treats open with his nose. *Little shit.*

"My biggest worry is who is there for her right now," I say. "I know this is harder on her than it is for me, and I worry that she's so used to being on her own that she's suffering alone pointlessly. That breaks my heart. It keeps me up at night."

And fuck her mom while we're at it.

"How do people who fall in love more than once survive this multiple times?" I ask. "I'm not sure I could ..."

Georgia

"My third day of work went so well," I say, a little brighter than I have the past two days. "I was on my own for a few tasks and didn't need help. It felt really good to be productive and use my skills. The paycheck will be nice, too."

I pour myself a glass of sweet tea.

"I still haven't talked to my mother. Honestly, I haven't even tried. Every night when I go to bed, I think I'll wake up the next day and feel calmer and know what to say. But every day when my eyes open and Ripley isn't here, I'm angry all over again."

My drink sloshes around in the glass as I move into the living room.

"Ripley answered my good morning text right away today," I say, sitting on a chair. "I wanted to call him on my break at work, and at lunch, and on the way home, and right now ... but I can't. I'm just so damn embarrassed. What would I say to him? He's defended me so many times that I can't possibly talk to him without being able to say—hey, I had your back like you had mine."

I lay my head back and look at the phone. I'm so weary.

"What I think even more than that, though, is that I'm afraid that I'll go back into it, only to have something happen—with my mother, or otherwise—and he'll decide I'm too much for him and just not worth it. I'm not sure I could survive that."

I take a sip and feel the cool liquid slide down my throat. Then, out of nowhere, a round of tears fills my eyes.

"Hell, I'm not sure I can survive this. I miss him so fucking much."

―――――

Ripley

> Me: Four days without seeing you is killing me.

> Georgia: Charmer.

> Me: Are you okay?

> Georgia: Truth or a lie?

> Me: Truth.

> Georgia: No. I'm not. But I will be.

> Me: Tell me how to fix this. How can I help you?

> Georgia: I got it. I have to do this on my own.

> Me: No, you don't.

> Georgia: 🍑

> Me: 🍑

I stare at the screen for a long time. Then I turn my camera on and press record. But when I open my mouth, nothing comes out. So I turn it off.

Chapter Thirty-Two

Georgia

"No, but I see what you mean," I say. April my new coworker stands on the other side of my desk, showing me a draft for a promotional packet we've been working on this week. "I don't like it either. It doesn't grab attention or evoke any emotion." I look up at her. "I think we can reject it and have the art team try again."

"I agree." She sighs, smiling at me. "I love having you here. My gosh, it's so nice being able to collaborate with someone this easily. They usually hire men who think they know it all, and then I'm left doing all the work and redoing it the way it should've been done in the first place if they would've listened to me."

I fold my hands on my desk. "I'm really loving it here, too. Everyone is so nice and welcoming."

"You're a perfect fit." She taps the paper against her hand. "I'm going to officially reject this design and then grab lunch from the sandwich shop on the corner. Want anything?"

"No, thank you, though. I brought my lunch."

"Suit yourself. See you in a bit."

"Hey, will you close my door on your way out?" I ask.

She nods and pulls it shut behind her.

I put my desk phone on Do Not Disturb and grab the applesauce I brought for lunch. It's all I've been able to keep down all week.

I'm stuck. I'm stuck, and I don't know how to get myself unstuck. I can't force myself to reach out to my mother, which is completely childish and immature. But if I call her first, she'll come to the conversation with a victim mentality, believing *she* was in the right all along. If that happens, I might really snap on her.

No one needs that.

But I'm not sure if she'll ever come to me first. It's never happened before. She's never apologized to me for anything. I don't even think she's ever acknowledged that she was wrong. I don't need a big production made of it, but I do need her to accept some responsibility—both for herself and for our relationship.

I simply can't, and won't, do it anymore.

I peel open the applesauce and find my plastic spoon in my bag. As soon as it's in sight, my chest squeezes, and tears fog up my eyes. *Ripley and his Dora backpack.*

A solitary tear streaks down my face, rolling over my cheek, lips, and off my chin.

My God, I miss him.

Ignoring the spoon, I take out my cell phone instead and find his name.

> Me: I miss you.

> Ripley: You have no fucking idea how much I miss you.

Another tear drips down my cheek.

> Ripley: What do you need?

"You," I whisper.

> Me: Nothing you can help me with. I need to figure out how to talk to my mother without killing her. I'm so angry with her, Ripley. SO MAD. I can't get beyond it. And it's doing to me what holding on to my anger at you for all of those years did—it's delaying my happiness. But I just can't apologize to her. I can't lose her, either. I don't know what to do.

I start to put my phone away, not expecting an answer. But just before I drop it into my bag, it dings.

> Ripley: That's all you had to say. 🍪

"What does that even mean?" I ask before typing a cookie emoji back to him, then turning off my phone.

I swing back to my applesauce and notice a file sitting on the corner of my desk. *What's that?* I slide it over and open it to see where to return it.

The first line catches my attention and causes my jaw to drop.

"What do the Downings have to do with the Brewer family?" I ask aloud, scanning the document.

I go line by line, feeling dirty for reading something that isn't mine. But the fact that it involves Ripley's family, naming Gannon intentionally, makes it feel like my business.

It's an old document, dated a year ago, discussing a lawsuit between the two families. By the looks of it, my employer lost.

Notes behind the first few pages detail their case and why they thought they were owed the money—because Reid Brewer promised, but they never received a kickback for a deal that I can't make sense of but looks illegal based on the attorney's language.

My brain scrambles as I process this information.

If I'm understanding this correctly, the Downings are unscrupulous. *The Downings tried to embezzle the Brewers?*

Fuck.

What the hell do I do with this?

My heart races as I weigh my options. I love this job, and everyone here has been very fair and generous. And, quite frankly, I need the money.

But what would it say to Ripley if I stayed?

You were out of work for months, Georgia. It took so long to find a job that fit. *God.*

I bite my lip and glance into my bag at my phone.

"Then why didn't you just let him talk shit?" A softness drifts across Ripley's face. "Because it was about you."

I shove away from my desk and grab the folder, then make my way into the hallway. My heart picks up its pace with every step I take, and my palms sweat against the papers in my hand.

Mr. Downing sits behind his desk with the door open and looks up just as I arrive.

"Ah, hello, Georgia," he says, leaning back in his chair. "What can I do for you?"

I march into his office and lay his folder next to his pen. "You left this in my office."

"Thank you." His brows pull together as if he's concerned. "I would've been looking for that this afternoon."

"I also need to let you know that I'm leaving, and I won't be returning. Thank you for the opportunity, but I quit."

Confusion riddles his face. "I'm sorry. You're quitting? Is that what you said?"

"Yes. Effective immediately."

"Did something happen?"

"Yes, Mr. Downing, something did happen. My loyalty lies elsewhere. I'm sorry."

"I don't understand."

I give him the best, most professional smile I can muster. Then I turn on my heel, grab my bag from my office, turn off the light, and leave.

Chapter Thirty-Three

Ripley

The sun is hot, and beads of sweat roll down my back. I recheck the address on the mailbox. *Matches the one Nick found for me.*

I knock again, the wood of the doorframe scratching my knuckle.

This could be a giant fucking mistake. But I have to try. If Felicity isn't going to protect her daughter and do what is right, I will. I'll try, at least.

I lift my hand to knock again. The door swings open slowly just before I make contact.

Here goes nothing. I hold my breath as Felicity's eyes find mine. A guard immediately slides over them.

"Hello, Ms. Hayes. I wondered if we could talk for a few minutes."

"I have nothing to say to you."

"That's fine."

She puts her hand on her hip, much like Georgia does when she's irritated.

"You have a lot of balls coming here," she says.

"Trust me. I'd rather be doing a million other things besides this."

She lifts a brow. "Then why are you?"

My heart races. *Please let this work.*

I choke back the hateful things I want to spew at her. I swallow the accusations, the insults, and the assumptions. None of those things will help me, and more importantly, they won't help Georgia. And that's why I'm here.

"I want you to know that I understand your contempt for me," I say. "You hate me. I get it."

"How could you possibly understand that? How could you know what your father did to me? What he probably did to countless other women? He swooped into my life, saying all the right things, declaring his love for me. Promised to take care of me. When, in reality, he had a beautiful wife and family at home with no intentions of leaving them. Again, how could *you* possibly understand that?"

"Well, for what it's worth, I wish he had left us. It would've been a hell of a lot easier."

Her eyes widen, but she says nothing.

I shift my weight from one foot to the other, the wooden boards beneath me creaking. My brain is empty, forgetting the speech I prepared on my way over here, leaving me standing in front of Felicity fumbling like a fool. It's not the look I was going for.

"My father hurt a lot of people," I say, my voice even. "Every day I carry his last name—a name I should be proud of. A name that came from men and women who did remarkable things. It's my mother's last name—a woman who's intelligent and strong. It's my sister, Bianca's, name. She's one of the most brilliant women in the world. And my four brothers and nephew share it, too. They're kind and hardworking. Men who I look up to and revere. Yet we all share a name tainted and soiled by the man who should've protected us. We can never shake that attachment from him."

Felicity opens the door and steps onto the porch.

"You have memories of him being nice to you," I say. "That's more than I have. My father broke my nose, tried to kill my mother and my sister, and gave me all kinds of hangups that nearly ruined my life. Like the one that told me I wasn't good enough for your daughter."

Her eyes narrow as if she's still working through this whole situation. I just keep talking. I don't know what else to do.

"I'm sorry for what he did to you," I say. "I'm sorry for what he did to all of us. But all I can do is move forward, be a better man, and try to bring respect and dignity back to my family's name."

I take a deep breath, reminding myself to keep calm. This is my one shot. Quite possibly my only opportunity to talk to Felicity.

"Ms. Hayes, your daughter loves you more than anything in this world. I know you have to love her the same. How could you not? I mean, she is a little mouthy sometimes, but that's her only real flaw."

Her lip twitches as if she wants to smile, but she doesn't. *That's where Georgia's stubborn nature comes from.*

"I would never want to hurt either of you or come between you," I say. "My family is my foundation, and I know how long and hard we hurt when our father tried to tear us apart. Thankfully, we rallied and are stronger than ever. I could never be the reason that Georgia doesn't have you ... even if it means that I have to give her up."

She places a hand on the house to hold her steady while tears gather in the corners of her eyes. My heart breaks at the thought of having to follow through with walking away from the love of my life.

"I haven't really talked to her since I saw you at her house the other day," I say. "I'd imagine she's trying to figure out how to fix things between the two of you, and between us. You and me. And that's not her place, Ms. Hayes. It's not her role to speak for me or take on my troubles. I've given her the space she asked for, but now, I can't stand the thought of her being alone and weighed down by this mess that's ultimately created by my asshole father."

Felicity wipes a tear with the back of her hand. "He is an asshole."

I nod. *Yes, he is.*

"Please don't let Reid Brewer get between you and your daughter," I say. "Be angry with me. Hate me. It's wrong, but I can bear that. But there's no reason in the world that your beautiful daughter should be paying for the sins of a man in prison who she's never met."

She wipes a tear from her face. "This isn't what I expected of you."

We watch one another as if we don't quite know how to proceed. I'm completely in the dark with this.

I notice how Felicity's eyes are the same warm honey color as Georgia's. She nibbles her lip when she's pensive. There's a fire in her eyes that keeps me on my toes.

The words she slung at me the other day—telling me I'm not important in Georgia's life, and I'm my father's child—sting as they come to the surface again. But this isn't about me. I have to brush those words off if I want to move forward.

And I have to find a way to do that. There is no other choice.

"If she ever needs anything—anything at all—please call me. That goes for you, too," I say.

"Why can't you tell her that yourself?"

I smile sadly. "Because she's not exactly talking to me right now."

"Aren't you mad?"

At you? Yes. "No. I'm upset that she feels alone, and that she's hurting and freezing me out. But I'm not mad at her for it."

"Why would you include me in that offer?" she asks.

"Because you may hate me, and we may never be ... friends, so to speak. And from the looks of it, I might not get to spend a lot of time going forward with Georgia either." *Please, God, don't let that be true.* "But I've spent my entire adult life separated from her and it's never changed the fact that I would do anything for her. I'll still hang the moon for her even if she asks me to in a year from now—even if she decides that you're right and I'm not worth her time."

Felicity takes a deep breath, and it's the first real sign I've seen that she's comprehending someone else's point of view. Georgia didn't believe she'd ever come around, and I can see that, too. But something with Felicity has shifted. She's no longer holding her head high as if she's untouchable.

I don't know her well enough, but I wonder if it's shame that has caused her shoulders to drop just now. So I continue, hoping I'm reading her correctly.

"Because she's important to me, and you're important to her, then that means you're important to me, as well. Even if you hate me." My throat scratches, leaving my voice raspy. "And that's all I came here to say."

I turn to leave before I shout or cry or get on my knees and beg this woman to wake the fuck up and grow the fuck up. But I'm stopped before I even take the first step.

"Ripley ..."

I look over my shoulder to see a tired, broken, scared woman crying behind me.

Oh hell.

"She won't talk to me," she whispers. "She always calls when we fight. Or she just shows up here like nothing's wrong and it's all fine. But we're five days in now, and I haven't heard from her. I was hoping you were her."

"She should be at work right now."

Felicity laughs sadly, wiping away the onslaught of tears streaming down her cheeks. "Of course, you knew that."

I'm not sure what that means, so I just wait.

"I've really done it this time," she says, her voice breaking. "I thought I was doing the right thing by trying to keep you away from her." She closes her eyes and shakes her head. "I also was ... scared, I guess, that you were going to take her away from me. I know the dazzle of the Brewer name. I fell for it once. How can I compete with that?"

"You don't have to compete with me. *You're her mother.* She only gets one of those."

She smiles at me through her tears. "Georgia said a bunch of things to me after you left and I haven't been able to forget them. She said some terrible, awful ... *truths*," she says, spitting out the word. "And I don't know how to act. I didn't realize she felt this way." Her lips quiver. "I didn't realize I was acting that way."

"That's between the two of you. I can't speak for Georgia, either. She has a voice that she's capable of using." I can't help but roll my eyes. "And we know she doesn't usually have a problem doing that."

Felicity chuckles, still wiping her tears away. "Does she know you're here?"

I shake my head. "She's not talking to me much, either. A text here and there is really it."

"Then why did you come?"

I slide my hands into my pockets and feel the twisting of my heart.

My lungs burn from the struggle to breathe, and my stomach aches from being unable to eat much over the last few days.

"I came because putting Georgia in the middle of this is unfair to her," I say. "She did nothing wrong. If you want to be upset with someone, let it be me. I'm a Brewer. Georgia's just caught in this crossfire and is slowly becoming yet another one of my dad's victims. And that is so wrong. It's unacceptable. You have to see that."

Slowly, she nods her head.

"I hope, and pray, that she'll come back to me," I say, emotion gathering in my throat. "And I also hope that the two of you can find a way to heal your wounds. In the meantime, if you guys need anything ..."

"She deserves an apology from me." Felicity stands taller as if she's accepted her fate. "But I don't know how to do that."

"Admit your mistakes."

"I'm afraid she won't talk to me. I wouldn't talk to me."

Her head falls forward, her body heaving with sobs. I suppress a groan as I reach for her and pull her into a hug. It only makes her cries louder.

It's such an odd predicament to be in—comforting the woman who has caused the woman I love so much pain. I want to tell her to grow up, buckle up, and be a mother, but maybe she doesn't know how. Maybe she deserves a little grace.

God knows I don't always have the answers.

Finally, she pulls away, her eyes filled with gratitude. "I was wrong about you. I'm sorry, Ripley."

I smile at her. "Thank you. Apology accepted."

"Now I need to figure out how to do that with my daughter. It's going to be a lot more complicated with her."

I take a deep breath. "Would you like my help?"

"Would you do that?" She balks, stunned. "Would you help me fix things with Georgia?"

She looks as shocked by my offer as I feel. *I need to learn to think before I speak.*

"I can't guarantee anything, obviously," I say. "She has her own reasons and feelings, and they're valid—even if they're hard to hear."

"I know."

"But if you'd like someone to sit with you while you talk to her, I'll do that."

"Let me figure a few things out, and then I'll call you this afternoon. Deal?" I ask.

She smiles the way Georgia does when she thinks things might be all right. "Deal."

I nod and step off the porch, my mind reeling.

Peaches, I hope to see that smile on your face again soon. Very, very soon.

Chapter Thirty-Four

Georgia

"It's been an eventful day," I say, looking into the camera while stopped at a red light. "I quit my new job because, unbeknownst to me, there is some very bad blood between the Downings and the Brewers. Well, it is worse than just an argument or clash of characters. But, while I don't know where I stand with Ripley right now, I'd never do anything to hurt him. My loyalty lies with him."

I tap my fingers against the steering wheel, thinking.

"Mom asked me if I'd talk to her today," I say. "She sent me a text as I was walking to my car after quitting my job. I wanted to be a brat and tell her no because I don't want to hear a bunch of excuses, really. And God forbid she actually takes responsibility for anything." I frown. "Myla, let's not use any of this, okay? I just need someone to talk to."

I need Ripley.

"Ripley also called. It was the first time we've really spoken since the whole showdown with Mom in my driveway. He asked if I could swing by his house this evening and, of course, I said yes. Am I nervous? Yup.

Do I know what he wants? No. Am I tired of living without him? Absolutely. I just hope he doesn't get me over there and try to let me down gently. I don't *really* think that's what will happen, but he has to have had second thoughts about getting involved with my life's drama."

My heart aches as I consider the idea of not having Ripley in my life. Of not being his. I only got a taste of it, and it's all I can think about. I just know that he isn't like the other guys I've dated, because if Ripley breaks things off with me? I'll be ruined. I've never felt that way before, even when I've blown dates off. Knowing he has that power over me is terrifying.

"Okay," I say as the light switches to green. "That's it for now. Wish me luck!"

I toss the phone on the passenger seat next to the purple gloves Ripley gave me, and head toward his house.

———

Ripley swings his front door open before I'm even on the sidewalk. He steps onto the porch, gripping the railing as if he might fall off it if he doesn't.

His eyes are alight, yet tired. They're without their usual sparkle and mischief, and to see a part of him be lost to this mess kills my heart.

And it makes me resolved to find a solution—and that solution begins with me.

My steps quicken as I grow closer. I practice saying a casual *hello* in my head. Instead, I fall into his arms without thought.

He pulls me close, so close that I can almost not breathe, and buries his head in my hair.

I close my eyes and feel him around me, and for the first time in days, I feel like I can relax. I'm not alone. For the moment, at least, I'm safe and don't have to carry everything by myself.

"I've missed you," he says, kissing my forehead before pulling back and searching my face like he hasn't seen me for much longer than a week. "How are you? You look tired, Peaches. And thin."

"Well, it's hard to eat when you're upset."

He pulls me into another hug.

I press a kiss to his chest before leaning back, needing the safety in his eyes.

It occurs to me that this is the place where I'm the calmest. The happiest. The most untouchable. Along with those feelings comes a fear that it'll be robbed from me. It'll be taken away. I'll be discarded. Never called again because I'm not worth the effort or loved unconditionally.

Still, I hope, because I have Ripley. I need to have hope.

Because I love him.

I'm not afraid to name the feeling that's been fluttering in my heart lately. It's been growing and changing, twisting into a sensation that takes up my entire being.

How can you not love someone who goes so far out of their way for you? Who has your back when you don't know you need someone watching out for you? Who takes punches for you?

He loves me in all the ways he knows I need loved—in ways I don't even understand. And I'm not sure he even realizes that he loves me. But it doesn't matter. His actions speak louder than his words ever could.

But that doesn't mean I don't want to hear them.

He holds my face in his hands and kisses the tip of my nose. "Before we go inside, I have to tell you something."

My spirits plummet.

"Today, I went and saw your mom," he says.

My mouth falls agape. "You did what?"

"Don't be mad."

"I'm not mad, I'm just ..." I laugh in disbelief. "At least you're still alive. Is she?"

He grins. "She's sitting inside at the table, waiting on you."

Excuse me? "I'm sorry. Did you say my mother is in your house?"

He nods.

"*Your house?*" I ask. "This one? She's here?"

He nods again.

"Holy shit. Did you kidnap her? That's illegal, you know."

His laughter fills the air, and it's music to my ears. It might be the music just before his perp walk, I don't know, but it's music anyway.

ADRIANA LOCKE

"I'm glad you're entertained by this," I say. "But I need more of an explanation."

His feet straddle mine as he brushes a strand of hair out of my face. "She and I had a talk. We talked about my dad and what a monster he is. I told her that I understood she was leery of me, and that I wouldn't get between the two of you. But also, that I would always be there for both of you."

I bury my face in his chest again, fisting his shirt in both of my hands. He sways back and forth with me in his arms.

"She asked me to help her apologize to you," he says softly.

I jerk back. "What?"

"She's nervous. She's scared. And you don't have to accept anything she has to say—that's why we're doing it here. I can kick her to the curb so fast she won't see straight."

I laugh nervously. "She's really in there?"

He nods.

"Wow."

"I don't want you to feel tricked," he says. "It all happened so fast, but I didn't want you worrying while you came here. When you think of coming here, I want you to eventually feel happy. Like you're coming home."

Tears well up in my eyes.

"And I thought that if I could catch you outside, I could give you the option of seeing her or not," he says. "You can go. You don't have to do this. I'm on your side always and forever." He kisses me softly. "But I don't want you to leave. She knows that. She knows that I'm doing this because ..."

His cheeks flush. *Ripley blushing? That's a first.*

"Because what?" I ask him.

"Because I love you."

My breath hitches as the tears I fought to contain spill down my face. "Are you serious?"

"I'm totally serious. I've loved you for a long time, I think." He smirks. "Not when you were arguing with me about the existence of pickles. Or about how many steps are in Jeremiah's house."

I laugh, elated at hearing those three words from him.

"I didn't tell your mom that I love you," he says. "I wanted to tell you first, although I think she got the picture."

His hands find mine, and he strokes my palms with his thumbs.

This is the feeling I never knew if I'd ever experience. I didn't know if this kind of thing was out there for me. But it was—it is—and it was right in front of me the entire time.

"I love you," I say, smiling from ear to ear.

His brow pinches together as if he didn't hear me clearly.

"I love you," I whisper again.

"You do?" He laughs, almost as if he's in disbelief. "You love me? Really?"

I laugh, too—also out of disbelief. *How can this crazy man not see how lovable and amazing he is?* "Yes, I love you. Of course, I love you, Ripley."

"Thank God." He pulls me in for another hug. "Now, what do we do about your mom?"

I take a deep breath and step away from Ripley, but my fingers instinctively grasp for his.

"We should video this for the show," I joke. "It has the potential to get super high ratings."

"Not that high. I'll remove her before it gets that froggy."

I wish we were going inside alone. The only place I want to be is in his arms somewhere ... maybe with food. And a nap. *Heaven knows that I need both.* But I need to take care of this situation with my mom because our patterns of behavior are unhealthy. And then the enormity of what Ripley just said hits me.

"When you think of coming here, I want you to eventually feel happy. Like you're coming home. I'm on your side always and forever. Because I love you. I've loved you for a long time, I think."

Coming home. To Ripley. To the man I love. To the life I once dreamed of and now dream of again.

One that I never thought was possible.

I want this so much—more than anything.

It's time to move forward ... by letting go of the past.

"Let's get this over with," I say, leading him inside.

He rushes to open the door for me. *Always the gentleman.*

"Waffles!" I say, laughing as he leaps in circles like a ballerina. "Hey, buddy."

He barks before jumping so high he nearly makes it into my arms.

"Don't jump on people," Ripley says, shaking his head. "We're working on that."

I bend down and pick him up, and he licks my palms. Then he scurries up my chest and puts his little nose in the crook of my neck and sighs.

Yeah, buddy. I'm happy to be back, too.

Ripley leads me into the kitchen with his hand nestled in the small of my back. I don't feel like a stranger here anymore, nor do I feel like a visitor. I belong here. I feel it in my bones. *Home.*

We round the corner, and I spot my mom standing at the windows overlooking the valley. Her arms are pulled over her stomach, and when she turns to me, I see the sadness painted on her face. It kills me.

But I have to stay strong.

"Do you want me to stay here or go into the other room?" Ripley whispers in my ear.

I grab his hand and hold it, signaling for him to stay. He doesn't move a muscle.

"Hi, sweetheart," Mom says, her tone uneven.

"Hi, Mom."

She drops her arms and sighs. "I hope you're not upset that I'm here. I'm second-guessing everything now, and I don't know whether it's right to be here."

"It's fine. But why are you here?"

She glances over my shoulder at Ripley as if she gets strength from him, too.

"Georgia ... I'm sorry," she says simply. "I'd like to list all the things I'm sorry for, but I'm pretty sure I'd wear out my welcome before I got through them all."

"Probably," Ripley mutters just loud enough for me to hear.

"Honey, I'm going to start seeing a therapist next week," she says.

My eyes widen.

"There are a lot of things I need to unpack, as they call it." She grips the chair in front of her. "And I need to do it before it ruins a lot of lives."

"I think that's smart," I say carefully.

"You deserve better from me," she says. "And, truth be told, I'm not sure if I even realize all the ways that I've probably failed you. I'm sort of numb right now."

I snuggle Waffles, feeling his little breaths against my neck. "What changed? I want to believe you, Mom, but this is quite the one-eighty."

She's never been this self-aware, which is painful.

She holds her hands out to the side to emphasize her point. "I have nothing. Just like you said. I don't have a man in my life. I have no friends. No real job. No future. And I'm on the verge of not having my daughter, either." She frowns. "When you didn't call like you always do, it gave me some time to think about the things you said. It hurt to hear that, but I needed to."

"I'm sorry for hurting you. I want to say it wasn't my intent, but that might be a lie."

"I understand. If I had a good man like you do and someone tried to chase him off, I'd probably be a little mean, too." She winks. "You can be a little mean anyway. But you learned that from me."

My lips twitch, almost forming a smile.

"I'd hung up the phone to the therapist's office when Ripley knocked on my door," she says, looking at him. "I understand why you love him. He's really hard not to like."

He squeezes my hip softly as if he's uncomfortable with the fuss about him.

"Yeah, he's hard not to like," I say, tilting my head back and smiling at him. "He's really hard not to love."

He places a sweet kiss on my lips.

"I don't want to keep you two," she says. "I know you have a lot to talk about, too. But I hope you'll accept my apology, Georgia." Her voice cracks. "I love you, sweetheart."

I set Waffles on the floor, much to his chagrin, then I embrace my mother.

Her body shakes as she cries. This is a woman who feels the depths of losing everyone she loves. My heart hurts for her. She might have caused all of the things that have happened to her lately, but everyone deserves a second chance.

God knows I've been given enough of them.

"I love you, Mom."

She pulls away, her eyes wet with tears. "Honey, you have no idea how much I love you."

"I have a little idea." I smile at her, holding her at arm's length. "We'll be okay. We'll figure this out." I hug her again. "Why don't I call you tomorrow and we can make plans to have dinner?"

"I'd really, really like that."

She presses a kiss to my cheek. "I have a car picking me up soon, so I'll see myself out. Enjoy your night."

"You can stay," I say although I hope she declines. I need time alone with Ripley.

Mom chuckles. "I need to go." She gives Ripley a quick hug, whispering something in his ear that I can't hear. It makes him laugh. "Goodbye, you two."

"Bye, Mom."

Waffles barks at her.

"Goodbye, Ms. Hayes," Ripley says. "Would you like me to walk you out?"

"You stay here with my daughter, or I'll snap right back to mean Felicity."

We all laugh. It feels very, very good.

She goes down the hallway, and we don't say a word until the door closes. Together, we let out a sigh of relief.

I take a step toward Ripley, but he takes one back.

My heart skips a beat.

"I have something I want to ask you before you touch me," he says, giving me a soft smile. "And it has to be in this order because, if not, it'll take me far too long to get back to this. Because I'm going to have a hard fucking time letting you go."

"Hurry then. You're wasting time."

He grins. "The last time this was proposed to you, you left the guy who asked, so I know I'm taking a risk by bringing this up. But I love you, Peaches. And I've been trying to figure out how to prove to you that I'm in this for the long haul. *For forever.* I don't want there to be a second in your life when you have room to remotely consider that I'm not serious about this. About you. About us."

I force a swallow, my anticipation growing. I don't know where he's going with this. Part of me says to run—but a bigger part demands that I stay.

"I did a little renovation to one of the bedrooms downstairs this week," he says. "I turned one of them into a reading nook. I didn't know exactly what that was supposed to look like, but it turns out Bianca had tons of ideas." He rolls his eyes, making me giggle. "I hope you love it."

"You built a reading nook for me? Here?"

He nods. "Because I hope you'll consider moving in with me."

"*What?*"

My brain hadn't had the chance to think this far in advance. I didn't dream of him asking me to move in with him. I'm caught off guard, and I don't know what to say.

"I'm not pressuring you," he says, "I've waited over ten years. I can wait a few more. Theoretically." He winks. "But as far as I'm concerned, we both live here. The only reason I'm not asking you to marry me is because I know you'll say no. But I hope that one day, you'll say yes."

"Ripley." I blow out a breath, surprised. "I don't know what to say."

"The word *yes* would be good."

I consider his request. *Is it too fast? Is it the right choice? Do I want to do this?*

Slowly, the answer becomes clear.

This is my dream—the one thing I've been too scared to even dream of. But Sutton apparently manifested this for me. *How can I say no?*

I won't. I'm going to say yes. But I can't give in that easy.

"I have demands," I say.

"Name them."

"Pancakes. I want a puppy named Pancakes," I say, thinking on my feet.

"Fine."

"No more hiking. Ever."

He snorts. "Trust me. That's already done. I'll never hike with you again."

"Sugar." This one will get him riled up. "I need sugar in my life, Ripley."

He grins mischievously, folding his arms across his chest. "It's terrible for you."

"So? I've been eating it for thirty years. I think stopping sugar at this point would probably shock my system and make me die. Do you want to be responsible for that?"

"Maybe we can find some healthy candy and snacks."

I shake my head. "No. I want real candy. Chocolate. Sugar for my coffee."

Waffles paws at me until I follow him to his snack drawer. *He's such a smart little thing.*

"Some chips—not all the time," I say. "And chicken nuggets. Oh! Frozen pizzas are literally half of my diet. I can't just never see one again."

I pull open the drawer where Waffles's snacks are kept and get him a treat.

"Do you want a drink?" I ask Ripley.

He shakes his head, amused.

"So where do we stand on this food issue?" I ask, needling him until he responds. His lack of participation in this conversation is no fun.

"We can barter."

"Grab me some sunflower seeds, will ya? I just bought a new bag."

"Sure. Sunflower seeds aren't a bad snack, but they're not really a snack. I think we just need to redefine what a snack is to you."

I open the pantry and burst out laughing. "No, you did not!"

Then I open the refrigerator and freezer and laugh even harder.

Tears flow down my cheeks in a mix of humor, surprise, and love.

Not only are there cookies, but there's a bag of real sugar. Fruity cereal. Frozen pizzas and chicken nuggets.

All of my favorite things are here—including my most favorite of all. *Him.*

"Looks like I'm moving in," I say, dropping the phone as Ripley grabs me into a hug.

"It pains me to have that junk in my house, you know."

"You'll get used to it."

Waffles barks at the commotion, making me laugh.

Ripley's mouth is on mine. His hands are on the waistband of my shorts, and then his lips trail down the side of my neck as if he has to touch me everywhere immediately.

"Hey," I say, giggling as he kisses the crook of my neck. "You better stop filming, or this is going to turn X-rated really quick."

He pulls back, smiling from ear to ear. He picks up my phone and hands it to me, and then I shut it off.

"I love you, Ripley Brewer," I say, beaming with happiness.

"Not as much as I love you, Peaches Hayes."

Chapter Thirty-Five

Georgia

"This bothers you, doesn't it?" I take a large bite of a white chocolate macadamia nut cookie and then lay my head in the crook of Ripley's arm. "Cookies in your bed. I bet you're dying a little inside."

He hums against my hair. "After going all week and not seeing you and not being certain I ever would again, you can eat whatever the hell you want to eat in our bed as long as you're in it."

I grin at the *our bed* line. All night, he keeps slipping little things like that into our conversations. It's *our bed. Our home. Our puppy, Waffles.* It's so damn cute, that's what it is.

Ripley ran us a bath after he properly welcomed me *home*, and we sat in the gigantic tub for over an hour just being together. I agreed to let him help move my things tomorrow, which is much faster than I anticipated when I said yes. I hesitated and almost pushed back. Then I remembered that life's too damn short to keep waiting. *Waiting for what, anyway? Time to overthink things? Time to scare the shit out of myself? Time for something to go wrong?*

No, thanks. I'm done with all of that.

"Think it's too soon to ask for a week's vacation?" he asks, chuckling against my cheek. "I really just need a few days with you."

"Oh! That reminds me. I quit my job yesterday."

I stuff the rest of the cookie into my mouth.

"What? Why?"

"Well," I say, cookie crumbs toppling out of my mouth. *Oops.* I pause to swallow. "It's a long story."

"One I want to hear."

It's his tone that says what he means, not the words. He's worried. He's concerned. He thinks something happened, and he's two seconds from getting off this bed and going to take care of it.

I'm not sure what, exactly, to tell him. I don't want to lie to him. And he needs to know what I saw just in case it matters because I don't know the whole story between the families, nor do I want to. It's not my business. But this could be awkward.

I sigh. "Well ..."

"Well ..." he repeats, coaxing me along.

"My boss left a folder on my desk. It was an accident; he didn't mean to do it. I didn't realize it was there until I was trying to choke down some applesauce at lunch."

Ripley tenses beneath me but doesn't interrupt.

"Coincidentally, it was a folder about the Brewer family," I say, wincing.

He pulls away, urging me to sit up and face him. So, of course, I do.

His features pull together, puzzled. "What are you talking about, Georgia?"

"It was a legal case, I think. They were suing your family, but I think it was resolved."

"Babe, who were you working for?"

"Todd Downing."

Ripley's eyes almost fall out of his head. "You're fucking kidding me."

"Nope. I'm not."

He scrubs his hands down his face.

"I don't know the situation between you, but I got that it wasn't friendly," I say.

"So what happened? You found the file. Looked through it, I take it. Then what?"

"I found it. I snooped. I didn't mean to snoop, exactly. It could've been ten people's files because my office was the gathering place for a media packet we were working on. But, yes, I opened it and saw Brewer Group at the top. That caught my interest. Then I saw the details of a court case and notes and ..." I frown. "Then I took the folder into Todd's office, placed it on his desk, and told him I quit."

I smile nervously.

It takes Ripley a few seconds to get his wits together. Still, I don't think he can fully process the events.

"Yeah, I'm unemployed again," I say. "But I'll find a job. I won't be dead weight around here."

A small grin tickles his lips. "I could give a fuck if you ever work a day in your life again."

"Oh, I'm working."

"If that makes you happy, then good. But everything you ever need is already taken care of. You know that, right?"

My cheeks flush and I start to speak, but he cuts me off.

"You really quit your job because of the folder?" he asks.

I shrug. "Of course. I'm not working for the enemy."

"But we weren't really together."

I laugh. "First, you know that's not true. We were together, just not ... together. And second, even if we weren't together, my loyalties lie with you. And I told Todd that."

He moves so quickly that I don't anticipate it. I'm flipped on my back before I know what's happening. Waffles, who is not supposed to be on the bed, lifts his head from the bottom of the mattress as if to tell us to stop being so loud.

Ripley hovers over me, his eyes twinkling. "You are one of a kind, Peaches."

"I know. You used to hate me for that."

He grins. "There's a thin line between love and hate, you know."

"I know." I run my hands along the lines of his shoulders. "I'm just really happy we crossed to the other side."

Waffles barks, making us laugh.

"There's a piece of cookie stuck to my arm," Ripley says, side-eyeing me.

I giggle. "Just remember how badly it hurt not seeing me all week."

"You're rotten."

"I'm yours."

He buries his face in the crook of my neck, making me squirm.

"You're damn right you're mine." He places a kiss behind my ear. "And I'm all yours."

"You're damn right you are."

Epilogue

Ripley

A month later ...

"Slow that thing down," I yell out the window, laughing as a shirtless Tate rolls Jason's golf cart to a stop beside my car. "You're going to kill yourself in that thing."

Mimi, Jason's wife's grandmother, sits in the passenger seat, grinning like a loon.

"You stay out of this, Ripley." Mimi laughs. "This is the highlight of my week."

"I'm just mad you're cheating on me with Tate."

She winks. "Don't talk about me like that in front of Georgia. She'll get jealous."

Georgia laughs from the seat beside me. "Hi, Mimi."

"Hi, sweet girl. Your mom and Chloe are already cooking. The two of them stress me the hell out," Mimi says.

"Me, too, Mimi. Me, too," Georgia says.

Tate hits the gas, and the golf cart lurches forward, then speeds down the street in front of Jason's house.

The sun is especially bright this Saturday, and the air not too hot or too cool. It's the perfect Tennessee afternoon. These weekend days are quickly becoming my favorite.

It's been four weeks since Georgia moved in with me and Waffles. It's been a learning experience. She hates mornings, loves cheap frozen pizzas, and I'm considering ordering another king-sized bed just so I have room to sleep.

But I wouldn't have it any other way.

"When are we supposed to go to Canoodle to film our final scene?" Georgia asks, her hair blowing in the breeze.

God, she's gorgeous. And she's mine.

It's still hard to believe sometimes.

"Tuesday," I say, pulling up next to Jason's car. "They're creating fake search terms for us to pretend we used for the basis of us being totally matched together."

"Do we have a say in the terms?"

"I don't think so."

"Darn. Could've been fun."

"They also want us to try to recreate our hiking date. Apparently, they think that footage of us running through the rain would be great for the show."

"Oh, I'm sure it would. Speaking of the cabin, did you leave your card there that day? Whatever happened with that?"

I turn off the ignition. "I did not. Instead, I made a donation to the park."

"A generous one, I'm sure."

I only grin.

"Also, speaking of the cabin, I have some news for you," I say. "I wanted to wait and tell you in front of everyone because I think your reaction will be hysterical, but the segue right now is too perfect."

"Why does this scare me a little?"

"Because you know me." She giggles. "Guess who got a job?"

"I'm guessing you."

"Guess what I'm going to be doing."

There's no way to even guess what this little firecracker has gotten herself into. She could tell me she's running for governor, and I wouldn't be surprised. I'd be more surprised if she lost the race.

"A pinup model," I say, throwing out the first random thing that comes to mind.

"*A weatherwoman.*"

I recoil. "What?"

"I'm going to be a weatherwoman."

"You're kidding me." I laugh. "There's no way."

She bounces in her seat. "I can't call myself a meteorologist because clearly, I don't have that degree. But I can be a weatherwoman because I'm just reading the weather on the morning newscast."

I burst out laughing but pull her in for a hug. "That is amazing. I … I'm actually speechless."

"Why? I'm good at the weather."

"You're reading the weather, not predicting it. Don't get confused. If you go on the air and start freeballing the forecast, you'll be unemployed again."

She leans back and takes off her seat belt. "I'll dazzle them with my abilities, and they'll see what I'm capable of."

"I'm sure," I say with as straight of a face as I can manage.

"Is everyone coming today?"

"Everyone but Gannon."

She wrinkles her nose. "Are you going to tell me what's going on with him?"

"I would if I knew."

"Fine." She checks her nose and teeth in the mirror. "Let's go in and see everyone. I hope Arlo is here. I could use some baby snuggles."

I give her a quick kiss. "Go on inside. I'll be there in a second."

She climbs out of the car and dashes into Jason's house. Seeing her so happy makes me happier than I ever thought possible.

We may have had a rough road getting here, but I wouldn't change a damn thing about our journey. Every little piece of our lives made us who we are so we would be ready for this moment together.

And every one for the rest of our lives.

. . .

Have you read Renn's book, The Proposal, and Jason's book, The Arrangement? Both are available now.

Keep reading for a bonus scene from The Invitation, and then the first chapter in Flirt, the first book in the Carmichael Family Series ....

Bonus Scene

Ripley

"That was amazing," Mom says, smiling proudly. "Ripley, honey, I always knew you'd be a star."

"*A star* is a little much," Tate says, rolling his eyes.

Georgia beams beside me, her cheeks pink from blushing.

When Jonah called last week to thank me again for helping him out of The Invitation's bind, he also mentioned how pleased he was with the results. This confirmed what Sutton had been telling us since we wrapped filming—Canoodle Pictures had a hit on their hands. The post-production team called the footage '*magic*'.

If only they had some of the scenes we didn't film. They'd really see magic then.

"Thank you, Rory," Georgia says to my mom. "It was fun."

"It sure looked like it," Mimi says, wearing a little smirk she learned from Tate. "I'm sure they're gonna have people signing up left and right to be on that show. I mean, you walked away with Ripley, and he walked away with you. If they have The Invitation: Geriatric's Edition—I'm in."

Everyone laughs.

My living room is full of our friends and family, here to watch a

BONUS SCENE

special edit of the show that Jonah ordered for us as a display of gratitude. He said since the show ended in our relationship, it was only fitting that we get a special cut of the film. So, we invited everyone to our house for a movie night and watched The Invitation: Season One—Special Cut together.

"The office chatter seems to think we'll get signed on for at least two seasons," Sutton says from her spot on the floor beside Jeremiah. "Who knows? Maybe we can do one with a more mature heroine."

"More mature?" Tate snickers, petting a sleeping Waffles on his lap. "Have you met Mimi?"

"Are you saying I'm not mature?" Mimi asks him.

Jason shakes his head. "You tried to get me to take you to toilet paper old man Sammy's house last weekend because he sat by someone else at Bingo."

Georgia leans against my side. I pull her against me, wrapping my arm around her back.

"That old fart not only sat by Big Mouth Berta, but he wiggled his tongue at me like he was taunting me," Mimi says. "Not only are her pies not as good as mine, but I'd be better in the sack than her, too."

Another round of laughter fills the living room. *This is the way life is supposed to be.*

"And we didn't go toilet papering his house, did we?" Mimi asks Jason. "See? I was mature."

"Meems, didn't you have Tate drive you around the neighborhood shirtless yesterday?" Chloe asks. "And didn't I hear you tell him to slow down as you went by Sammy's?"

Mimi sighs. "Yes, I did. Because two can play the jealousy game but only one of us can win. There's nothing about Big Mouth Berta to be jealous over. But look at this stud muffin." She grips Tate's biceps and squeezes. "I win."

"Easy on his ego," Jason says. "He won't be able to fit his head out the door if you keep it up."

"I'm just worried about how Tate will handle it when Mimi finds a guy of her own," Renn says, holding a sleeping Arlo.

"Oh, it's going to happen," Mimi says. "I'm on the hunt for a sugar daddy."

"You mean Tate's not your sugar daddy?" Gannon asks with his tongue in his cheek.

Tate fires him a glare.

"Gannon, *don't*," Mom says.

"That really was beautiful," Felicity says from across the room. "It's fun to watch the two of you fall in love." She pauses to look at the plethora of Brewers surrounding her. "And I'm really blessed and thankful that my daughter and I have gotten to know all of you."

A comfortable silence descends around us as we look at one another.

I'm not sure if Felicity and Mom have discussed Dad, nor do I know if Mom knows that Felicity and Dad had an affair. Something tells me Mom suspects it, at least. Regardless, she has embraced Felicity into our family with open arms. That has allowed Felicity to heal some of her wounds and be a better mother to Georgia.

That's all I really care about.

"So, explain this to me," Renn says. "Did they really look at your search history, or was that just a gimmick on the show?"

"Hell, no," I say, chuckling. "I told Jeremiah that was a hard limit."

"That will be the premise of the show," Sutton says. "But if we do get the show picked up by a network, we will sort of stage the search histories. No one is really going to let you see what they're looking up."

"That would be interesting, though," Georgia says. "Can you imagine?"

"I want to see Gannon's," Tate says, snickering. "Stocks, bonds, and bondage."

Mimi sits up. "Do tell me more."

A burst of laughter falls across the room once again. I lean down and press a kiss against the top of Georgia's head, then wave at Jeremiah as he and Sutton sneak out to the front door. He has to catch an early flight in the morning. We knew they couldn't stay long.

Mom and Felicity get up and head into the kitchen, chatting animatedly about wine brands—one thing the two of them have in common. Gannon types away on his phone. Mimi and Tate make plans for tomorrow. I heard the words shirtless and golf cart before their voices hushed. *God be with them.* Renn and Blakely move into the guest

BONUS SCENE

room to change Arlo's diaper, and Jason and Chloe chat with Bianca via Facetime.

I sit quietly, appreciating the moment and thinking about how far we've all come ... and about how we got here.

When Dad was making our lives miserable, and trying to kill Mom and Bianca, I wasn't sure what our family was going to look like on the other side. There were moments when I was certain we would fall apart. I knew the stress was going to break us. I expected the worst; I couldn't see any other result.

Yet, we're here.

And, most importantly, I'm here with Georgia.

I'm not sure when we'll get engaged, married, or have kids. I'm not sure when I'll have the nuts to even ask her. All I can do is let the universe do its thing.

It's been right every time so far ... even when I questioned it.

Like when I was certain I hated Georgia.

Chuckling, I kiss the top of her head.

"What?" she asks, looking up at me with her honey-hued eyes.

"I was just thinking."

"About what?"

"I don't know. Isn't this all crazy when you think about it? Me and you? Mom and your mom? *Renn has a baby.*"

She smiles softly. "It just goes to show that we don't always have things figured out, even when we think we do."

"That's true."

"I've been thinking about that a lot."

"Really?"

Her face flushes.

"What do you mean?" I ask her, curious.

"I just mean ..." She slips a hand under my shirt and spreads her fingers against my abs. "I thought I would always be someone who would be terrified to settle down. I'd expect the worst. I'd always be looking for the sparkle to wear off." She reaches up and kisses me gently. "But you keep the cookie jar full, if you know what I mean."

My chest shakes as I chuckle. "I'll fill more than that for you right now, if you know what I mean."

"We have a house full of people." Her eyes twinkle as she looks around. "Do you think they'd notice if we slipped away for a few minutes?"

I grab her hand and pull her to her feet behind me. "I don't know, but we're about to find out. "

The end. 🍪

Chapter 1: Flirt

WANTED: A SITUATION-SHIP

I'm a single female who's tired of relationships ruining my life. However, there are times when a date would be helpful.

If you're a single man, preferably mid-twenties to late-thirties, and are in a similar situation, we might be a match.
Candidate must be handsome, charming, and willing to pretend to have feelings for me (on a sliding scale, as the event requires). Ability to discuss a wide variety of topics is a plus. Must have your own transportation and a (legal) job.

This will be a symbiotic agreement. In exchange for your time, I will give you mine. Need someone to flirt with you at a football party? Go, team! Want a woman to make you look good in front of your boss? Let me find my heels. Would you love for someone to be obsessed with you in front of your ex?

I'm applying my red lipstick now.

If interested, please email me. Time is of the essence.

CHAPTER 1: FLIRT

**Chapter 1
Brooke**

My best friend, Jovie, points at my computer screen. The glitter on her pink fingernail sparkles in the light. "You can't post that."

I fold my arms across my chest. "And why not?"

Instead of answering me, she takes another bite of her chicken wrap. A dribble of mayonnaise dots the corner of her mouth.

"A lot of help you are," I mutter, rereading the post I drafted instead of pricing light fixtures for work. The words are written in a pretty font on Social, my go-to social media platform.

Country music from the nineties mixes with the laughter of locals sitting around us in Smokey's, my favorite beachside café. Along the far wall, a map of the state of Florida made of wine corks sways gently in the ocean breeze coming through the open windows.

"Would you two like anything else?" Rebecca, our usual lunchtime server, pauses by the table. "I think we have some Key lime pie left."

"I'm too irritable for pie today," I say.

"*You* don't want *pie*? That's a first," she teases me.

Jovie giggles.

"I know," I say, releasing a sigh. "That's the state of my life right now. I don't even want pie."

"Wow. Okay. This sounds serious. What's up? Maybe I can help," Rebecca says.

Jovie wipes her mouth with a napkin. "Let me cut in here real quick before she tries to snowball you into thinking her harebrained idea is a good one."

I roll my eyes. "It *is* a good one."

"I'll give you the CliffsNotes version," Jovie says, side-eyeing me. "Brooke got an invitation to her grandma's birthday party, and instead of just not going—"

"I can't *not go*."

"Or showing up as the badass single chick she is," Jovie continues, silencing me with a look, "she wrote a post for Social that's basically an ad for a fake boyfriend."

CHAPTER 1: FLIRT

"Correction—it *is* an ad for a fake boyfriend."

Rebecca rests a hand on her hip. "I don't see the problem."

"*Thank you*," I say, staring at Jovie. "I'm glad someone understands me here."

Jovie throws her hands in the air, sending a napkin flying right along with them.

Satisfaction is written all over my face as I sit back in my chair with a smug smile. The more I think about having a *situation-ship* with a guy —a word I read in a magazine at the salon while waiting two decades for my color to process—the more it makes sense.

Instead of having relations with a man, have situations. Done.

What's not to love about that?

"But, before I tell you to dive into this whole thing, why can't you just go alone, Brooke?" Rebecca asks.

"Oh, *I can* go alone. I just generally prefer to avoid torture whenever possible."

"I still don't understand why you need a date to your grandma's birthday party."

"Because this isn't *just* a birthday party," I say. "It's labeled that to cover up the fact that my mom and her sister, my aunt Kim, are having a daughter-of-the-year showdown. They're using my poor grandma Honey's eighty-fifth birthday as a dog and pony show—and my cousin Aria and I are the ponies."

"*Okay*." Rebecca looks at me dubiously before switching her attention to Jovie. "And why are you against this whole thing?"

Jovie takes enough cash to cover our lunch plus the tip and hands it to Rebecca. *Perks of ordering the same lunch most days.* Then she gathers her things.

"I'm not against it in *theory*," Jovie says. "I'm against it in *practice*. I understand the perks of having a guy around to be arm candy when needed. But I'm not supporting this decision ... this *mayhem* ... for two reasons." She looks at me. "For one, your family will see any post you make on Social. You don't think they'll use it as ammunition against you?"

This is probably true.

"Second," Jovie continues. "I hate, hate, *hate* your aunt Kim, and I

CHAPTER 1: FLIRT

loathe the fact that your mom makes you feel like you have to do anything more than be your amazing self to win her favor. Screw them both."

My heart swells as I take in my best friend.

Jovie Reynolds was my first friend in Kismet Beach when I moved here two and a half years ago. We reached for the same can of pineapple rings, knocking over an entire display in Publix. As we picked up the mess, we traded recipes—hers for a vodka cocktail and mine for air fryer pineapple.

We hung out that evening—with her cocktail and my air fryer creations—and have been inseparable since.

"My mom is not a bad person," I say in her defense, even though I'm not so sure that's true from time to time. "She's just ..."

"A bad person," Jovie says.

I laugh. "*No.* I just ... nothing I can do is good enough for her. She hated Geoff when I married him at twenty and said I was too young. But was she happy when that ended in a divorce? Nope. According to *her*, I didn't try hard enough."

Rebecca frowns.

"And then Geoff started banging Kim and—"

"*What?*" Rebecca yelps, her eyes going wide.

"Exactly. Bad people," Jovie says, shaking her head.

"So your ex-husband will be at your grandma's party with your aunt? Is that what you're saying?" Rebecca asks.

I nod. "Yup."

She stacks our plates on top of one another. The ceramic clinks through the air. "On that note, why can't you just not go? Avoid it altogether?"

"Because my grandma Honey is looking forward to this, and she called me to make sure I was coming. I couldn't tell her no." My heart tightens when I think of the woman I love more than any other. "And, you know, my mom has made it abundantly clear that if I miss this, I will probably break Honey's heart, and she'll die, and it'll be my fault."

"Wow. That's a freight train of guilt to throw around," Rebecca says, wincing.

I glance down at my computer. The post is still there, sitting on the screen and waiting for my final decision. Although it is a genius idea, if I do say so myself—Jovie is probably right. It'll just cause more problems than it's worth.

I close the laptop and shove it into my bag. Then I hoist it on my shoulder. "It's complicated. I want to go and celebrate with my grandma but seeing my aunt with my ex-husband ..." I wince. "Also, there will be my mother's usual diatribe and comparisons to Aria, proving that I'm a failure in everything that I do."

"But if you had a boyfriend to accompany you, you'd save face with the enemy and have a buffer against your mother. Is that what you're thinking?" Rebecca asks.

"Yeah. I don't know how else to survive it. I can't walk in there alone, or even with Jovie, and deal with all of that mess. If I just had someone hot and a little handsy—make me look irresistible—it would kill all of my birds with one hopefully *hard* stone."

I wink at my friends.

Rebecca laughs. "Okay. I'm Team Fake Boyfriend. Sorry, Jovie."

Jovie sighs. "I'm sorry for me too because I have to go back to work. And if I avoid the stoplights, I can make it to the office with thirty seconds to spare." She air-kisses Rebecca. "Thanks for the extra mayo."

I laugh. "See you tomorrow, Rebecca."

"Bye, girls."

Jovie and I walk single-file through Smokey's until we reach the exit. Immediately, we reach for the sunglasses perched on top of our heads and slide them over our eyes.

The sun is bright, nearly blinding in a cloudless sky. I readjust my bag so that the thin layer of sweat starting to coat my skin doesn't coax the leather strap down my arm.

"Call me tonight," Jovie says, heading to her car.

"I will."

"Rehearsal for the play got canceled tonight, so I might go to Charlie's. If I don't, I may swing by your house."

"How's the thing with Charlie going? I didn't realize you were still talking to him."

She laughs. "I wasn't. He pissed me off. But he came groveling back

CHAPTER 1: FLIRT

last night, and I gave in." She shrugs. "What can I say? I'm a sucker for a good grovel."

"I think it's the theater girl in you. You love the dramatics of it all."

"That I do. It's a problem."

"Well, I'll see you when I see you then," I say.

"Bye, Brooke."

I give her a little wave and make my way up Beachfront Boulevard.

The sidewalk is fairly vacant with a light dusting of sand. In another month, tourists will fill the street that leads from the ocean to the shops filled with trinkets and ice cream in the heart of Kismet Beach. For now, it's a relaxing and hot walk back to the office.

My mind shifts from the heat back to the email reminder I received during lunch. *To Honey's party.* It takes all of one second for my stomach to cramp.

"I shouldn't have eaten all of those fries," I groan.

But it's not lunch that's making me unwell.

A mixture of emotions rolls through me. I don't know which one to land on. There's a chord of excitement about the event—at seeing Honey and her wonderful life be celebrated, catching up with Aria and the rest of my family, and the general concept of *going home*. But there's so much apprehension right alongside those things that it drowns out the good.

Kim and Geoff together make me ill. It's not that I miss my ex-husband; I'm the one who filed for divorce. But they will be there, making things super awkward for me in front of everyone we know.

Not to mention what it will do to my mother.

Geoff hooking up with Kim is my ultimate failure, according to Mom. Somehow, it embarrasses *her,* and that's unforgivable.

"For just once, I'd like to see her and not be judged," I mumble as I sidestep a melting glob of blue ice cream.

Nothing I have ever done has been good enough for Catherine Bailey. Marrying Geoff was an atrocity at only twenty years old. My dream to work in interior architecture wasn't deemed serious enough as a life path. *"You're wasting your time and our money, Brooke."* And when I told her I was hired at Laguna Homes as a lead designer for one of their three renovation teams? I could hear her eyes rolling.

The office comes into view, and my spirits lift immediately. I shove all thoughts of the party out of my brain and let my mind settle back into happier territory. *Work.* The one thing I love.

I step under the shade of an adorable crape myrtle tree and then turn up a cobblestone walkway to my office.

The small white building is tucked away from the sidewalk. It sits between a row of shops with apartments above them and an Italian restaurant only open in the evenings. The word *Laguna Homes* is printed in seafoam green above a black awning.

My shoes tap against the wooden steps as I make my way to the door. A rush of cool air, kissed by the scent of eucalyptus essential oil, greets me as I step inside.

"How was lunch?" Kix asks, standing in the doorway of his corner office. My boss's smile is kind and genuine, just like everything else about him. "Let me guess—you met Jovie for lunch at Smokey's?"

I laugh. "It's like you know me or something."

He chuckles.

Kix and Damaris Carmichael are two of my favorite people in the world. When I met Damaris at a trade show three years ago, and we struck up a conversation about tile, I knew she was special. Then I met her husband and discovered he had the same soft yet sturdy energy. All six of their children possess similar qualities—even Moss, the superintendent on my renovation team. Although I'd never admit that to him.

"I swung by Parasol Place this afternoon," Kix says. "It's looking great. You were right about taking out the wall between the living room and dining room. I love it. It makes the whole house feel bigger."

I blush under the weight of his compliment. "Thanks."

"Did Moss tell you about the property I'm looking at for your team next?" Kix asks.

"No. Moss doesn't tell me anything."

Kix grins. "I'm sure he tells you all kinds of things you don't need to know."

"You say that like you have experience with him," I say, laughing.

"Only a few years." He laughs too. "It's another home from the sixties. I got a lead on it this morning and am on my way to look at it now."

CHAPTER 1: FLIRT

"Take pictures. You know I love that era, and if you get it, I want to be able to start envisioning things right away."

"You and your visions." He shakes his head. "Gina is in the back making copies. I told her we'd keep our eye on the door until she gets back out here, so it would be great if you could do that."

"Absolutely," I say, walking backward toward my office. "Be safe. *And take pictures.*"

"I will. Enjoy the rest of your day, Brooke."

"You, too."

I reach behind me to find my office door open. I take another step back and then turn toward my desk. Someone moves beside my filing cabinet just as I flip on the light.

"Ah!" I shriek, clutching my chest.

My heart pounds out of control until I get my bearings and focus on the man looking back at me.

I set my bag down on a chair and blow out a shaky breath. "Dammit, Moss!"

He leans against the cabinet and smiles at me cheekily.

"We're going to have to stop meeting like this," he says. "People are going to talk."

Flirt is available now.

Acknowledgments

Returning to the Brewer world has been an absolute blast. This family is one of my absolute favorites. Every time I write a Brewer hero, I'm convinced he's my favorite and no one will ever outdo him. Naturally, I'm saying the same thing about this hero, Ripley.

I always say that I want to write stories that make readers feel good. I want you to piece up one of my books, knowing you're in good, trustworthy hands. And I want you to walk away with a smile on your face. That's truly how I felt while writing The Invitation; I wore a smile on my face every single minute and I hope you enjoyed it as much as I did crafting it.

As always, my first thanks it to my Creator for the many blessings in my life. Like Ripley and Georgia, I've learned over the years to trust the process. It's not an easy lesson to learn, but it's one of most rewarding when you finally get it.

I started my writing journey because my husband dared me to give it a try. I never wouldn't tried to write the stories floating through my brain down if he hadn't believed in me first. That's book boyfriend material, isn't it? I'm so grateful for him.

Our four sons supply tidbits to my books without knowing it. Tales they share about their lives, the wild things they say back and forth, and the immense love I have for them all play a part in my storytelling. They are my best work, now and forever.

I'm so lucky to be surrounded by a group of amazing women who help support me and my stories. Whether it's brainstorming sessions, writing sprints, or text updates, these women keep me motivated and inspired: Mandi Beck, S.L. Scott, Jessica Prince, Dylan Allen, Anjelica Grace, Kenna Rey, and Lulu Moore.

Thank you to Marion Archer, Jenny Sims, and Michele Ficht for your hand in edits. You three understand me and have a knack for knowing what I mean, even when it's not really what I say. I'm in awe of you.

Kari March created the perfect man cover for the ebook and paperback. Books and Moods outdid themselves with the magical special edition paperback cover. I'm smitten! Thank you both for your creative genius!

While I'm writing, there are a team of amazing women who keep the ship sailing smoothly. Thank you to Tiffany Remy, Jenn Hess, Kaitie Reister, Stephanie Gibson, Jordan Fazzini, and Sue Maturo. You're the best team ever.

And thank you to the entire team at Valentine PR. You show up each and every day with your pom-poms, thinking caps, and patience. (Lots and lots of patience.) I appreciate each and every one of you.

Finally, to my readers—this book celebrates ten years of writing for me. That's so mind-blowing! You've stuck with me, supported me, and loved me and my characters like no other! I'm so grateful to you. You'll never know how much.

Xo, Addy 🖤

About the Author

USA Today Bestselling author, Adriana Locke, writes contemporary romances about the two things she knows best—big families and small towns. Her stories are about ordinary people finding extraordinary love with the perfect combination of heart, heat, and humor.

She loves connecting with readers, fall weather, football, reading alpha heroes, everything pumpkin, and pretending to garden.

Hailing from a tiny town in the Midwest, Adriana spends her free time with her high school sweetheart (who she married over twenty years ago) and their four sons (who truly are her best work). Her kitchen may be a perpetual disaster, and if all else fails, there is always pizza.

Join her reader group and talk all the bookish things by clicking here.

www.adrianalocke.com

Made in the USA
Columbia, SC
24 April 2025